A ROARING LION

CARL RICHARDSON

Matador
9 Priory Business Park,
Wistow Road, Kibworth Beauchamp,
Leicestershire. LE8 0RX
Tel: (+44) 116 279 2299
Email: books@troubador.co.uk
Web: www.troubador.co.uk/matador

ISBN 978 1784622 961

British Library Cataloguing in Publication Data.
A catalogue record for this book is available from the British Library.

Printed and bound in the UK by TJ International, Padstow, Cornwall
Typeset in 11pt Aldine by Troubador Publishing Ltd, Leicester, UK

Matador is an imprint of Troubador Publishing Ltd

Brethren, be sober, be vigilant; because your adversary the devil,
as a roaring lion, walketh about, seeking whom he may devour …

1

At the sound of the key in the front door, Helen froze. It was the sound she had been waiting for for five days, and yet now that she heard it, momentarily, she was disconcerted, even afraid. The luminous hands of the bedside clock showed it was a quarter past three; but she didn't need to look at the clock. She had lain awake all night, unable to sleep, and unable to think clearly either. She had formed a half resolution to go to the police in the morning, in the hope that such a decision would allow her at last to sleep, even though she knew that John would be coming back, and would be angry if she had involved the police. On the previous occasions, he had at least told her in advance that he was going away; this time he had simply disappeared, leaving just a short, scribbled note, and he had been away for longer than ever before. She ought to have been angry, not just at being treated in such a way by her husband, but at how blatantly he offended against her. But her overwhelming emotion was gladness that he was back, and that she would see him again, and perhaps even a pathetic pleasure that, even if there was another woman, if that was what it was, he had at least come back to her. The anger would come later, when there was time for her to reflect without the immediate pressure and confusion of uncertainty. On the previous occasions, he would not say where he had been, and although she could not avoid the suspicion that there was someone else, she had failed to bring matters to a head. For one thing, John did not look to her like a man who had just fallen in love again. For some time he had been almost constantly depressed, worried and irritable; and what made it worse for Helen was that he had been unable to confide in her. The mysterious disappearances, which he would not explain, only added insult to injury, and although his mood and spirit seemed to be revived somewhat for a while following each return, there was a strangeness about it which she could not account for in terms of the conventional explanations of the behaviour of wayward husbands. And so, until now, she had held her peace.

She sat up and switched on the bedside light. She could hear John moving around downstairs, and she had almost got out of bed to go down and greet him when she heard him coming up the stairs. Then he was standing framed in the bedroom doorway, and for a minute they just looked at each other in silence. He looked terribly drawn and gaunt, and yet with an air of grim determination rather than hopelessness: that certain strangeness which she did not understand. He carried a suitcase, which he slowly set down on the floor.

"It's been five days, John. I've been worried sick. Where have you been, and why are you doing this?"

John did not speak, but simply shook his head in a gesture of unutterable weariness.

"Could you not even have told me you were going away? Can you not see how unfair it is on me? I can't stand much more of this, in God's name I can't. When will it end?"

"It ends tonight." His voice was flat and grey. He picked the suitcase up and put it on the bed. "It ends now. There will be no more of this."

He had opened a bedside drawer and was taking out selected personal belongings and putting them into the suitcase. Helen stared at him, uncomprehending at first, then with growing dismay as she took in what he was doing.

"Are you not staying? John, what are you doing? Are you ..."

He stopped what he was doing and came and sat on the bed.

"Helen, I can't explain very much, not here – it isn't safe for me to do so. You'll have to accept what I tell you on trust for now. I hope I can explain properly later, but not now. All I can tell you is that I have to quit this place for good, and at once. These trips away have been a preparation for that, and at last, thank God, it's all arranged."

"You're ... leaving." There was disbelief in her face. "What have you come back for?" Her voice was barely more than a whisper.

"I've come back for you. You're coming with me. It's all arranged, as I said."

"Going with you? Going where? Why can't you explain?"

"I can't, not now. I'll explain when we arrive there, but not before."

"Arrive where?" She was exasperated, as much by her own tiredness from lack of sleep as by her husband's strange secretiveness.

"I'm sorry, darling, I can't even tell you that, not yet. When we're on our way perhaps, but not yet."

Helen rubbed her hands over her eyes and ran her fingers through her hair in a gesture of weariness.

"You're mad," she said, as much to herself as to him. "You're mad. You arrive here at half past three in the morning after being away for five days, and expect me to get dressed at a minute's notice and depart into the night with you for a destination you won't tell me of, and leave behind my home, my life, everything, for good. That's what you said, wasn't it, for good?"

"Yes. That's what I'm asking. And I'm not giving you much of a choice. You're my wife. I have to go. I have no choice. I'm asking you to come with me. If you don't come with me, what will you do?"

"Why do you have to go?" Her eyes were wide and dark, seeking the truth. "Have you done something wrong? Are you on the run from the police?"

"I have done nothing wrong. Nor am I on the run from the police – at least, not yet I'm not. But in a sense, I am on the run, and I have to leave at once, now that my preparations are complete. Will you come with me? You are my wife. If you won't, what will you do?"

She dropped her gaze, and for a minute, stared at nothing. What would she do? She had no job. She might be able to get a job, but not one that would allow her to keep on the house if John left. She would have to find somewhere else to live, at least. And what of the rest of her life – her mother and father, her friends, her little social routine . . ? But how quickly one's perspective shifted. Ten minutes ago she had been able to think of nothing but his return, and the rest of her life had been of no account. She would have forgiven him almost anything if he would come back to her, under almost any circumstances; and yet, now he had come back, it was not as she had expected. She still doubted his sanity, and yet she was his wife. What was she to do?

"You're determined to go to this place, wherever it is?"

"I'm determined to go. All this, all these trips away have been in preparation for this."

"And when we get there, wherever it is, would it be possible ever to return here?"

"For you, I expect it would be possible, yes. For me, it would not. I have no choice."

He waited for her to answer. She closed her eyes and for a minute said nothing. Was the beginning of yet another suspicion forming in the back of her mind? If only she could sleep! She caught herself wool-gathering, and it was only a slight rustling noise from John's coat that brought her back to herself. She looked up at him wearily.

4

"I'm pretty well done in. I've had very little sleep." It was manifestly true, but she was also clutching at straws.

"Neither have I; but we must be clear of here by daybreak. You can sleep a little on the way, and when we get there, you can sleep as much as you like."

He was willing her to come, and for a moment, she was aware of the strength of that will. She felt driven by it, surprised by its fierceness, and almost as helpless in her surprise and tiredness as a leaf blown before the wind. Slowly and deliberately, she pushed aside the bedclothes and climbed out of bed.

In an hour, they were ready. The sky was pale with dawn as the front door of the house closed behind them with a click, and with two suitcases each, they started along the road to the station. Even at that hour there were quite a few people about: shift workers on their way to Trafford Park or the city centre, office cleaners, delivery roundsmen. For them, it was just another Saturday morning: another day's work, or half a day if they were lucky. Manchester United would be playing at Old Trafford that afternoon in one of the first games of the new season, and the luckier ones would be there; and whether one was lucky or unlucky, it was one of the main topics of conversation. Most of those who had time to buy an early morning newspaper turned straight to the sports pages to read what was being said about the match that afternoon. The news of the momentous events in Moscow and Berlin that filled the front page might be read later, or not at all. Such things were unreal, and only fools wasted time worrying or even thinking about them. Reality was work, if you were lucky; the noise of machines on the shop floor; the clock; the foreman; the ever-present threat from the men in suits behind the frosted glass doors upstairs marked 'Manager'; the journey home, to the welcoming arms of a wife if you were lucky; Saturday nights; and on Saturday afternoons, Manchester

United. Crammed with such distressful bread, few of those abroad at such an hour had a second glance for the somewhat forlorn-looking middle-class couple laden with suitcases. The ticket clerk at the railway station noticed them: they might have been holidaymakers if they had not had the slightly desperate, exhausted look of refugees.

"Doing a midnight flit, I'll bet," he said to himself.

At Oxford Road station in the city centre, they boarded the Liverpool train. Helen kept falling asleep; but there was little respite yet. At Liverpool, they took a taxi from Lime Street station to the Pierhead, and the offices of a shipping company. Here, there was a longer wait in a drab waiting room, but at least it was a chance to sleep for a while. Helen found John shaking her awake again.

"Helen. Helen, wake up. This one's ours."

There were long corridors, and then a long room with a long bare counter on which suitcases were placed for men in uniform to make chalk crosses on.

"Anything to declare? Anything to declare?"

More corridor, then open quayside, a gangplank, the side of a ship. For a moment, Helen hesitated, the sight of the ship seeming to shake her out of her lethargy, as if she understood the nature of the journey for the first time. Even if it was not to be a long voyage, to cross the sea, to put the sea between oneself and home for the foreseeable future, perhaps forever, was more than, in that moment, she could bear. She stopped and looked back. It was only Liverpool – the grey, many-storeyed facades of the Royal Liver Building, the Custom House and the Cunard Building rising in municipal sobriety above the functional, single-storey quayside buildings, and beyond them, the haze of an industrial city; and yet … and yet … it was hard to turn away, perhaps forever. But she could not stop on the gangway. People were already starting to push past her. John looked back for her, smiled and held out a hand.

"Come on, I've booked a private cabin just for us. You'll be able to sleep there."

When she awoke, it was the movement of the ship that woke her, or rather, the absence of the steady pitch and roll to which she had become accustomed, even in sleep. Her eyes met John's, and he gave her a wan smile.

"We're nearly there," he said.

They looked out of the little porthole. Their cabin was on the port side, amidships, and the view from the porthole was limited; but to the right and already very close, a grey silhouette of land loomed out of the mist. Reluctantly the land revealed its details from the shadow – strange objects that broke the skyline materialised as factory chimneys, cranes, towers. A large buoy, green with seaweed and orange with rust suddenly appeared close alongside and drifted past; the beat of the engines quickened as the ship manoeuvred in the channel; a lighthouse appeared, then a long, high stone quay that seemed to go on forever, until the ship edged into its berth. John and Helen left their cabin and, clutching their suitcases, made their way up to the boat deck. There was an endless quarter of an hour until the exit gates were opened; then they were walking down the gangway. John was first onto the quayside. He walked forward a few yards, set down the suitcases he was carrying, and turned to face Helen as she came up to him. He took her suitcases off her and set them down, and then flung his arms around her in an embrace so fierce that she felt she was being crushed. She was bewildered and overwhelmed, not just by his embrace, but by the strength of emotion that it revealed. He was shaking as he held her, and when he released her, she saw that his eyes were bright with tears.

"We made it," he said, his voice little more than a whisper. "Welcome to Ireland, my love."

She smiled uncertainly, not yet understanding what had

happened. They went through the customs hall, and after a short wait, a bus took them into the centre of Dublin. From College Green they walked to Westland Row station through streets that were starting to become busy again with people returning to the city centre for a Saturday night out. Lights were appearing in the windows of public houses, and queues were forming outside cinemas. This might almost have been Manchester: the Free State had existed for nearly twenty years, but the streets of Dublin still looked very familiar to British eyes. But in Manchester, in England, beyond the darkness of the streets, beyond the darkness of the darkest night, there was that other darkness which deepened as the certainty of war drew close: the shadows of the mass graves of Flanders and northern France that haunted all who remembered the last time. In Manchester, even the most riotous celebrations of United's victory at Old Trafford would not dispel it – in the small hours of the night, in the sobriety of Sunday morning, it would return like the memory of a tragedy; and for all who remembered, the future was opaque, a blankness without the possibility of hope. In Dublin, it was hard to define the difference unless one was alive to it; but for John, it was as striking as that between night and day. In the Free State at least, there would be no 'next time'. Publicly, it was one in the eye for the British; and that was something everyone could approve of. But beneath that, there was a certain lightness of heart in the expectation that normal life would continue; that one could make plans for the future; that the great issues of the day would still be the price of beer and the income tax, as they should be; that men would not be going away, and women would not fear the sight of a telegram; that here at least, there would be sanity. It was a small thing to be grateful for, but without it, as John knew, there could be nothing else.

They got off the train at the little seaside town of Bray. It was nearly nine o'clock, and the light was beginning to fade rapidly into a summer night. Helen nearly rebelled when she learned that there was still a long walk ahead; but as there was no transport of any kind to be had in such a place at such an hour, they had no choice. From the edge of the little town, a country lane ran south-westward up into the Wicklow Hills. A little under a mile beyond the town along the lane, they came to the cottage. It was a long, single-storey building in whitewashed stone, standing a little off the lane in a walled garden. The garden was knee-high with grass and looked more like a hay meadow than a garden. Standing waiting while John fumbled for the key, Helen was not sure whether to be dismayed or delighted by what was evidently their new home. In truth, she was too tired to care at that moment. As long as there was a bed … There was, in a low-ceilinged room at the back of the cottage. Helen couldn't get into it fast enough.

When she awoke, she did so reluctantly in the way one does after profound sleep, savouring the sweetness of rest. At first, she was only aware that it was day – when she eventually looked at her watch, she saw that it had stopped at twenty past ten, and as the daylight looked well established, it was presumably late. She was next conscious of the fact that she was alone in the big double bed that she and John had fallen into, exhausted, the previous evening. John was not in the room. It was an old-fashioned room. The ceiling was low and beamed – an oil lamp hung from a hook on one of the beams. Opposite the bed, a modern fireplace had been set into the original massive chimney breast. To one side of it stood a wash stand, with bowl and pitcher. The only other attempt at modernity was the William Morris wallpaper above the high skirting boards, which looked as if it was probably original. There was a wardrobe and a chest of drawers in dark-stained wood of distinctly rough carpentry, and a thin carpet covered the stone-flagged floor. The silence was almost absolute – not even a bird sang, and the only sound was the occasional creak of the house timbers as they expanded in the warmth of the day. Bright sunlight streamed into the room through gaps in the curtain, creating splashes of light and colour on the walls. Helen might have found this warm stillness oppressive; but there seemed to be something in the air which forbade it – a laziness that was at once soporific and sweet, with the inconsequentiality of a butterfly in a sunny garden. It had been so long since she had been touched by it that she did not at first recognise it. She got out of bed and walked over to the window and pulled aside the curtain. The window was at the back of the cottage and looked out over the hay meadow that served as the back garden, stretching up towards the summit of the low rise on which the cottage was built. Here the pattern of hedgerows formed a green horizon, the dark green of late summer, ripe and mature with the fruit of the season of life, flaunting its fertility at the sun. She opened the window and let the summer in to envelop her. The hay meadow was shot through with countless wild flowers – larkspur, coltsfoot, cowslip, campion – far more than she could ever know; and the warm air was tantalising with hints of their perfume, overlaid with the pungent, erotic sweetness of pollen. Butterflies and thistledown drifted uncertainly towards the still unfamiliar blue silhouettes of the Wicklow Hills.

The surprise was complete. It took her as unexpectedly as it had done twenty summers before on her first trip outside grimy Manchester to the countryside, in boundless joy that today was summer, and today and today and today a seven year old ran shouting to embrace the green stems with bare arms and bare legs and the juice of berries on sun-browned skin. The sun seemed to stand still in the sky and burned alike the seven year old and the twenty-seven year old in the same moment of green oblivion. In such a moment, time was forgotten in the discovery that the sunlight of twenty summers before, caught in the pure crystal of a child's eye, was not lost forever.

Somewhere in the depths of the blue vault above, a skylark began to sing, its elusive chirring filling the warm air and the green earth. Vainly she looked for it against the measureless blue, its ceaseless song as elusive in the air as the scents of the wild flowers.

She heard a voice calling her name. It was John. He had walked over to a neighbouring farm, and come back laden with milk, eggs, cheese and bacon.

"We won't starve here at least, even on Sundays," he announced cheerfully. They stowed the food in the pantry, then John lit the stove so that they could heat a kettle for tea. The kitchen was uncompromisingly old-fashioned. Apart from the stove, there was a massive range beside the fireplace; but it was far too warm a day, even within the stone walls of the cottage, to light the fire to heat the range. They fried eggs and bacon on the little stove, and drank unsweetened tea, because they had no sugar. Such makeshift improvisation added to the feeling that this was a new departure, a new beginning; one that would shape and define the rest of their lives.

Even in so short a space of time, the change it had produced in John was remarkable. The grim, careworn figure of forty-eight hours before, who had haunted her recent life like the ghost of Banquo at the feast was already a fading memory. It was as if the man she had married had been restored to her in all his youthful vigour and energy, infused, perhaps, with the procreative greenness of this place. Some great load had been lifted from his shoulders, and he was buoyant with happiness: there was even something triumphant about him in his exuberance. For Helen, caught as she was in a mood of indolent delight, this transformation was a culminating sweetness, and she was induced to surrender to its seduction. She did surrender, and it was blissful; but even in the most blissful extremity of surrender, she knew that still she did not understand.

Contrary to his word, John was not immediately forthcoming about the reasons for what had happened. He had got a job in Dublin as a teacher of English and history at a non-denominational secondary school. His income was considerably lower than the salary he had left behind in Manchester, but in Irish terms it was still comfortable, and for John at least, the sacrifice had been scarcely worth a second thought. They were solvent, and they were free, and he had asked no more of fate.

On the Sunday evening, John had gone through preparations to start work the following morning with a certain show of first-day nerves; but at the same time he had spoken with enthusiasm about the new job. Helen remained puzzled. If it was less well paid, what was the point? She still awaited an explanation.

Even after they had made love for the first time that night and were lying awake in the warm darkness, watching glimpses of an August moon chasing clouds through a gap in the curtain, the thought would still not leave her.

"I'm still puzzled," she said quietly into the darkness. "You had a respected position at the university, and you had prospects of advancement. To leave like this …"

"I know. Don't I know it. That only made it harder. But in the end, it wouldn't have made any difference. I wouldn't have been there much longer anyway." He sighed and stirred in the bed. He was still reluctant to say too much. He wanted to be vindicated by events, not by words, and he was sure beyond doubt that events, when they came, would obviate the need for any more words. He mused aloud, as much to himself as to Helen.

"I suppose from their point of view, it would be largely a matter of honour; whereas from my point of view, it's a matter of sanity and reason. I don't think I've lost honour, at least, not yet. Whether I will do so will depend on them."

It was Helen's turn to sigh.

"I do wish you wouldn't talk in riddles. I still don't understand."

"Oh, Helen my love, don't let's argue, not now. I need your support now, for tomorrow, not to argue. I promise you, you won't have to ask why for much longer. It'll become only too horribly clear soon enough. But don't let's talk about it now. Not now – not after today."

He reached out and touched her smooth soft skin, and turned towards her. Helen remembered the hay meadow and the sunlight, and she smiled, feeling his warmth in the darkness.

2

Early on Monday morning they kissed goodbye on the platform at Bray railway station. Even though Helen still did not understand, or approve of this retrograde step, as she saw it, she nevertheless wanted to be as positive about it as she could. He seemed to be so sure that it would make sense soon enough that, for the time being, she left it at that. And last night had been so good...

John had left her some money to buy essential groceries from the shops in Bray, and by mid-morning she was back at the cottage planning a campaign to clean the place from top to bottom. She started in the kitchen, which contained the cottage's only water tap. The range had not been used for some time and was filthy and clogged up with ash. It took her the rest of the morning and half the afternoon to clean it, and she still hadn't finished the kitchen when John arrived home, with the consequence that John had to wait for his tea. Not surprisingly, he was full of his new job, and he stood around the kitchen with his hands in his pockets talking enthusiastically at her back while she cleaned herself up and prepared their meal. She didn't mind, and found that, despite her reservations, she was interested. StMungo's, pleasantly situated in a genteel suburb of south Dublin, was technically a non-denominational secondary school. However, since all Catholic children went to denominational Catholic schools, St Mungo's was effectively a Protestant school for south

Dublin. Its pupils were Church of Ireland or Non-Conformist, or the offspring of the non-religious or of confirmed atheists – the dissenters of Irish society, which was a reason for its being regarded as somewhat less than respectable by the Catholic majority. The school even had one or two women teachers – and Helen found herself experiencing a momentary twinge of sympathy for traditionalist disapproval of these, if for a different reason.

The staff at the school, John had found even on his first day, were demoralised by division. The older staff could remember the time before the Great War, when the school's status had been very different. Then, the school had been part of the Establishment, a part of the fabric of British rule in Ireland, and members of the Anglo-Irish ruling class had sent their children to the school. Some of the staff had been on first name terms with such people, and some of the buzz of being close to the centre of events had rubbed off on the school. The late Lord Carson had been a patron of the school, and most of the staff at that time had shared his confidence that the worst would never happen. Now, seventeen years after the worst had happened, there were some at least, who had still not come to terms with it. It was a piece of Bolshevism whose continued existence threatened the very fabric of civilisation, or at least, of British civilisation. Some of them were Irish enough to see it, also without any sense of incongruity, as a treacherous reversal of the Glorious Revolution, as a victory for reactionary popery, three centuries after such matters had been settled forever. They walked about in a permanent cold rage, and the name of De Valera was abominable in their ears. But after seventeen years, it was inevitable that younger staff would see the matter differently. Even though still Protestant – the school had not yet abandoned all its standards – they were prepared to identify with the Catholic majority and see their future in the new

15

Ireland. What else was realistic? The British weren't coming back.

Strong views were held on both sides, but on the whole they had not been allowed to interfere with professional relationships – at least, not until recently. In the last year, John had been told, things had been different. Ever since Munich, and certainly since the events in Czechoslovakia in March, the prospect of war looked inevitable: inevitable, at least, for Britain. For the old guard on the staff, it was unthinkable that the young men of Ireland should not flock to the colours and go to fight for Britain, King and Empire. Some of them were tactless enough to make it clear that they were referring to their younger colleagues, and on a number of occasions the sanctity of the staff room had been violated by bitter arguments which usually descended into the most deplorable personal abuse.

John was both apprehensive and rather excited by this discovery: apprehensive because soon, perhaps very soon, he would have to defend himself; excited because for the first time he would have allies, among whom he need not feel ashamed. He did not describe any of these feelings to Helen – he was still waiting for events to justify his actions – only, that it was not the happiest of occasions to join a staffroom so deeply and bitterly divided. He was nevertheless pleased that he had been enabled thus to introduce the matter of his own position and motives indirectly, in a way which placed them in a wider and more objective context.

On the Wednesday of that first week, John arrived home on a bicycle he had bought at a second-hand shop in Dublin. It was essential to have one's own transport, living in such an out-of-the-way place, he announced. The following morning he again walked into Bray, setting off early; and in the evening, he again arrived home riding a bicycle – this time a lady's cycle, which he had bought for Helen. Helen was more amused than grateful, and as it was rather an old model, she made gentle fun of it, calling him an old lady riding an old lady's bicycle. He laughed at the joke; but after tea, as it was such a lovely evening, they cycled down to the sea at Greystones, and walked along the beach hand in hand as the sun cast a broad pink highway across the sea to the horizon as it slid behind the soft grey summits of the hills. It was a fulfilment, a consummation of peace and contentment in a way that even John could not have foreseen, even then. As they stood and looked out over the sea towards the distant coast of Wales, dimly seen on the edge of vision, watching while the pink highway dissolved gently into silver-grey, it seemed that over that farther shore there loomed a greater darkness than the darkness of the approaching night: a darkness visible in the minds of men. Between, there was only the sea, which now lapped gently at their feet in a summer calm.

John squeezed Helen's hand.

"Are you happy?" he asked her. He himself was idyllically happy, and was quite unable to conceal it. His happiness was infectious, and Helen squeezed his hand in return and smiled at him.

"Yes," she said, "I'm happy too."

But her smile was still a little bemused, as though she humoured him in some secret that was part of a game they played, a game which was not yet played out.

The time for dreams and games, however, was already over. The following morning, John arrived at St Mungo's earlier than usual, having cycled from the station for the first time. It felt good having the independence of the bicycle, and it was now possible to catch a later train into the city as a result. From the station, it took him about half the time to reach the school than it had done on the previous mornings. On this Friday morning, other things were different, too. The staff usually had a quiet quarter of an hour or so in the staff room to prepare themselves before issuing forth to meet the barbarian hordes in the classrooms. There was rarely any general conversation – individuals sat by themselves, or in twos and threes, talking quietly over a cup of coffee. Even as a newcomer, John was aware of the difference on that morning as soon as he walked in, and he shared in the general feeling of excitement and apprehension when he learned the reason. The German attack on Poland, which had looked increasingly likely over the last couple of months, had apparently begun. There was nothing in the morning editions of the newspapers, but those who had wireless sets reported that the news had been on both Irish radio and the BBC.

John got himself a cup of coffee, then stood staring out of the staffroom window, across the curved driveway to the school gates. In his mind's eye, he saw another, grander entranceway from a wider and grander street in another city. It was still less than two weeks since he had last walked through that other entrance, a memory now darkened to a great remoteness by all that had happened since. What would he have done if he had still looked on that place now? Who did still look on it, and with what coldness in their hearts? If ever there was a moment when he ought to have rejoiced, when he might have fallen down on his knees and given thanks, it was this; especially as it seemed that he had only just made it in time. One of his concerns had been that the British authorities might have imposed travel restrictions immediately on the outbreak of war, at least for men of military age. But he felt nothing – or almost nothing: perhaps just a slight sadness for what had been lost because of the stupidity of others.

"Penny for 'em," said a voice at his elbow. It was Carter, the young science teacher.

"Oh!" John smiled ruefully. "Just … memories."

"England?"

John nodded.

"Are you maybe sorry you came, now; or just homesick?"

John could not help laughing at that.

"No, I'm not homesick. I haven't been here long enough for that. Nor am I sorry I came – most emphatically not."

"All the same, things aren't going to be easy here now, either. Not after the way they've been."

Carter was still not sure of him.

John continued to gaze out of the window.

"There's no reason for anyone to lose his dignity over the matter," he said. "Especially as we're likely to have right on our side now." He glanced sidelong at Carter, who was looking puzzled.

"We? Whom do you mean by we?" Carter was still cautious.

"Oh, come on. You've just said yourself that things aren't easy here. I've only been here a few days, but it's not hard to see why. All this patriotic claptrap from these closet unionists."

It was Carter's turn to laugh.

"My word, you haven't been slow in picking up our bad habits. You may not be homesick yet, but you've certainly acclimatised quickly enough. Well, you take my tip and keep your voice down when you're talking about patriotic claptrap. The unionists here certainly aren't in the closet, and frankly, I'm fed up with seeing the staff room turned into a bear garden by grown men bawling insults and abuse at each other. The kids know all about it, and it just demeans us in their eyes."

"I've no intention of getting involved in brawls in the staffroom – or anywhere else. It just isn't necessary – that's what I was trying to say."

Carter patted him on the shoulder.

"I'm sure your heart's in the right place, but you won't find it as easy as that, I'm afraid. For one thing, you're British."

"Meaning?" John raised his eyebrows.

"Meaning that you're not going to find it so easy to stay aloof from the brawling. Whether you like it or not, what you decide to do will be a focus of interest. You'll be expected to do one thing by one side, and you might not get too much sympathy from the other. After all, it wasn't too long ago that some of us were fighting the British."

"And whom do you mean by us?" John looked at him in dismay. "How old were you in 1922?"

"Oh, don't take it to heart." Carter looked slightly embarrassed. "I wasn't speaking personally, of course. If there are any raving republicans here, then I'm not one of them. But if you were thinking that, because you're here now, you won't have to concern yourself about the war, assuming there is one, well, I don't think it will be as easy as that."

"But everyone knows that Ireland will be neutral."

"Oh, Ireland will be neutral, all right. But that won't apply to everyone in Ireland. There's the first bell – I'll have to go. I'm taking 3A for physics first period. I'll see you later." He gathered his papers together. He paused and looked back as he was walking away. "By the way, you'll be glad to know that I was seven in 1922."

At lunchtime, John went out to buy a newspaper. The evening papers had rushed out early editions to cover the war news; but at that stage there was very little hard news to report – most of it was rumour and speculation. He felt unsettled by Carter's ripostes, but decided that they had been a warning rather than a gibe. If Carter had had enough unpleasantness already, he would not be relishing what was to come, and was presumably trying to steer him away from trouble. Well, if Carter was worried by the prospect of trouble, then he was not. He almost relished it. If there were any white feathers from this lot, then he would have an answer for them.

The end of school that day was the end of the first week in his new post, and he had expected to enjoy a little celebration to mark the occasion; but the events of the day had almost completely overshadowed it. It was by chance that as he cycled through the streets of the city, he had a momentary image of Helen standing in the sunlight in the hay garden, waiting for his return, and an understanding that the celebration would be for her; and because it was she who was his joy and his love, his fear and his dread. Without her, his new life here would be hollow.

He stopped at a flower shop and bought as large a bouquet of flowers as he could conveniently carry on his bicycle. The evening editions of the papers had little of substance to add to what had appeared in the lunchtime editions, and he travelled home in a mood of apprehension. This was the moment he had fretted over countless times in his thoughts during the dark weeks and months of preparation and waiting. It was a point of no return, the second of the two great gates which he must pass through if he was to find the place he sought for himself and Helen. If he could not take her with him now, it was all in vain.

He was not good at decisions – the more important the issue, the worse was his torment lest he should make the wrong choice; and even as he opened the garden gate and wheeled his bicycle up the path to the cottage, he still did not know how much he should say, and how much he should leave unsaid. Would she know? Would she guess? Would she despise him? She was his wife, and he did not know.

He went through into the kitchen, but she was not in the house. Then he glimpsed her through the kitchen window in the hay meadow, and he went out to her, still clutching his bouquet. She was standing almost exactly as he had seen her in his mind's eye an hour earlier, the high grass almost up to her waist, her back to the cottage as she looked up at the westering sun sinking towards the distant hills. She turned at the sound of his voice and smiled.

"You're home early."

"It's Friday. They let you out earlier on a Friday." The bouquet was crushed as they embraced, and he had to rescue it so he could present it to her.

"They're beautiful. And they're for me?"

He nodded, still full of indecision. "I've just completed my first full week in the new job. It's not gone badly at all, and I was so pleased I bought you these on the way home."

"They're lovely." She kissed him again. "They shall have pride of place. I've picked a lot of flowers this afternoon. I finally finished cleaning the cottage today, and I wanted to have fresh flowers in every room. Did you see them when you came through?"

He hadn't noticed them in his preoccupation. "Come and show me," he said.

Helen had found old jamjars and receptacles of all kinds to put bunches of wild flowers in at every window, filling the cottage with the fragrance of late summer. In the late afternoon, the rooms were dark in contrast with the strong sunlight outside, and one was drawn towards the windows and the light, and the scents of the flowers. In such Arcadian tranquillity, John's resolution failed him again, and he followed Helen into the kitchen, where the principal fragrance emanated from a dish of hot-pot in the oven. He helped her to prepare the meal.

"I was wondering," she said, once they had sat down, "if you would dig over some ground at the back for me tomorrow or Sunday. I've decided it would be a good idea to have a vegetable garden, and perhaps even one or two flower borders as well. I know the meadow looks beautiful, but I would like some garden flowers as well. You wouldn't have to dig it all over; just enough for a smallish plot."

John laughed. "Dig it all over? No chance of doing that between now and Sunday."

"A smallish plot, I said."

"Well, how small is smallish?"

"Not too big, but enough for a couple of rows of potatoes, a row of cabbage, and a row of carrots and onions. And if you're feeling very energetic, perhaps a small patch for some annuals as well."

"I didn't know you were a gardener."

"Well, I suppose I'm not really; but ever since Mum and Dad moved to the country, I've been rather envious of their garden, and now we've got an even bigger one than theirs, I thought I'd like to try my hand."

"But your dad doesn't grow vegetables – or not many. It's mostly roses he goes in for, isn't it?"

"Yes, but I expect he'll be growing more vegetables too, now." She gave him an enigmatic look. "When I went shopping in Bray this lunchtime, I heard the news about Poland. I thought that if there's going to be a war, we'll need to be able to grow our own food. Food's always scarce during a war. Have you heard the news? Do you think there will be a war?"

He hadn't expected things to happen this way, and was momentarily taken aback. He could not assess her mood, and found that he could only wait on events. He nodded slowly.

"It looks as if there will be."

"You heard the news, then?" She seemed to want confirmation of the point, so he went and fetched the newspaper he had bought in Dublin. Helen pored over it with interest, unfolding and refolding it so she could read it on the table. She frowned as she continued to read, and at length she muttered the word 'British' two or three times, in tones which indicated that she was puzzled by something. She unfolded the newspaper so she could read on, and evidently caught sight of the front page.

"Oh! This is an Irish newspaper."

She was starting to understand. John held his breath.

"Yes," he said slowly.

"I mean," she went on, "in here they keep referring to the British as though they were… separate; I mean…" she groped for the words "as if Britain was… another country."

He felt he needed to say almost nothing: that the newspaper, as an external reality, would say it far more eloquently than he could.

"Well, I suppose, from their point of view… I mean, after all the trouble of twenty years ago…"

"Oh!" Helen was slowly digesting this discovery. As with most women, her knowledge of politics was limited, largely through lack of interest. Such a deficiency is often mistaken by men as a sign of dullness or subservience, whereas in truth it is mainly a consequence of a natural human desire to concentrate one's attention on what matters to one most. Men had constructed numerous arenas in which to compete for the material things of this world, so that in turn they could compete for the favours of the fairer sex. Politics was only the largest of such arenas, and how men chose to make fools of themselves in the world was not a matter of general interest to most women. It was only occasionally that politics intruded into ordinary life in such a way as to require one to focus one's attention on it. For Helen, as for many during that weekend, this was such an occasion.

"But," she said after a pause, "if there is a war, Ireland will be on England's side." Her face wore a concerned expression as she looked at him.

"Well, I don't imagine that Ireland will be on Germany's side. But it's very possible that Ireland won't be on anyone's side. I think that most people in Ireland would prefer to stay out of it altogether."

"But won't they have to choose sides?"

He shook his head. "Not necessarily. There were neutral countries during the Great War – Switzerland, Sweden, Holland. It looks as if America will be neutral this time, too."

He had at one stage thought a lot about America. It was so much bigger and with so much more opportunity than a backwater like Ireland. But its very size meant that it was also more risky, more uncertain; and in the end, the distance, the cost, and the disruption involved proved to be beyond him. He could not have taken Helen to America. He was still far from certain about Ireland as he waited for her response.

"If Ireland is neutral, what will happen to us?" she asked.

He shrugged his shoulders. "Nothing in particular. Life here will carry on as normal, I imagine. It usually does in neutral countries."

"And if there is a war – what will you do?"

She had reached the heart of the matter by a circuitous route, but she had at last reached it. On this first occasion, he avoided the issue, and temporised.

"I don't know. At the moment I'm not worrying about it. We'll just have to wait and see what happens first."

"But if there is a war …"

He stopped her by putting his fingers to her lips.

"Wait and see what happens," he said gently.

She was still an unknown quantity, even to herself. The events of the last few days had been so rapid that she had not had time to adjust and form a perspective on them, and John sensed that he should not say any more.

"One thing I will do, whether there's a war or not – I'll dig over a vegetable patch for you."

The following morning they lay in late, and at lunchtime, cycled into Bray to go shopping. The Saturday morning editions of the newspapers were again full of the war; but again, there was little real news. There was to be a British ultimatum; the French were wavering; but nothing had actually happened yet. The only thing the editorials seemed to agree on was that the question of whether or not there would be a general war would be decided within the next twenty-four hours. John felt philosophical. There was nothing more he could do, and the best thing would be to forget about the outside world until Monday morning.

Instead of going straight home, they went in search of a nursery where they could buy some seedling winter vegetables for the vegetable plot. They took directions in a greengrocer's shop in Bray, directions that proved to be extremely vague. After about an hour, they reached Greystones without having found it. They had a late lunch in an hotel where the waiters wore bow ties, and the walls were covered in oak panelling, and the floors creaked, and there was a quasi-religious hush; and they felt slightly ill at ease in their casual cycling clothes. But Helen was delighted at having found such a place, which she felt more than made up for their tiredness and disappointment at not finding the nursery. They stayed until nearly four o'clock, falling asleep in huge armchairs in a lounge whose walls were covered in vast, dim landscapes by long-forgotten early-nineteenth-century painters.

They did not remember about the nursery until after they had returned home, by which time they were too tired to care. John advised against going to look for the nursery again the following day, since, it being a Sunday, it would not be open. He would get some seed from a florist in Dublin, or they could try again the following Saturday. Even the sight of the discarded morning newspapers could not disturb John's equanimity. Everything was still in limbo: everything might still be lost, and yet …

Sunday was a glorious late summer day. Just before lunch, John walked over to the neighbouring farm and came back with milk, eggs and a chicken. Helen prepared the chicken for the oven while John started digging the vegetable plot. Digging was hard work in the sun, and Helen had to keep breaking off what she was doing to make lemonade for him to quench his thirst. When she called to him that dinner would be ready in ten minutes, he leaned on his spade and surveyed the results of his labours. The vegetable plot was almost finished. There were two deep furrows for the potatoes, with the earth banked up high in between, and several shallower furrows for the other vegetables. At first, his only feeling was one of satisfaction with the evidence of work done; but then it seemed to him that the ordered furrows jarred somehow with the rest of the garden; that it was as if a piece of English regimentation had been imposed on the wild anarchy of an Irish meadow, marring its natural beauty, emphasising the fact that they were strangers here. He told himself this was a lot of fanciful nonsense. It was just a vegetable plot in their back garden. But, of course, it was also a reminder of Helen's foreboding about the war, and with that thought, his pessimism returned.

"Dinner's on the table," Helen called accusingly. He put the spade away and went indoors.

3

Monday brought a return to routine. For Helen, it was wash day, as it had been on every Monday of her married life. However, as she had already discovered, heating water for the dolly tub on a wood-burning stove was something of an art form, one which kept her preoccupied all morning. It wasn't until she had the first wash out on the line, and was sitting down for a break, that she remembered about the war. She came across the discarded newspapers from the weekend and read them again with interest. She wondered what was happening about the war at that moment. John had continued to be reserved about the reasons for their move to Ireland, but it was becoming increasingly clear that it had to do with the impending war. He had always taken an interest in politics, although it had never been very clear to her what his interest was, since, as far as she knew, he didn't take part in any political activity. Many men took such an interest in politics for no very good reason: she might even have been apprehensive earlier if she had thought that John had a particular reason for such interest. As it was, she still had to guess, and it was because such guesses led to a limited number of not very satisfactory conclusions that, however happy she was in their new home, she retained a residual feeling of doubt. The temptation was there to be idyllically happy, such was the nature of the place; but as with many essentially placid people, Helen found that she did not like it when basic assumptions about what was normal were called into question, however obliquely. Matters had certainly not reached such a stage yet, but the signs were not encouraging. Not that anyone welcomed a war. The whole business was wretched. And Ireland was so beautiful, even if it was rather primitive. No doubt she would hear about the war that evening from John.

For John, routine was temporarily forgotten. The morning edition of the *Irish Times*, bought at Bray railway station, had some real news at last. Britain was at war with Germany – had been at war for nearly twenty-four hours. He would have been about to set out for the neighbouring farm to buy the chicken for their dinner at the moment when the British found themselves at war. He had hardly been thinking about the war at all at the time. Even during that weekend, when everything had hung in the balance, or so it seemed, and there was no certainty as to whether he would be able to stay in Ireland, he had found it impossible not to daydream about the future. If they stayed, they might go on a second honeymoon, down to the south-west perhaps, Killarney and Cork. They could make improvements to the cottage, modernise it, make it more comfortable to live in, so they could entertain friends there; and they would have a baby. The path he had been following crossed a field of barley, and he had stopped amid the sea of rich dark green and looked up at the sky where blazing white cumulus contrasted with summer blue. What was there about this place? There was something almost unworldly which seemed to charge the air, to move in the wind that bent the trees and the corn and brought the rain over the soft hills to Wicklow in eternal westerlies; something which taunted mortality; something which no man could capture, however many might try.

Mortality? Was that all it was? A fantasy created by the knowledge, the hope, that here, sanity would prevail? Mortality was the oldest of the gods, and the one who prevailed in the end. In the blinding whiteness, he saw an image of Helen, smiling and naked, her skin creamy soft, her body big with child, her breasts heavy with milk. When he touched her, her big round belly was gentle against him, her shoulders soft, her mouth warm and sweet – the sweetness of life. Why should any man be ashamed to want such sweetness? Why should any man be ashamed to have shared the life of his child, to have kissed his infant brow and shared his schooldays, to want no less for him in his life; and why should a child feel ashamed to have a father who bore him such love?

He saw his father's name on the plinth beneath the memorial outside the town hall. On that last night, before returning to the house, he had stood looking up at it for a minute, the letters barely discernible in the dim lamplight. There was no other memorial, no burial place; just a name on the plinth among 117 others; and a widow with a child in arms who did not understand what he had lost – the presence, the absence of the young man in uniform whose photograph had pride of place in the drawing room. It had been a last opportunity to say goodbye.

De Valera was keeping Ireland out of the war. It was the other main story on the front page, and he read it through again and again, savouring and weighing every word, judging it with doubt. But there seemed little room for doubt. Behind the statesman, and the politely turned phrases, there was, clearly discernible, the ghost of the old IRA man with a score to settle. There was much debate about the war emergency, but there was no doubting De Valera's determination to keep Ireland out of the war and neutral. It was just the way he had hoped it would be; but to see the real thing in newsprint on the front page of the *Irish Times*… The real thing: he raised the folded paper to his mouth and gently kissed it. Perhaps there were few who could have understood how he felt at that moment – the artist who has made good the creative idea; the refugee who has found sanctuary; the sinner who has been forgiven; the prophet who has been justified. He had played the world at its own game, and he had won. It was a rare delight. The Dublin train clanked into the station, and he wheeled his bicycle towards the guards van.

At St Mungo's, the atmosphere was subdued, but tense. The tension was inevitable, because of the general expectation that the headmaster would have to make a statement to the pupils and the school about the war. For a statement to be issued at all would be seen by some as partisan – only the British were at war, and only the unionists would expect a statement about it. But because the others saw no need for a statement made it all the more likely that one would be issued. The headmaster, Mr Crosby, was taking the matter seriously, and had spent the weekend drafting his statement. He was equally determined that a statement was necessary. At sixty-four, and as a product of Trinity College, he would, if asked, have described himself as British; but on another level, as Anglo-Irish. The distinction was a subtle one. It meant that he was not neutral – this was his war, and his loyalty was still to the crown. It was a loyalty tempered, however, as with most Anglo-Irish, by a certain contempt for the British. He had not forgotten the anguish he had felt as a teacher, at seeing boys whom he had known since they were eleven, leaving the school at eighteen as young officers and going straight to their deaths in France. They had all been volunteers; and they would be volunteers this time, too, De Valera's Eire notwithstanding. Any boy who chose not to go this time simply from cowardice would be diminished in his eyes as being unworthy of the school. But now the school was divided. Not all the pupils shared the same loyalties. During that weekend, Crosby realised that he no longer had the stomach for controversy. The endurance of the Free State, against expectation, had shaken the old certainties, and more parochial

31

interests had taken on a new value in consequence. Ireland was not in the war, and Crosby did not like to see his school divided. As with many who become tired of old prejudices, he took the view that compromise was morally superior. But he proved to be unequal to the task. He sought to broaden the basis of his appeal by asserting that it was not merely a matter of patriotism, but a war of reason and civilisation against barbarism and fascism. Criticism of Irish neutrality was thinly veiled.

"This is a war," he said, "in which every one of us is involved, because the values we hold dear, of our ancient freedoms and our democracy, are under attack. It is a war of civilisation against barbarism; of democracy against tyranny; of justice against injustice; of good against evil. The enemy we face is utterly determined, and only a united and unstinted effort by all those on the side of civilisation will enable us to prevail against this threat. There may be some who feel that they can sit back and let others defend civilisation. But my message to you today is that any from this school who do volunteer to serve will bring honour not only to themselves, but also to the school ..."

Afterwards, as John was leaving the hall, Carter stopped him in the corridor.

"What did you think of the old man?" His thin face was alive with interest.

"Well, it seemed mild enough, given that he felt it necessary to say something."

"Mild? It was a disaster. The old man's lost his touch completely. He was trying to avoid trouble, and he's just brought it on himself all the more. The unionists are seething because he didn't go far enough, and I know that some of the republican sympathisers will be issuing their own statement in the classrooms, telling the kids that the war is nothing to do with Ireland. There'll be trouble when the others find out about that – a lot of trouble." He paused, and looked at John quizzically. "What will you do?" he asked.

John affected surprise.

"Why should I be expected to do anything? I really can't see what all the fuss is about. It won't change anything."

"It might change things in here. Some of the sixth-form boys have already declared an intention of volunteering."

"On their own initiative?"

"Don't be daft man – it's glory; it's adventure; it's what every boy dreams of."

"Well, what do you expect me to do about it?"

"I didn't quite mean it that way."

"What way did you mean it, then?"

"Well …" Carter paused, somewhat embarrassed. "There's likely to be a general expectation that, as you're British, you'll set an example by volunteering yourself."

"General expectation?"

"Look, I'm not being personal. I'm telling you this for your benefit. You still seem to think you have nothing to do with all this."

"I think you've got the whole thing completely out of proportion. I'm a teacher, not a recruiting officer. And I thought you were supposed to be a republican sympathiser."

"And so I am, which is generally known. What isn't generally known is where you stand."

"I don't see that it's anyone else's business."

"Just like a bloody Englishman. You still haven't seen it yet, have you? There's a great deal of malice in this – more than, as an outsider, you probably imagined."

"Or, as an outsider, I might reasonably expect."

Carter shook his head. He seemed exasperated as much as anything else.

"You English divided this country, and we have to try and make some sense of it. That's where the malice comes from."

John was equally exasperated.

"I can't help you. You seem determined to make an issue out of something which is of no consequence."

Carter turned to go. "Well," he said, with a lugubrious look, "you said you were a teacher, not a recruiting officer. Could you be a teacher against a whispering in the classrooms that you're a coward because you haven't volunteered? That's what I mean by malice."

"That's outrageous. Even if I don't volunteer, it's nobody's business but mine. The speech by the Head was a long way from being a licence for that kind of prejudice."

"That's why some people are so dissatisfied. Sooner or later you'll have to take this seriously. The malice is a part of our way of life. You'll have to adapt to it or go under." He looked at his watch. "I'll have to go. I've got a class. I'll see you at lunch."

But John had mentally dismissed Carter as either a sensationalist or a troublemaker. How could he possibly be intimidated by these people? They were living in the past. If these were Irish republicans, he would have expected more of them than this carping fecklessness. Perhaps that was why the Irish had never amounted to anything – stabbing each other in the back had become too much of a way of life. St Mungo's was hardly representative of the new Ireland, and yet it contained the essence of the Irish dilemma – a little stronghold of patriots still loyal to a country which had forgotten their very existence, and would despise them if it knew of them. For they were also Irish – tainted, irredeemably tainted, with the land in their blood; with the damp, rain-laden Atlantic winds; with Derry, Drogheda and Kilkenny; Napper Tandy, Emmet and Wolfe Tone. They were a part of the whole, even if the whole was no longer theirs. Outside the gates, Ireland was Catholic, Celtic, republican and fecklessly anti-British: John carried with him that slight contempt that the English have for the Irish. He had no doubt at all that when the killing started in earnest, there would be a good deal of sober reflection on the virtues of neutrality.

4

Helen was ironing when John arrived home that evening. Outside the back door, lines of washing were still billowing in the wind, the remains of the last wash. The kitchen was hot and full of steam. Helen had had the stove going all day, first to heat water for the washing, then to cook the evening meal, and also to heat the iron warmer. Her face was flushed, and her forehead gleamed with sweat, but when John kissed her he noticed that she had the sweet clean smell of newly laundered linen. He had bought some lemonade in Dublin, and they both stood outside the back door drinking it, watching the washing billowing towards them over the vegetable patch, giving glimpses of the hills beyond. All the good weather they had had was having a beneficial effect on John. Helen gulped her lemonade, and not merely from thirst.

"I can't stand here, I'm afraid," she said. "I'll have to go in again, otherwise the meal will burn to a cinder."

John felt very relaxed, and after a minute, walked over to the washing and began to take down the items which had dried in the wind. He brought them into the kitchen and folded them into the orange box which was serving as a laundry basket, while he looked hungrily at the stove.

It was only after the meal that Helen asked about the war. She had even forgotten about it during the heat of the washing. It had not yet assumed for her the importance it held for John, and she did not yet perceive it as having impinged on her personally. It was still part of the outside world, an event larger than reality. But it could not be ignored.

John showed her the newspapers he had bought.

"How will it affect us?" she asked at length.

"It won't affect us at all particularly, at least, not at the moment." He pointed to the item containing De Valera's statement. Their previous conversation on Friday evening had ended inconclusively; this time, John felt he was on much firmer ground.

"Yes ..." She glanced through it again. "But ... won't you be called up?"

He shook his head. "I can't imagine so, at least, not as things are at present. As long as Ireland is neutral then it's most unlikely that they'll introduce conscription for their army. It's such a small country that it would hardly be worth the disruption. I'm sure it would be much better to rely on neutrality."

"Oh, you mean the Irish army." She gave a little laugh. "I don't think I even realised that they had one. No, I meant the British army."

"Oh, no, certainly not the British army. They can't conscript people in Ireland any more, at least, not in the Free State. That's one of the consequences of the Free State becoming independent. So, as long as Ireland remains neutral, it's unlikely that the war will have any direct effect on us."

"Will you join up anyway?"

John affected surprise.

"What on earth for? After all, we've only just got here. We're just starting our new life." He put his arms around her. "Aren't you happy here?"

"Oh, yes, it's wonderful. I've been very happy. After all the grime and greyness of the city it's like paradise. But won't everyone be feeling much the same? I mean, even if they're less fortunate than us, they won't want to have their lives disrupted by the war; but if there has to be a war to stop Hitler and his tyranny, then everyone will have to make sacrifices. I suppose most people would rather stay at home if they had the choice, but ..."

He kissed her lightly on the forehead and smiled broadly.

"You're quite right, my dear," he said, still smiling. "A lot of people will be making sacrifices and there will be a lot of disruption; but for the great majority of men in Britain, there will be no question of joining up. They won't be given the choice: they'll be conscripted. I'm quite certain that most of them wouldn't go if they weren't conscripted; but unfortunately for them, that's the price they have to pay for acquiescing in bad and venal politicians. It's not necessarily the fault of every one of them individually, but it's their bad luck to be living under such a government at a time like this. What I'm trying to explain is that it's different for us because we don't live there now. This is Ireland, not Britain, and our lives are here now. I'm sorry about the war, and I'm sorry for the people who have to take part in it, but I can't spend all my time being sorry. We have to get on with our own lives and make our own plans for the future."

He kissed her lightly again, and smiled again. Her responding smile had a little nervous resignation in it. He was very confident. She had not been sure quite what his response would be: she had not expected such a confident and reasoned response, and she realised that if she was to raise the matter again, it could only be after considerable thought. For the time being, evidently, the subject was closed.

September saw the return of Irish weather. The balmy days of late August were replaced, by the middle of September, by grey skies and seemingly endless rain. The long grass of the hay meadow became wet and dank and the cloud hung in lowering banks over the hills. The change affected Helen in particular, who was spending all day alone in the cottage with nothing but the now bleak-looking countryside to look out on. Some days she cycled into Bray to go shopping, but even Bray seemed chill in the rain – there was a tight, closed-up feeling in the wet streets where people hurried to get out of the rain, and hurried to get home. Helen had never thought that she would feel homesick for Manchester, but now there were times when she did. She missed the sensation of being enveloped in a city large enough to defy the elements, where the routine and bustle of a million people created a current of life that transcended that of the individual, and had the ability to lift the individual above herself by a power of communal spirit, real or imagined. In other moments, Helen knew she was romanticising. Even the war could not disguise the dark side of the city, and the war would also bring its own darkness. It did not do her any good to think about the war. She had an idea, as yet ill-defined and unfocused, that she and John ought to be playing their part instead of disappearing into the depths of the Irish countryside. What her part should be she could not have said; but there would be war work of some sort for women, she was sure. It would be disruptive of life, and possibly unpleasant, but at least she would once again be part of the community she was starting to feel homesick for. She had not immediately realised that being in Ireland would cut them off from all that. Her interest in and knowledge of Irish politics and history being almost nil, her view of Irish neutrality was essentially one of contempt.

John was quickly sensitive to her mood. It was not unexpected, and he did what he could about it. They started going to the cinema two or three times a week. There was a small cinema in Bray, but most weeks, especially on a Saturday evening, they would go into Dublin and visit one of the big cinemas in the city, and perhaps have a meal at a restaurant afterwards. This was not every week, as John could not have afforded it; but at least the visits to Dublin kept Helen in touch with the big-city life which she seemed to miss. In Dublin, they could watch the latest films, which would take a long time before they reached Bray. They saw *Stagecoach*, *Wuthering Heights* and *The Man in the Iron Mask*; they also saw newsreels which suggested that, following the fall of Poland in September, the war in Europe had pretty much fizzled out, and that Britain, France and Germany were left with a state of war which nobody wanted much, except the British and French politicians. John had a healthy respect for the stupidity of the politicians, however, and saw no reason to doubt the wisdom of the move to Ireland, or to regret it. He did, nevertheless, find grounds for a certain optimism in this state of affairs, particularly in relation to the effect of the war on Helen. He relaxed his natural caution to the extent of deciding to buy a small portable wireless to help relieve the monotony of Helen's daytime hours. He had previously been against the idea of a wireless because of the expectation that it would exacerbate the tensions between them that the war had produced, given that Helen would certainly listen to the BBC. But now the benefits seemed to outweigh the risks.

The wireless proved to be an undoubted success. Helen was delighted with it. She would often have it on in the evening as well as during the day, and while John did not find the endless dance band music and inane light entertainment which seemed to make up most of the BBC's output entirely to his liking, it did make the cottage more cheerful, particularly as the nights lengthened, and the darkness started to draw in as the autumn advanced. He tried listening to Irish radio, but that was no better. They did listen to Irish radio, however, particularly in the evening when John influenced the choice of listening, especially to hear the news programmes. He found the contrast between British and Irish coverage of the news both interesting and useful. The BBC was now subject to an official censor, but the insidious effect of this was only apparent when one contrasted the BBC with Irish radio, which broadcast reports from both sides in the war. John took care to make sure that Helen noticed and understood the difference and the reasons for it. She listened mostly to the BBC during the day, and he was concerned to ensure that the negative effects of British propaganda were undermined as far as possible by the sobering comparison with Irish objectivity.

Not that Helen was entirely idle during the day. In addition to housework and shopping, their vegetable garden was starting to bear fruit, so much so that it was producing more than the two of them could consume. Helen even took some of the surplus into Bray, piled high on a tray fastened to the luggage rack of her bicycle, to try and sell it to local greengrocers; but she had limited success, and ended up virtually giving it away. There was no shortage of food in Ireland, and certainly no shortage of vegetables. John derived a certain private satisfaction from this when she told him about it, despite her evident disappointment. The effects of wartime restrictions in Britain were becoming increasingly evident, even in the eternally optimistic bonhomie of the BBC; and to have the abundance of food in Ireland demonstrated to Helen in so pointed a way was, John felt, another small victory in a good cause.

The war would not go away, however, and eventually it intruded in an unexpected way. Since they had moved to Ireland, Helen had continued to correspond, as she had done before, with her parents. Having lived all their working lives in Stretford, where Helen herself had been born and brought up, Helen's parents, and principally her father, had started out as people of no consequence, and had retired as people of some consequence, at least financially. They had bought a retirement home in the country, in Cheshire. Retiring to the country was not just a status symbol, although it was that too.

Certain places were fashionable and had become blighted with retirement houses for the undiscerning; but some, like Helen's parents, became genteel in their retirement, and their main motive was to get away from the unpleasantness of living in close proximity with the lower classes. Although the city had its prosperous suburbs, the only sure way of getting away was to get right away, into the depths of the countryside. They had found their refuge in rural south Cheshire, on the outskirts of Nantwich, in a place where they were as likely to be troubled by the unclean denizens of Stretford as by the German air force. The advent of war, however, had brought about the unlikely. It had taken the authorities some little while to work their way down to Nantwich, but when they did reach it, the distress signals were immediately forthcoming. On a Thursday morning in late October, Helen received a letter from her mother describing how, with virtually no warning, they had had a woman and three children from Salford quartered on them as evacuees. They were of the worst sort – the children being particularly obnoxious; but the evacuation officer had been unsympathetic and uninterested in the protests of Helen's parents that in their failing state of health they were quite unable to cope with the noise, the rowdyism and the violation of their privacy. He merely threatened them with prosecution if they contravened the evacuation order. By the time Helen's mother wrote to her daughter, she was already nearly at the end of her tether.

Helen read the letter in horror. All the unsettled feelings she had had about being cut off from her community, and not playing her part in the war, were brought into focus for the first time by this letter. She felt that she could sit by no longer. It was almost as if she had been woken from a great sleep, and at first she was confused, and was not sure what to do. Initially, her distress was such that she would have quickly packed a small bag and left immediately, to make her way back to

England as best she could. By the time she had packed the bag, however, she was calmer. She could not just leave and allow John to arrive home and find himself abandoned. Also, she would need money. Even if they waited until tomorrow to travel, it would not make a lot of difference. They would go tomorrow. Early in the afternoon, however, she had another piece of inspiration – she could send a telegram. Within five minutes of having the thought she was on her bicycle on her way to Bray post office. 'Your letter received. Am coming at once. Helen.' she telegraphed. She could not let them down now. Back at the cottage, she packed a bag for John, too, so that there might be no delay in case it might be possible to travel that night. Then she impatiently awaited his return. It was only shortly before four o'clock that she decided that, whether they travelled that night or not, it would be best if they ate first. She was still preparing the meal when John arrived home. By this time she was much calmer and more settled – she could see the matter clearly in her own mind, and was more confident as a result. It was John's turn to be confused and anxious, although at that moment, he could not tell her the real reason for this. Helen was less than tactful, however.

"We'll have to go back to England at once – something dreadful's happened," was how she greeted him. She thrust her mother's letter into his hand, and went back to what she was doing while he read it. John scanned the letter with a sinking heart. This was something he was not prepared for. He had mentally anticipated the likelihood of trouble at some stage, but he was not prepared for the suddenness of this. His worst fears had burst upon him in a moment, and for a moment, he felt defeated.

John made himself a cup of tea, and took the letter into the living room where he sat down to peruse it again. The nature of the plight of Helen's parents made it all the more

43

difficult. He had genuine sympathy for the obvious horror they were suffering; but at the same time, everything he heard about what was now going on in England, this included, only confirmed the wisdom of his decision to get out. In England itself, things had got worse more quickly than the last time, and although the killing had not really started in earnest yet, that would no doubt follow before long. Large numbers of men were now being conscripted, and if he had not already been called up, his call-up would be imminent. It would not be safe for him to go back to England. He had managed to get out, and he must now stay out, whatever happened. The position was simply stated. What was he to say to Helen? She was apparently intending to go to England at once, presumably on the morrow. He was uneasy and unhappy about the idea, even though he understood the necessity of it. Indeed, if she was to go at all, the sooner she went, the sooner the matter could be sorted out. But he had to tell her that he could not go with her.

Helen came into the living room. "Well?" she asked expectantly.

He nodded slowly. "It's a bad business. But then, everything over there seems to be a bad business now. The whole country seems to have gone mad."

"We must go to them at once. Tomorrow. They're old people and they can't cope with that sort of thing. It's cruel that they should be expected to. We must go tomorrow."

He nodded again. "I agree, the sooner they get help, the better. But we'll have to put our thinking caps on for this one. It's important that we have a fairly clear idea in advance of how we're going to deal with the problem."

"What do you mean?"

"Well, your mother says here that the evacuation officer threatened them with prosecution if they contravened the order. We can't just ask these people to leave – they've

44

apparently now got a legal right to live in your parents' house. That's what I meant about the country going mad. We'll have to think of something a little more devious. Give me an hour or so, and I'll try to work something out."

"Alright. But can't we do that on the way?"

"It's best to work out as far as you can what you are going to do beforehand. I'll have to tell you what I think is the best way tonight. You must go back to England tomorrow and get to Nantwich as soon as you can. I can't travel with you tomorrow. I can't just abandon my job. I've not asked for leave tomorrow, and it's unlikely I'd get leave on compassionate grounds."

"Oh!" Helen had evidently not considered this aspect of the matter. "How soon will you be able to get leave?"

"I don't know. I haven't taken any leave yet, so I don't know the procedure. At the university you had to give at least a week's notice, unless it was on compassionate grounds. That usually meant the death of a close relative."

"Wouldn't they count this as compassionate grounds? It's awful what's happened."

"I know. But it's not a death, and it's happening to thousands of people. It's just part of the war."

"It's not happening to thousands of people in Ireland," she said, in a flash of inspiration.

He sighed. "It's not Ireland's war. Look darling, at the moment I don't know when I'll be able to get leave. It might be the day after tomorrow. It mightn't be until next week. You can't wait for that. You must go tomorrow. I'll figure out the best plan of action if you'll give me an hour or two to think."

"Well, alright. But I hope it's not going to be two weeks before you can get any leave."

"I honestly don't know what the position is until I ask tomorrow."

"Suppose you were to join the army," she said suddenly.

45

"We could both go tomorrow then. You could join up straight away, and then you could just forget about this job."

He looked at her angrily. "That's about the daftest thing I've ever heard you say. First of all, I wouldn't be able to help you at all if I was stuck in an army camp somewhere hundreds of miles away – and the army certainly wouldn't give me leave for something like this." He waved the letter at her. "Secondly, after the war, if there was any afterwards, I would very likely be blacklisted for employment if I'd just walked out of this job without even giving notice. Employers don't like that kind of thing, and it would be remembered."

"Even if you'd fought in the war for your country?"

"There was no shortage of unemployed ex-soldiers after the last time, and there won't be after this lot either. I've no intention of being one of them. Also, this job is important to me, and I've no intention of just walking out of it, so any suggestion of that sort is completely out of court."

"So you won't be coming tomorrow?"

"I can't come tomorrow. You must go, however. What I will do is to try to think of some way of getting these people out of your parents' house without incurring some legal penalty."

The subject was closed. John felt that, on balance, he had won this round also, but at a cost. This time there had been a price to pay, and it did not bode well for the future.

5

They were both up very early the following morning, so that John would have time to see Helen off before going into work. It was a tense parting outside the shipping offices. John could not help but see it as the unravelling of what he had achieved. He was still the victim of his own indecision, reluctant to face the weakness at the centre of their relationship: that he did not trust her to accept him as he was. His only distinction was that he had chosen this way rather than the way of the majority. If that, thrown in the balance against him, was to outweigh everything else, then he was estranged indeed – a dreamer for whom love was an earthly paradise, requiring only that the love of another should be unconditional to be complete in itself. If it were not so, then everything was ashes.

For Helen, the nightmare of the journey began almost at once. The ferry to Liverpool she had booked for was due to sail at 9 am. It eventually sailed at twenty past three in the afternoon, because of a scare about German submarines in the Irish Sea. When the ferry reached Liverpool, it was the early hours of the following morning, and the ship didn't berth until dawn because of the blackout regulations. Even then it was not over. Tired, and suffering the after-effects of prolonged seasickness, Helen found that to travel the forty or so miles to Nantwich would be a major operation. Trains were either cancelled or running so late that timetables ceased to have any meaning. It would be a matter of luck if she could find a train going to somewhere she wanted to go to, and even greater luck if there was a connecting train. The war seemed to have produced a paralysis of bureaucracy in the name of military efficiency and security. She was challenged, by people who seemed no better than busybodies, because she did not have a gas mask or identity documents, which apparently had been issued to everyone while she had been away. She had come home to find that she was a stranger, even an alien, in her own country, and she found that disturbingly unsettling. She was not sure whether to give way to exasperation because of the chaos, or to blame John for having separated her from the mainstream of the life of the country, however unpleasant, by taking her to the backwater of Ireland.

When she reached her parents' house it was early afternoon, and she was well-nigh exhausted. She hesitated at the gate. She felt quite unequal to the prospect of dealing with some foul-mouthed harpy from the back streets of Salford, especially one who had been given the idea that she had some power over Helen's parents. She drew a deep breath. She had pleasant memories of this house, and she was not looking forward to seeing the place violated. But when the door was opened in response to her knock, to her surprise, it was opened by John's cousin Henry Stanford.

"Hello, Helen."

"Henry!"

She had hesitated for a moment, doubtful of whom it was. She hadn't seen Henry for some time, and she had only met him a few times. He was about five years older than John, but he had much more than the advantage of five years. He worked for Refuge Assurance on Oxford Road in Manchester, had been married twice, and now lived with his second wife in a big rambling detached house on the outskirts of Bowdon. Being very much better off than she and John were, and moving in different circles in consequence, he was not someone they saw very often; but Helen had always liked him.

"Henry – it is Henry, isn't it?"

"It is. You look worn out. Come on in."

He reached forward and took her suitcase off her and ushered her through the door. The next minute she was in the living room and in her father's arms.

"Helen! Oh, my love, I'm so glad to see you!"

"Dad!"

"We got your telegram. You've no idea how much it meant to us."

"How are you?" She looked at him with concern. He did not look well. "Where's Mum?"

"Your mum's upstairs in bed. She's been hit bad by this business, and she's going to need time to get over it."

"Can I go up and see her? But ... Where are the ... ?"

"They've gone," said Henry.

"Gone – you mean for good?"

"I think so, yes."

"What happened?"

"Well, to start from the beginning, I received a telephone call from John yesterday – that was Friday. He was speaking from Dublin. He told me as briefly as he could what had happened, said he wasn't able to leave at such short notice, but that you would be coming over, and asked me if I would go down to see what I could do to sort things out."

"Did he say why he couldn't come at such short notice?" Helen asked.

"No." Henry was obviously surprised by the question. "Didn't he tell you?"

"Oh, yes. He gave me his reasons."

Henry was still looking at her curiously.

"I just wondered if he'd explained it to you, that's all," she said.

49

"Well, no – he was trying to be as brief as possible. They charge for telephone calls from Ireland at international rates these days. His main concern was to explain the problem, and to ask if I'd come down here to sort it out."

"Which you have done."

"Well …" Henry was all modesty. "It was no great matter in the end. I think your mum and dad allowed themselves to be over-intimidated by the evacuation officer. I made one or two checks before I came down, and it seemed to me that, with a bit of luck, it wouldn't be all that difficult; and so it proved. Technically, they may have had a right to be billeted here with a minimum subsistence, but that didn't mean that we didn't have a right to charge them for extras such as hot water, laundry service, additional heating, and also breakages. Those brats she brought with her were appalling, but their tendency to break things was their undoing. When they broke the crystal vase that was kept on the dining room sideboard, I demanded compensation from the woman – threatened to take her to court if she didn't pay. Of course she couldn't pay and it frightened her, and that did the trick. They must have done a bunk in the night – they were gone by this morning."

"And you think that's the last of them?"

"I'm sure of it."

"You don't look too sure," Helen said, looking at him.

Henry opened his hands in a gesture of exasperation.

"It's not so much about them, as about the position for the future. This sort of thing didn't happen in the Great War, and one wonders what else might befall. It's not that I'm being unpatriotic – we all have to do our duty now the country's at war; but one does wish that there could be a little compassion shown where there's room for it."

Helen nodded emphatically, but her father gave a wry smile.

"It may not be as bad as you think, lad," he said. "It may be that the way it's turned out is for the best after all."

They both looked at him expectantly.

"Well, for a start, you're wrong about the Great War. It did happen then – only then, it was mostly soldiers, not civilians. There wasn't very much of it, I grant you, because most soldiers were sent to the front – certainly nothing like the scale of this business – but in a way, that meant it was resented all the more by those who had to suffer it. And there was no scaring soldiers away like this woman with her kids."

"You didn't have soldiers billeted on you, did you?"

"Oh, no, we didn't, but we knew of people who did. But what I meant just now was that, although I found this woman obnoxious and hated her being here, I'm pretty certain that she felt much the same way. She only came because she'd been ordered to, and she was afraid of the law. A lot of these lower class evacuees feel lost away from their own back streets, however squalid – away from their own community. I'm quite sure she's gone straight back to Salford, and was glad to get back. She won't say anything to the authorities because she'll be afraid of being punished for breaking the evacuation order. That may mean that, if she's officially still billeted here, the authorities won't billet anyone else on us."

"You've been thinking it all out, haven't you, you old rascal," Helen said with a smile. She kissed him again; but suddenly he stood back, his face changed and serious.

"Now, don't misunderstand me," he said. "I can't deny that I'm extremely grateful for what Henry has done; in fact, I don't know how we would have carried on if those people had stayed. But that doesn't mean that we're trying to avoid our responsibilities. We'd still be prepared to take in a decent, genteel person, if the authorities would have the sense to put like with like, instead of trying to force quite unsuitable people together, regardless of whether they will get on."

"I quite agree," said Henry. "We all have to do our bit to help win this war, but that doesn't mean the authorities shouldn't use a bit of imagination as well."

Helen suddenly felt self-conscious. The fact that she and John had been languishing in Ireland since the beginning of the war had not so far produced any comment; but she was conscious of a sense of loss at not having shared the experiences of these last weeks and months with her family and her community. She was conscious of resentment against John for having put her into such a position, and of embarrassment about having, in effect, evaded her duty, as she now saw it.

It was not until later that the subject came up in conversation. Henry was to stay overnight, and so would dine with them that evening. Helen's mother did not feel well enough to come downstairs, so there were just the three of them at dinner.

"You've not said very much about yourself, Helen love," said her father. "How are you managing in Ireland?"

"Oh, not too badly. We've got a cottage just outside Bray, which is south of Dublin on the coast." (This for Henry's benefit.) "It's a bit isolated, and it gets lonely during the day sometimes, especially now the bad weather's coming with winter. But, all in all, we're happy enough, I suppose."

"John's teaching at a school, I believe," said Henry.

"That's right. St Mungo's School in south Dublin. It's a private school for non-Catholic children – rather an exclusive school, actually."

"But not the same as the university, surely."

"No, no … I suppose not. But it's what he wanted to do."

"It seems a strange move, nevertheless. Do you know what the reason for it was? I mean, was his position at the university in doubt?"

"Oh, no. It was nothing like that."

She remembered the night when he came back to the

house; when they left for Ireland – the fear, almost terror of that night. But that terror was still a private matter between husband and wife. She could not speak of it here.

"The reasons were on his side rather than the university's. He wanted a complete change of scene, and this was what came up." She was still protecting him, and she felt ashamed.

"But he'll be coming back for the war, presumably." Henry did not seem inclined to drop the subject. "I mean, it looks as if Ireland's going to stay neutral in all this – trust the bloody Irish to stab us in the back. So, he'll be coming back here fairly soon to join up, I expect?"

Helen didn't know what to say. Here in England, Henry's sentiments sounded perfectly reasonable, and here at least, she found that they were her own sentiments also. It was in part a matter of pride, particularly in the eyes of other women, as well as those of her family, however apprehensive she might be about the prospect of widowhood. It occurred to her then that John had not really taken her point of view into account: he was only concerned about his own reasons for being in Ireland, and however persuasive they might seem over there in his presence, over here they seemed less and less honourable. She knew intuitively that John would not be coming back for the war, and she had to think quickly about what she should say. If she could just say enough to avoid any embarrassment about the matter, perhaps that would be enough.

"I expect he will, yes. To be honest, he hasn't said very much about it, but I expect he will in due course."

"And will you stay in Ireland when he does come?" her father asked. "Would you be able to manage over there on your own? I don't have to tell you that there's always a home for you here, love, and you'll always be welcome. It'd be easier for John, too, when he was home on leave, than having to go across to Ireland to see you."

"Oh, yes, I suppose that's right. I hadn't thought of it that way." She was nervous and flustered, and she hoped it didn't show. "As I said, we haven't talked about the war very much. It's not seen as being so important over in Ireland because we ... I mean, Ireland, isn't in the war. People just don't talk about it in the same way as over here."

"Well, I hope you'll not let John forget his duty – although I'm sure there'll be no need for you to remind him," said Henry.

"Oh, I'm sure," said Helen, brightly. "Have you joined up yet, Henry?" This with a tiny bit of malice for the embarrassment of the last few minutes; but there was no catching Henry in that way.

"I have indeed. I volunteered for the navy in September, and I'm waiting for my posting to come through. You're given some choice when you volunteer – you should mention that to John, too – and I asked for a posting in destroyers. I reckon there's more chance of action and promotion in the small ships than in the battleships and cruisers, so I've gone for a destroyer posting. Perhaps you could recommend that to John, if he's interested in the navy. We might even be posted to the same ship."

"Oh, I'm sure he'd like that," Helen said, still with the bright smile.

Later, however, when she and Henry were alone for a few minutes, Henry was more frank.

"Look, Helen, I hope you don't mind my having made a bit of a thing about this earlier, especially at a time like this. But, to tell you the truth, I've been a bit concerned about John. I was more than a little surprised when he suddenly left the university to go to this teaching post in Ireland, which must have been something of an unknown quantity, especially with the outbreak of war following on so soon afterwards. Make no mistake, John had a good position at the university, and if you want to keep a position like that, and have a chance of advancement, you have to do the right things. I'm afraid that a move like this, to this backwater of a place in Ireland will have harmed his career considerably – in fact, under normal circumstances, it would have finished him. People remember things like that, and they're held against you. A university may seem like a quiet, cloistered existence, but behind the cloisters it can be as cutthroat as an advertising agency, and under normal circumstances, a move such as John's just made would be virtual suicide, career-wise. So you see, John's been very lucky that the war has come when it has. Everyone will be going into the army or the navy or the air force, and what happened before won't matter so much. A good war service record should put John back on his feet again. Now, you'll not fail to make the point to him when you go back, will you?"

"Oh, no, indeed, I entirely take your point."

"I'm sure John won't mind a bit of good advice, coming from me. He'll know I have his best interests at heart. The other point is that, as I said before, it does make a difference if you volunteer. It doesn't just mean that you have a choice, to a certain extent, of what you do, but it also makes a difference to your service record. It won't do John any good at all if he waits until he's called up. It'll look far better on his record if he volunteers. Really, he's waited rather too long already, and the longer he waits, the more it'll look as if he's skulking in Ireland hoping the war will go away or end before he gets involved, and, well, I don't need to tell you how bad that would be. So, you see how important it is for you to come back to England as soon as possible?"

"Oh yes, I do see, and I shall speak to John about it," she said, maintaining the bright tone in her voice.

"Well, I'm sure you will do. I hope you don't mind me having made a bit of an issue about this. It's just that I wanted to be sure you'll pass on what I've said to John."

55

"I'll certainly speak to John and tell him what you've said."

Helen's thoughts were in confusion. Instead of being able to unburden herself as she had expected, she found herself tongue-tied by a desire to protect John, even though she herself agreed with everything that Henry had said. It was still a private matter between John and her, and would remain so at least until she had seen him again.

Helen remained with her parents for a few days to ensure that they had recovered from their ordeal. Henry had returned home on the Sunday afternoon. His parting words to her had been: "Tell John to look me up as soon as you get back to England, and I'll see what I can do for him – but don't leave it too long!"

The journey back was as much of an ordeal as the journey out had been. This time, she booked a night crossing; but the ferry was still delayed for three hours because of a scare about enemy submarines. In addition to the physical discomforts of the journey, she had the burden of what she would have to say to John when she got back. The experience of having been cut off from her community by their sojourn in Ireland was still a strong influence on her; but even more atavistic emotions had been brought out by the experience of the past few days. Helen was a conventional woman, and entirely shared the conventional view of a woman's place in society. Women were quieter creatures than men, less inclined to exchange certainty for excitement, and the lot of women was therefore entirely acceptable. For those poor souls whose craving for excitement would not let them accept their lot, then the opportunities were there if they wanted them badly enough – they usually had the choice. Men didn't have such a choice, and it was right that they should not have. Helen's view of a woman's place and a woman's role was complemented by an equally conventional view of a man's place and a man's role in society. She was beginning to understand that her feelings for John were based on an assumption that he would naturally conform to those conventions; and the idea that he might not was causing her increasing disquiet.

Helen arrived back at the cottage on the Thursday morning of that week. John would have left for work a couple of hours earlier, and so the cottage was empty. She had been away for nearly a week, and she looked round for evidence of how he had fared while she had been gone. The cottage had an un-lived-in feel about it, as though it had been waiting for her to come back and fill it with her warmth and her life again. There was little evidence of John having been there at all while she had been away. It was as if he had reverted to what he would become without her almost as soon as she had gone: a single man, or a man on his own is a very transitory creature.

She made herself a cup of tea, and then went to bed, as she was very tired after the journey. She slept for several hours, and woke feeling refreshed; but the remembrance of the matter between her and John returned and settled on her like a millstone. She felt increasingly nervous and tense as the usual time of John's homecoming drew near. She prepared the evening meal and set the table, then sat down to wait. She tried to read a newspaper she had bought on the journey that morning, but she couldn't concentrate on it and put it aside. It was only at such moments that she could focus on the reason for her apprehension – that she was being forced to question the basis of her marriage, and she could not foresee the outcome. She felt miserable about it, but it was equally clear that there was nothing else she could do.

At the usual time she heard the click of the latch on the front gate, and a minute later John was coming in through the back door, stamping his feet on the mat and pulling his gloves off. He seemed pleased to see her – they embraced, and he kissed her.

"I've missed you," he said. "How was the journey?"

"Oh, pretty rough. There were endless delays because of scares about enemy submarines, and coming back it was a rough crossing."

"Well, you're back now, anyway. What about the problem – the evacuees?"

"That's been sorted out. I'll tell you about it over tea."

Helen didn't say anything at first about her conversations with Henry. She described how the evacuees had been got rid of, and how her parents had been; but from the start, she was full of praise for Henry. She wanted to build him up with praise before broaching the subject she had discussed with him.

John heard about Henry's success with the evacuees with satisfaction. He felt that it provided justification enough for his decision to remain in Ireland. He was not, however, ingenuous enough to think that that would be the end of it. He had guessed fairly shrewdly about the kind of experiences Helen would have on her return to England, and the likely effect on her. It was sobering for him to realise that he still did not know her well enough to be sure of what her reaction would be, but he had taken the whole business very seriously indeed. He had to come up with something positive to counter what he expected her to say. The idea was simple enough. What gave him the confidence he now felt was the luck he had had in giving it substance.

"I've got a surprise for you," he said as they were having coffee after the meal. Helen was feeling at her most tense – this was her moment to speak. She did not want to be distracted now, but John seemed in buoyant mood.

"I've been thinking a lot about how unsatisfactory it is for you to be cooped up here all day, especially in the winter. You've said yourself that you've found it depressing at times, and I think it would be good if you could get out during the day. In fact, what you could do with is a job, and that's exactly what the surprise is. I've managed to get you a job."

"Me – a job?" She was somewhat taken aback.

"Yes. I'm sure it'll do you the world of good. Take you out of yourself."

"What sort of job is it?" She didn't want to go down this road at all.

"It's a library assistant at the public library in Bray. It's only part time, so it won't tie you down too much."

Helen still didn't know what to say.

"Well, it's very kind of you, dear, because I know you'll have gone to a lot of trouble; but I do think you might have consulted me first. After all, I may not be ready for this yet."

"No, no, that's alright." John waved a conciliatory hand. "I haven't presented you with a *fait accompli* or anything like that. I mean, I've not signed you up for anything. I got to know about this job through a contact at the school – that's the way these things usually happen." (It had in fact been rather more complicated than that, but this was not the time for such details.) "I said I thought you'd be interested, so what I got unofficially was the chance for you to have first refusal of the job, if you want it. If you don't, well, there's no harm done. It's entirely up to you, love."

"Well…" At least it was a way in to what she wanted to talk about. "Well, I do appreciate what you've done very much, and if things had been different, I would be delighted about it. But, if I were to take this job, it would increase our commitments here at a time when we should be preparing to return home."

"Return home? I don't understand. This is home."

"I mean, return to England."

"Now, Helen, I thought we'd been over all this."

"I know, but, I feel I know more about it all after the visit I've just made."

"Go on."

"You perhaps don't realise how much has changed in England, even in the short time since we left. It's no longer just preparation for war. Now that the war has actually started,

59

it totally dominates everything. There are soldiers and policemen everywhere, and there are all kinds of wartime restrictions and regulations. Everyone's supposed to carry a gas mask and a National Identity Card, and you're constantly asked to show your Identity Card or other documents. I had a dreadful time, particularly on the journey out, because I don't have any of these things. I suppose because I'm obviously English, they gave me the benefit of the doubt; but there's widespread alarm, almost paranoia, about German spies and fifth columnists. But, in spite of the unpleasantness of all that, I also felt that I was missing something positive, which has also come out of the war. There's a tremendous spirit of community which has been brought out by the war. The war affects everyone and all aspects of life, and because the war now dominates everything, the shared experience has brought people closer together, into a real community again. I felt very much that I'd missed that because I'd been out of it over here. I felt that, at a time like this, we should be with our own community, sharing the experiences with them."

"I think you've forgotten the reason why you went back to England. It seems that this community of yours is all very fine and cosy as long as it doesn't involve too close an acquaintance with the back streets of Salford and the like."

"You're twisting what I said. You know what I mean."

"Are you saying that we should return to England merely to enjoy a bit of community spirit?"

"You shouldn't make fun of it. I think it's important – perhaps more important than you realise. But it isn't the only reason, no. There's something else."

"Something else?"

She told him then about her conversations with Henry, and what he had advised John to do.

"So, you see," she concluded, "if we don't go back soon, you won't be able to volunteer, and an important opportunity will be lost. We must finish here and go back to England as soon as possible. You do see why that's important, don't you?"

John walked over to the window, and looked out over their back garden, now gloomy in the last of the twilight. The ordered rows of vegetables looked shaken after their first encounter with the autumn gales; and beyond them, the long grass of the meadow brooded sullenly in battered, unkempt Irish wildness. The distant hills were a dim silhouette under an oppressively dark sky, cold with a cold wind shot with rain. It looked a drear place; indeed, he could not have imagined, when he had first seen it back in the summer, that it could look so drear. Yet this was his refuge, the only place he could look upon as a refuge. But now, there was something beyond that. There was something about this place, this landscape, even in the dreariest light of autumn, which spoke to him. Something deep inside him had been stirred by it, and he knew, without being able to put the feeling into words, that this was where he belonged.

His mind was already made up. It only remained to see what Helen's choice would be.

"Have you some idea of what you would do? If you went back, I mean."

"I don't ... I'm not sure ..."

She was disagreeably startled, not only by his question, but by the tone of his voice.

"If you go back to England, Helen, you go back alone. I have no intention of going back. I didn't come here on an idle whim. I have particular plans for my life, and I've come to Ireland because, as things have fallen out, Ireland is the only place where I can fulfil those plans. Those plans do include you. You play a very important part in them. They're based on the assumption that you will be my wife. My plans include things I want to achieve in the world: books I want to write, ideas I want to explore. They include time to get to know as

61

much as I can of the great works of literature and philosophy, theatre, music, art; time to find out more about the world and its splendours. My plans also include some very ordinary aspirations: to be a father; to have a child, perhaps two children; to know the happiness of family life; to know the pleasure of being able to hug my wife and children; to watch my children grow up, and share in all the stages of their lives; to have the memories of all those times as well as their real presence as a source of strength and comfort in my old age. These are my plans; plans which any normal, sane, civilised man might have. I offer them to you as my wife, to share with me, in the hope that you are also a sane and civilised human being. You must know, having just come back from there, that it's no longer possible to pursue such plans in England, because England is no longer a sane and civilised place. It's a place which, as you've seen yourself, has gone mad – a place afflicted with the madness of war. Let me make it clear to you, Helen, as clear as I possibly can, that I have no intention of spending years of the best part of my life living like an animal among the rats and the filth and the degradation and the fear of the trenches in France, eventually to be mutilated or killed, ostensibly for the sake of some distant country I know nothing of and care less about. I don't intend to throw my life away just because some idiot politicians have decided they want to have a war. So, I have no intention of returning to England."

"Then they'll say you're a coward. And how will I be able to hold my head up when I'm taunted that my husband is a coward?"

"Is that all you can think of? And how dare you throw that accusation at me? You know very well that if we went back to England, you wouldn't have to face the horror of the war; but you seem keen, almost eager, to consign me to it. Do I mean as little to you as that? Are you more concerned about your social reputation than about your husband?"

"That's not fair. And nor is it reasonable. Millions of men, ordinary men, as you put it, will be going to the war, many willingly like Henry, because they know it's their duty to fight for their country."

"Fight? What are they fighting for?"

"To defend their country, of course. And to stop Hitler."

"No-one's threatening their country at the moment, not even the Germans. And I've nothing against Hitler – he's never done me any harm. The only thing I've got against the Germans is that they killed my father; and I don't hold the Germans as being anywhere near as responsible for that as I hold the British Government, which sent millions of young men to death and mutilation in a useless, stupid, criminal bloody war, which achieved absolutely nothing and destroyed countless innocent lives. And now they're trying to do it again. Well, I'm afraid they've shot their bolt. Those of us who've still got the sense to think are wise to them this time, and we're not going to be taken in a second time. If Mr Chamberlain wants to have a war, then that's his business; but I've no intention whatsoever of fighting it for him. I'm staying here in Ireland because this is where my future is. Ireland is my country now, not England; and if England gets itself involved in a war, that's no longer anything to do with me. If you can't bear the thought of what that will do to your social reputation, then you'd better go. And if you are going, you'd better go now. I don't want to live with a woman who's ashamed of me."

He turned away from her and went into the hall and came back with his hat and coat. He stopped and looked at her as he put his coat on.

"I mean what I say. If you're going back to England, then go now. I'm going to the Queen's in Bray for an hour or two. If you're ashamed to be my wife, then I don't want to find you in the house when I get back. There's some money." He put some banknotes on the kitchen table. "You can put up in an hotel overnight."

He crammed his hat onto his head, and walked out into the windswept darkness.

Helen remained motionless where she stood for long after the sound of John's footsteps had died away. A tide of shock spread out from where it burned in the pit of her stomach, until it engulfed her whole body. At last, the pain of it forced her to move, and she paced round and round the kitchen table, as shock verged on panic. She did not even understand why she felt the way she did. She had perhaps expected John to be sullenly stubborn, or to acquiesce; indeed, she had even expected to prevail in the argument. She had not been prepared for this. Suddenly, she was staring into an abyss. It was an abyss of her own making, and yet her confusion stemmed in part from disbelief. She was a woman, and a woman had a right to certain expectations. John had roughly denied those expectations, in a way which had done violence to her womanhood, and her pride. Her pride was suddenly very important to her, and she had to decide now, before John came back, whether it would hurt more if she stayed or if she left. She understood John well enough to know that she would have to decide now. This was no tiff or tantrum – it was deadly serious. She had forced him onto the defensive in a matter which went to the heart of his being, and having done so, she could not now avoid the consequences of it. That was her abyss – she must deny her pride, or a part of herself.

She pressed her hands to her head, as if to try and control the turbulence of her thoughts. It was too soon; it was too sudden. She dared not look at the money on the table. It represented her pride – it also represented what she feared of the abyss. Would England be the same for her without John? All the men would be going away to the war. What would her position be then? She hadn't counted on the force of John's reaction, or its effect on her. She hadn't intended it to be like this. Once she left, she could not see how she could return – it would be a matter of pride. Indeed, everything would then be a matter of pride, and pride might prove a very thin gruel for subsistence for one in such a position. This was not how she had worked it out in her mind on the long journey back from England. The issues had seemed clearer then, and she was more sure of her position.

If she stayed, how would she live with the sense of wrong within her? How would she, if she stayed, greet John when he returned? If she was still there when John returned, he would assume that the subject was closed. He had given her a choice, and if she chose to stay, then it would be on his terms. The matter touched him so deeply that she sensed that he would not expect a word to be uttered about it – assumptions would be made, and they would carry on on the basis of those. But she knew that for her, in the end, that would not be acceptable. To continue their relationship on the basis that they were 'just trying to carry on' when something central between them had gone sour would, she felt, be impossible. Something would have to be said, at least. She did not know if she was capable of doing it, or of facing such a future.

She felt alone and resentful. If they had been in England, she would not be in this position. All the pressure would be on John, not on her. He would be forced to do his duty, or justify why he should not. Here, all the pressure was on her, or so it seemed.

Suddenly, she knew that it was impossible for her to decide the matter there, in that dimly lit kitchen, in that house. The place had suddenly become a prison, a hateful place where she was forced to break herself on a wheel of her own making – but in truth, of John's making. Without even pausing to get her raincoat, or to put out the lamp, she walked out into the night.

6

After the wind and the rain, John found the lounge bar of the Queen's Hotel a sudden haven of quiet. The Queen's was an old established hotel, and its lounge bar was much the sort of place John had found congenial in England. It reminded him somewhat of the lounge bar of the Midland Hotel in Manchester, where he used sometimes to go in the intervals of Halle concerts at the Free Trade Hall. Such places had plush seats, armchairs, prints of sailing ships on the wall, and the bar was brightly lit, with the light gleaming on glass and polished mirrors. Prices were usually higher than in the public bar, and the barman had plenty of time to polish the glasses. The lounge bar of the Queen's had been a welcome discovery shortly after he had arrived at the cottage. He would occasionally call in on his way home from work for a quiet half hour over a pint of mild; and sometimes he and Helen would call in on their way home from the cinema in Dublin on a Saturday night. It was one of the many small things of which a true civilisation is constituted.

John had arrived wet and cold, and after ordering at the bar, had hurried over to the fireplace alongside, where a peat fire hissed and roared in the grate. One of the fireside places was already occupied. A man sat sprawled in an armchair, his boots stretched out towards the fire, his jacket undone, his tie askew – he had the air of an old lag at ease in the place of his confinement. But a certain raffishness about him suggested that he was no common labourer or artisan.

"A wild night to be abroad, sir."

His accent was that of the far west of Ireland, of Connemara, but overlaid with something more educated and genteel, although such subtleties were still largely beyond John. John was not in the mood for conversation, and in any event, being English, would not normally have engaged in conversation with such a one. He wanted to brood, to try and bring some order to his thoughts, to prepare for what he might say to Helen when he returned – if she was still there. For that he needed space and silence. He almost regretted coming over to the fire; but he also needed to be warm. He nodded to the man and made a non-committal reply. The man seemed to sense John's reluctance to talk, and said nothing further.

John was shaking slightly as he stood in front of the fire, a reaction from shock as well as from cold. He had shocked himself as much as Helen by the force and the precipitateness of the threat he had made. It had been made on the spur of the moment; but once made, it could not be withdrawn. It was the unleashing of months of tension, of being so near to complete success, now released by Helen's stupidity and insensitiveness. In the end, it seemed, she did not understand his feelings or his fears, and she was too bloody selfish to care. It was anger which had driven him to do what he did; but beyond it, there was something darker and less easy to define. He could not reproach himself for anything he had done, or failed to do. What he had achieved was a success beyond his wildest dreams of a few months ago. He had brought Helen to a place which was, in its own way, a little paradise; and he had seen it in her also – the softness of summer, the warmth, the fruitfulness. She had been enchanted, at least for a while. She had felt as he had done, and he had seen it in her eyes, and felt it in her body. He had offered her love, tranquillity and security, and yet he had not cut her off entirely from the life she had known before. Had their positions somehow been reversed, he would have been entirely and utterly content. Such would have been the reaction of a sane and healthy man. But she not only wanted to leave this place, she also wanted him to leave her, for the war.

It would be easy to dismiss this as being no more than stupidity and selfishness, and this had been the cause of his anger. The unreasonableness of it was easy to see; but if that was so, then so also was the senselessness of it. If you loved someone, then you did not want to be parted from them; still less did you want them to face degradation, mutilation or death. But he could see that it wasn't as simple as that. If Helen had just ceased to love him, if she had just rejected him, then there would be no need for her to concern herself with him any longer – she would just leave. There would have been no need for her to come back to Ireland. It would have been much easier for her to have written to him from England, and to have stayed with her parents until the legal proceedings were completed, and she had had time to find someone else to make a new start with. But she had come back to Ireland, with demands and expectations. Was this merely vanity? Would she really be unable to live with her situation here in Ireland if she did not get her way, and they stayed? That might make some sense if they were in England; but not here. Even within the small oases of insanity that still existed here, such as St Mungo's, such views were strongly challenged; and outside the gates of such places, in the generality of Irish society, no-one held a man in contempt if he would not cross the water to join the British army and take part in Mr Chamberlain's war. Such things were still very much a matter of pride here, and Helen had been in Ireland long enough to be aware of that.

If it was not vanity, then what was it? What lay behind vanity? Human vanity was not empty: it was a veneer, a coat of many colours, a motley of suburban prejudices; a specious reassurance that what is proper is also right – that poverty is prosperity; that injustice is justice; that greed is honesty; that darkness is light. It was a deceit, predicated in order to justify the deceivers. And what, then, of those who were deceived?

John was afraid. Did every man then understand this? That which no-one ever quite mentioned, but somehow one could never quite forget: a half-imagined fear, only half understood, obscured in the jeers of schoolboys, the sniggers of youths and the knowing looks of young men; a fear never quite faced in full because for him, as for most men, things turned out to be alright in the end, or so it seemed; and the darkness under the mind, the sharp spectre of death without the immortality of the common man was put aside, and he deceived himself into believing he was one of the deceivers.

But no-one who had felt the spectre's breath ever entirely forgot it. When he was threatened in a way which called into question his value as a man and as a husband, and perhaps even his very masculinity, the doubt that never entirely left the innermost shadows in the mind of even the most contented man, came to the surface. On the surface, every man dreamed of his princess, while knowing that the dream was a vanity. Every man can love a woman for what she is and for that alone, even if she isn't very pretty – sometimes especially if she isn't very pretty. It is men's vanity that such love is reciprocated. It is their dark knowledge that it is not – that for a woman, love always has a price; and at the heart of every woman is a ruthlessness in exacting that price; and if a man cannot pay the price, or is no longer able to do so, then he can expect to be discarded. By their own ruthlessness, women create a trap for themselves from which they cannot escape. But for a man, love which has such ruthlessness at its heart is no love: it is the cause of that unbridgeable gulf between the sexes, and of that inner darkness which most men would rather forget, or overlay with their vanity.

There was nothing more. In a little while he would have to return to the cottage, and face the alien coldness that Helen had brought between them – if, indeed, she was still there. If she was not, the darkness would be complete.

John became aware that the raffish stranger was observing him carefully from over the rim of his glass. He could not say how long he had been standing there – perhaps that in itself might be cause enough for curiosity. John did not feel self-conscious or irritated by the other's gaze. He had reached the heart of darkness and found neither solace nor answer, and it would be futile to punish himself any more with it.

"It didn't look a particularly pleasant place." The stranger, having caught his eye, finally broke the silence.

"I'm sorry?"

"Wherever it was that you were in your thoughts just now, it didn't look a particularly pleasant place."

"Oh … no. No, I suppose it wasn't a particularly pleasant place."

"You were lost to this world, right enough. I've rarely seen anyone so engrossed as you were."

"Well, I'm sorry if I appeared to be unsociable. Perhaps I can buy you a drink?"

"You're very kind. I'll have another one of these. Charlie knows the score." He paused and sat forward. "Vincent Fitzgerald," he said, and stuck out his hand. John shook the offered hand, and introduced himself.

"John Stanford. Pleased to meet you."

When John returned with the drinks, Vincent Fitzgerald took a long and appreciative swig of his before he spoke.

"From the depths of your introspection, I'd have put you down as a financier or a politician; but you look more like a schoolmaster, if you'll forgive me the observation."

John laughed.

"Is it as obvious as that? You're quite right, that is what I am."

"Well, it was still a good guess. Do you teach here in Bray?"

John explained about St Mungo's.

"That must be a strange place to teach in, particularly at the moment," Vincent Fitzgerald observed.

"I'm afraid it is in some ways, yes. Are you a teacher yourself?"

"I was." Vincent took a reflective sip of his drink. "I was indeed. I was a schoolmaster for fifteen years in Galway. Just a village schoolmaster, you know. A little place called Kilkirrin, in the west of Galway."

"Did you enjoy teaching?"

"I did. I loved it. It was my life. You would perhaps have found it a little primitive compared with somewhere like St Mungo's; but I'm a Galway man, so it was different for me."

"But you gave it up?"

"Sometimes … things go wrong." Vincent gazed into the embers of the peat fire. "It isn't necessarily one's own fault, and if things had previously been going right up to that point, it can be very hard to accept. For me, it meant that I had to leave: leave teaching, and leave Galway, since there was nothing else for me in Galway."

"What was it that went wrong?"

"Oh, I'll not burden you with my troubles, at least not today. You've enough of your own by the look of it. Anyhow – I came to Dublin, as I suppose everyone does whose sheet anchor is pulled up by the force of events; and by one means or another, I ended up here in Bray."

"What do you do here?"

"I live by my wits, I suppose you might say. I write articles and stories for the *Irish Times* and other newspapers; and I supplement my income with various odd jobs during the summer season – whatever turns up. It might be said, perhaps, that it's a more interesting and cosmopolitan way of life than I was ever used to, and to that extent it has its compensations; but somehow it's a less … wholesome way of life. It's not what I was meant for, I'm sure of that."

"What were you meant for?"

"Oh, that's gone forever, I'm afraid. You can't return to the past, no matter how desirable that might seem to be. Your only hope is to try to understand why you're not at ease with yourself, if you find yourself in that position. Some men are driven by a demon within themselves, something they can no more help than the colour of their eyes, and they're as likely to hurt those around them as they are to hurt themselves. Some men are the victims of the selfishness of others, and whether that means that they lose the happiness that they had, or are denied the happiness that they desire, it's useless to wallow in nostalgia as a consequence. Your only hope is to understand the reasons for what has happened."

"Have you been able to do that?"

Vincent Fitzgerald smiled wryly. "I don't know. The truth is sometimes complicated, and you don't always understand what you do know of it. Perhaps the hardest thing to accept is that you yourself may also have been at fault." He took another sip of his drink. "What about you? Does any of this make any sense to you?"

John shook his head. "I don't know. Some of it does; but you spoke as if the crisis of your life was in the past and you were looking back on it. My crisis is now, and perhaps I'm too close to it to understand it yet."

"Well, if there's any help or advice I could give …"

"When the matter is resolved, whichever way it is resolved, I would be glad of a sympathetic ear to talk to. But I have to resolve it myself, and that's something which I can only do alone." John looked at his watch. "I'm afraid I'll have to go. It's been a pleasure to talk to you. Perhaps I'll find you in here again?"

"Most nights, I'm afraid. Most nights. One of God's punishments for my sins is to make me an inveterate denizen of saloon bars, and this one in particular, where my moral decline has been steady and irreversible. Charlie'll tell you all about it."

"Well, you owe me a drink, so I'll be back!"

Outside, the rain had stopped, and some stars were visible through breaks in the cloud. His bicycle was covered in glistening raindrops and he had to wipe the saddle and handlebars down with his handkerchief. It had been hard to break off the conversation with Vincent Fitzgerald. It was harder still to start the journey back to the cottage. He was mentally exhausted – his mind rebelled against any further travail that day. He knew that if Helen was still inclined to persist in her unreasonableness, and to confront him with it, he would have very little energy left to argue, and would be tempted to violence. The fact that he had reached such a point led him to feel, if not exactly sorry for himself, then a growing sense of injustice that Helen should have put him in this position. He had done his best, for her as well as for himself, and this was how he was rewarded. It was the best he could do to work himself into a combative frame of mind by the time he reached the cottage. He even regretted not having stayed longer talking to Vincent Fitzgerald. His English reserve had prevented him from saying anything of consequence to Fitzgerald about his present crisis, or even from allowing Fitzgerald to talk in more detail about himself. He was too middle class not to be instinctively suspicious of a character like that, alone and somewhat inebriated in a saloon bar. And yet, he had also been left with the impression that Fitzgerald might have been, in some sense, a kindred spirit, with whom he had more in common than he would care to admit, and that it was his loss that he had terminated their conversation when he did.

As he approached the cottage, he felt the first drops of rain on his face, which were the harbingers of another downpour. It seemed to be turning colder as well. From the front, the cottage seemed in darkness, but as he came round to the back along the path, he saw that light streamed from the kitchen window. Helen had evidently decided not to go after all. It was no use him trying to imagine what that might portend, or what lay in store. He put his bicycle away and walked quickly to the back door. It was only when he reached it that he noticed that the door was ajar. The kitchen was empty – the lamp hanging from the ceiling burned with a slight flicker in the currents of air which came in through the half-open door. He called Helen's name, but there was no reply. He took the lamp through to the bedroom and then the living room, but she was not there. She was not in the house. In the bedroom, he noticed that her clothes were still there, as were personal items which he knew she would have taken with her if she had decided to leave. In the kitchen, the fire in the grate was almost out, and he saw that the money which he had left on the kitchen table was still there.

He stood in the middle of the kitchen, perplexed. Surely she had not gone back to England without money, without possessions or even clothes? And in the middle of the night? There were no trains – she could not even have gone to Dublin. She had not taken her bicycle – it had been there when he had put his own bicycle away. He made another, more thorough search, and after twenty minutes had established beyond doubt that she was neither in the cottage nor the garden. He had half expected her to leave, but not like this. She could not have gone back to England – she had simply walked out into the night in the clothes she stood up in. He stood at the open back door undecided. Perhaps he should leave her to her own devices. If she had gone off in a temper or because she needed space to think, then she would return when she was ready. But he could not escape a feeling that something was amiss. The last traces of dusk were long gone, and the rain was now falling in a steady downpour. The air was cold with the chill of an autumn night, and Helen had not even taken a proper raincoat.

He put his hat and coat on again, and got out his bicycle. In deciding which way to go he assumed that he might have passed her if she had taken the road towards Bray, so he set off in the opposite direction. In the rain-laden darkness, the light from his bicycle lamp was feeble and uncertain. Even if she had taken this road, she would be very difficult to find unless she was directly in his path. He could only go slowly because of the darkness and the nature of the road, which was also mostly uphill. From time to time he called out her name, but there was no answer from the darkness. The rain continued in a relentless downpour, and he felt increasingly that he was on a wild goose chase. He didn't know that she had come this way, and there was little chance of finding her in the dark even if she had. She might even have returned to the cottage by now.

When the bicycle lamp suddenly went out, he stopped. He unclipped the lamp and shook it, but there was not even a glimmer of light from the bulb. Either the battery had given out, or perhaps there was water in it. He did not know how far he had come, or how long it had been since he left the cottage – in the darkness, he could no longer see his watch. It seemed like ages. He was wet through to the skin, the light raincoat he was wearing having proved unequal to the Irish weather. The rain had got under his hat, and even his shoes were full of water. Whether his attempt to find Helen had been justified or not, he could not do anything more that night. What madness had possessed her if she was abroad on a night like this? Without the light, the darkness was almost total, and he could sense rather than see the great weight of water pouring from the murky sky, as well as feel it as it stung his face and soaked through his clothes. Surely it was impossible that she should be here. He suddenly shouted her name into the darkness, but the only sound he heard in response was the steady hiss and splash of the rain. It was madness for him to be there: it was equally inconceivable that he should not be – if this was madness, he would fight it with all his strength. He turned his bicycle round and started back towards the cottage.

When he reached the cottage it was well after midnight. The rain had not stopped and he was completely waterlogged – all his clothes were wringing wet. He was also numb with cold. He put the bicycle away and hurried to get into the shelter of the kitchen. The cottage was exactly as he had left it. Helen had not returned. He knew then that his search had not been in vain and that something was seriously wrong: but for the moment, he had reached the end of his endurance. He needed to get warm and dry if he was not to come down with pneumonia; he needed food and sleep.

The fire in the kitchen had gone out, and he spent ten minutes re-lighting it and getting a blaze going before stripping his sodden clothing off and drying himself with a towel. He put dry clothes on, and although he was stupid with fatigue, he made himself go back into the kitchen to light the stove to heat some coffee and some food. It was while he was doing this that he considered what he should do. If Helen had spent all these hours out in the open, and was still there, then she would be in an even worse state than he: she might even be dead or dying. He ought to go into Bray and notify the police of what had happened, so that a search could be instituted. But the police in Bray consisted of a sergeant and two constables who, equipped only with bicycles, would have little more chance of finding Helen in the dark than he himself would. By the time they had managed to get a search organised, it would be nearly dawn. He might just as well rest until dawn and resume the search himself.

The truth, however, was that he did not wish to make known to others the shame of what had happened. From a stranger's point of view, either he had driven his wife out, or she had had a fit of madness and run out into the night with intent to injure herself. Such a thing would never be forgotten, and he would ever afterwards have to bear the shame of it. Life in a small community such as this would become untenable, and they, or he at least, would be forced to move away. He knew he would do a great deal to avoid such shame. For the sake of a few hours … But in those hours, of darkness and cold and icy rain, the price might be very high. He remembered her on a summer night when they were engaged, walking home after a dance, holding her in his arms, looking into her gentle eyes – his princess – his angel. He could not have conceived then that he could do such a thing – that he could contemplate leaving her out in the night, at the mercy of the elements, while he did nothing. For a minute he wept, the tears running silently down his face, until he dried them with the towel. It was as much self-pity as remorse; the burden of an overwhelming sense of injustice which was the result of the selfishness of others.

He consumed the hastily prepared meal, and then banked up the fire in the kitchen before retiring to bed. He was utterly exhausted. He awoke long after dawn. At first he did not know what time it was – his watch had stopped, as had the clock, which he had forgotten to wind. He switched the wireless on, to discover that it was well after nine o'clock. He was conscious of the fact that his absence from St Mungo's would already be the subject of adverse comment. He ought to go into Bray to telephone the school – he would be risking his job otherwise. But there was no time for that. The journey to Bray would have to wait until later: then he would be going to fetch a doctor – or the police.

His raincoat had largely dried out overnight in front of the fire. After the hastiest of meals, he banked the fire up again, and a few minutes later was on the road on his bicycle. It was still raining, but, as if the force of the seemingly endless deluge was finally spent, the rain had diminished at last to the merest drizzle, which was barely enough to dampen his coat. The air was still, humid and breathless, as it often is after prolonged rain which is reluctant to clear. The trees, the hedgerows, the fields were sodden, with a washed-out green colour, as if they had literally been inundated in a flood. Trees still cascaded water like heavy rain, and the road was covered in puddles brown with mud. It seemed as if he had never seen this countryside before, although he had cycled along this road many times. But now, in the cold grey light and pungent, heavy air, in the spattering raindrops, nature seemed to test him, to mark time on his mortality, at every turn of the pedals to squeeze a little more life out of him, to make him conscious of his frailty.

He was entering a strange country, a country of chaos and fear and isolation: the last of his life fell away as he cycled on – the cottage, the school, the dreams of summer, this very island of refuge. There was no longer a past or a future, only an endless lane through this waterlogged green maze. This was his punishment and just reward for fecklessness and cowardice, and for believing that he could thwart the designs of fate. What right had he to think himself more than a nonentity, if that was all he was? All his scheming had been nothing less than an affront to all that was proper and decent. A nonentity had no greater duty than to know his place, and those who were proper and decent would see to it that he was returned to it. He would lose all he had – but that was no more than it should be.

He shook his head as if to clear it. This was the chaos of insanity. He had come here in the expectation that, here at least, against all the odds, sanity would prevail; and despite everything that had happened in the last few days, he had not been disappointed. He must not lose sight of that now. It was his duty as an individual with a free will to do what he knew to be right, regardless of what the majority in England might think. Morality was not made by numbers, and if any were cowards, it was those of the majority who took refuge in the safety of numbers in order to persecute a minority they disliked – it was a safety which in the end was specious and vain. Nothing would ever obviate the crime these people were responsible for in the Great War: not even the blasphemy of turning the November 11th ceremony into a glorification of war. If, even in this refuge, they reached out to touch him with their corruption, he should not allow the miasma of it to overcome the citadel of his mind. Nor should there be any forgiveness for what they had done. They might destroy his happiness, but they would not destroy his integrity or his sanity.

He found Helen shortly before 11 o'clock. Her body lay on a grassy embankment just off the road, under a large tree where she had evidently attempted to shelter from the weather. She lay face down, her arms folded into a cradle for her head. It was a moment of such great tension that he felt no particular emotion. He was more than half prepared for this. The image of her still form seemed small, afar off, even as he knelt beside her, as if this last and nearest part of his life was also taken from him as the others had been, and he was finally detached from the world. The shock was not to confirm that she was indeed dead, but the discovery that she still lived. He gingerly turned her over to face him – her clothes and hair were soaking wet, and her skin was deathly cold, but as he turned her she made a little gasp. There was saliva running from her mouth which bubbled as she breathed. He was seized by panic. She still lived, and he still did not want to lose her. He called her name over and over again, but she was deeply unconscious and could not hear him. Even if she was not yet dead, she was near death, and the understanding of this left him nearly frantic with desperation. It would have been most rational to have cycled as quickly as possible into Bray to fetch help – the thought did not even enter his head. It was not the shame of the discovery of what had happened that governed him now. This was his Helen – his beloved. In his desperation at seeing her so near to death, he could not bear to leave her even for a minute, not here, like a dying animal under the sky. Without giving a thought to the risks or the ordeal involved, he lifted her up and carried her down to the road. Somehow he managed to sit her on the bicycle, while he took the weight of the upper part of her body on his back. He steadied her with her left arm draped over his shoulder. In such a fashion he was able to make progress. It was very slow progress however, with frequent pauses for rest. The physical strain, particularly on his arms and back, was enormous, and in time he reached a state of mental as well as physical exhaustion, in which his mind was reduced to a narrow, pain filled horizon of keeping the bicycle and its burden upright and keeping it moving forward under control. At no time did he even consider leaving Helen to go and get help on his own, despite the pain. He would not abandon her now. If anyone passed him on the road or spoke to him, he could not have said. His was, in any case, a private grief, which others had no right to look upon. It must have been a strange sight for any who did see him; but perhaps no-one did, even on that long and awful journey.

It took him nearly two hours to bring her home. The arrival at the cottage did not bring an end to his ordeal, however. He could not rest yet. There was still a fire in the grate in the kitchen, so he stripped Helen's clothes off there, and dried her as best he could with a bath towel. It would be best if she could be given a warm bath, but he did not have the strength for that at the moment. She was still unconscious, and he was now desperately concerned to bring a doctor to her as soon as possible. He got her into a dressing gown, and carried her into the bedroom and put her to bed. For the moment, he could do no more. He was trembling with fatigue. He sat down in front of the fire in the kitchen and remained there unmoving for nearly a quarter of an hour. Now that he had succeeded in bringing her back to the cottage, now that they were once again within the privacy of its shielding walls, the awfulness of what had happened was somehow lessened. At least now he would be bringing the doctor to her bedside, not to a roadside gutter where he would have nowhere to hide his shame – their shame.

As soon as he was able to move again, he heated some water in the kettle and made some coffee. He went through to see Helen once more before he left. She was still unconscious, but now showing some signs of life, stirring in her sleep, her eyes occasionally half opening for a moment, her skin beaded with sweat. She was clearly in a high fever. He dabbed her damp skin with a dry towel, noticing how hot she had become since he had put her to bed. He called her name softly, but she could not hear him.

At the doctor's surgery in Bray, he was made to wait. There were only three other people in the waiting room, but the receptionist made him wait his turn, despite his appeal that the matter was urgent. He did not have an appointment and so he must wait. The doctor, however, when John was eventually admitted and had described Helen's condition, responded at once. He opened his dispensary and put one or two items into his bag, told the receptionist that he was going out on a call, and led John outside to where a small car was parked in the rear yard. Within ten minutes they were back at the cottage.

When the doctor had finished examining Helen, he carefully gave her an injection in the arm. He sat back on the bed and regarded her for a moment before looking across at John.

"I'm going to arrange for her to go into hospital. I'm afraid she's got pneumonia, and it's quite serious. She needs a period of intensive care as well as the necessary medical treatment, and she can only receive that in hospital."

John nodded without speaking.

"Have you any idea what could have brought this on?" the doctor asked.

John nodded again.

"She was caught out in the storm last night – we both were; and we both got very wet and very cold before we were able to get back here to dry off."

"But it's affected her far more than it has you. Perhaps I'd better check your lungs as well."

"She had also just arrived back from a long and tiring voyage from England, and she was feeling pretty low both mentally and physically."

John pulled his shirt up so that the doctor could apply his stethoscope to his chest and back.

"Not a good idea, to be out in a storm like that," said the doctor, as he folded his stethoscope away. He gave John a quizzical look.

"No." John looked down at Helen's restless form.

"Well, it's none of my business I suppose. You haven't got pneumonia, but that's probably more to do with luck than constitution."

"Will she live?"

"With the care and attention she'll receive in hospital, she should have a good chance of pulling through. It's less easy to say whether her lungs will be permanently damaged as a result of this." The doctor continued to regard John with curiosity. What he didn't understand about the matter clearly intrigued him, not least John's unmistakable concern; but he was prevented by a sense of propriety from pursuing it directly any further.

"If she was ever … caught in a storm like that again, her chances would almost certainly be much less favourable a second time." It was as much as he would allow himself to say. Perhaps he would hear more about it in due course. One often did in such cases …

"I shall telephone the hospital from the surgery. I want you to wait here until the ambulance arrives."

"I wonder," said John, "if you would be kind enough to telephone my school. I'm a teacher. I haven't had the chance to contact them yet, and they'll be wondering why I haven't turned up today."

St Mungo's School … Doctor Grey was more intrigued than ever. It was presumably no more than a kind of class prejudice which made incidents, both tragic and otherwise, among the middle class, vastly more interesting than those among the lower class. It was more than merely rarity value – one could also see an image of oneself.

7

Helen remained in hospital for four weeks before she was deemed to be well enough to return home. During that time, John visited her every day, during the evening visiting hours, having had an evening meal at a pub or eating house before going on to the hospital. It was a very transitory bachelor existence, but the strain was emotional rather than physical. It seemed almost as if Helen, having found fulfilment from her visit to England, had fallen sick on her return, not with a physical illness, but with a sickness of him, and of the new home he had found for them both. He found that he had to rationalise this either as a fantasy, or as the sickness of an unnatural evil that is brought into contact with what is wholesome and good, and that in consequence he was fighting for Helen's soul as much as for the life of her body.

In truth, it was not easy for him to know how he fared in this struggle during Helen's stay in hospital. The lack of privacy in the hospital ward meant that conversations had to remain largely superficial. Helen's recovery, although steady, did not in any case allow for stressful conversation, and by the time she was able to talk lucidly again, these matters had been overshadowed by a new development. At the end of the first week, as John was leaving at the end of visiting hours, the ward sister asked him if he would have a word with the doctor in charge of Helen's case. John, tired and apprehensive, was not prepared for the doctor's question.

"Did you know if your wife was pregnant?"

"Pregnant?" John's surprise was manifest.

"We won't be certain until we get the results of tests in a few days, but on the basis of an external examination, the indications are that she's pregnant. I'd say she was about two months into the pregnancy."

Two months. It would have been the first night they had made love in the cottage, on the day after their arrival. That sleepy, sultry, late summer night, soft with her velvet darkness, drenched in the first sweetness of freedom, elated with triumph. If he had known then …

"How will … her illness affect her pregnancy?"

"I'm afraid I can't tell you that yet. We don't even have confirmation that she is pregnant, although I don't doubt it myself. But the point I wanted to make is that, if the baby was not expected, then you'll have to come to terms with the fact that the advent of the baby will necessitate considerable changes in your life. A baby is a great responsibility."

John felt himself reddening. That doctor from Bray had been talking, he was certain of it. Were doctors in Ireland subject to rules of confidentiality? He supposed that he could not stop doctors from talking among themselves. Well, they would have to draw their own conclusions.

"It's a responsibility which I know will bring me great happiness – and my wife also."

For the time being, everything was changed. John could have wished for this news to have come under happier circumstances, but he did not begrudge this. He could hope that Helen's unreasonableness was a temporary aberration, and that he could look forward to this fulfilment of both of their lives. He was still free; he had a new life; and now he was to have a child. Sometimes the fear overwhelmed him, but always he was able to beat it back. There was too much to hope for still.

He had good reason to be confident. The effect on Helen of the news that she was pregnant was profound. By the time Helen was ready to leave the hospital, it seemed as if his most optimistic hopes had been fulfilled. Fears that on returning to consciousness, Helen would return to irrationality, were not realised. She may not have abandoned her view about the war: the matter never really surfaced. All such things became peripheral for her as her horizons contracted to be filled, to the exclusion of almost all else, by her maternity. The travail of living was superseded by the imperative of life itself; and rather than being a diminution of her importance, it seemed to John that it was a demonstration of a fundamental power. At the same time it seemed as if a miracle had taken place in both their lives. The unnatural had been driven out by the natural; irrationality had been, if not dispelled, then at least scotched by a breath of sanity. For the time being a simple humanity prevailed, and replaced the sophistication of prejudice, at least in their domestic life. For the time being, it was a deliverance.

Unexpectedly, these events also brought relief for John in another quarter. On the day of the emergency, when he had brought Helen back to the cottage, he had resigned himself to the inevitability of losing his position at St Mungo's. Unauthorised absence from work was a cardinal sin, and with most employers normally resulted in immediate dismissal. This would be the case even for a 'first offence', and even if no other factors were involved. However, even before that day, John had found the situation at St Mungo's increasingly difficult. It seemed that, if it was allowed to, the war blighted everything it touched with its evil, so that John, having to face the evil both at home and at work, was on the point of despair. At St Mungo's, the unionists and the 'patriots' insisted on taking their position to its logical conclusion. If they were in the right, then anyone who took a different or contrary view of the war was in the wrong. Since the beginning of September, they had asserted their position with increasing belligerence. Elsewhere, such behaviour would not have been tolerated; but St Mungo's was tortured by its past, wedded to it by prejudices larger than itself, even though the perpetuation of such prejudices in such a place was the perpetuation of an unreality. At the heart of this rottenness was a headmaster who, while sharing the prejudices of the unionists, did not have the stomach to give effect to them, either by actively supporting the unionists, or by taking action against the targets of their belligerence. Such weakness meant dissention and disorder, not only among the staff, but also, increasingly, in the classrooms. John was at first a witness to this erosion of the normal standards of discipline, but as Carter had predicted, it became increasingly difficult for him to remain aloof from it. And if he was forced to take sides, he would have no choice in the matter, even if he had little sympathy with, and not a little contempt for the rather feckless response of the republican sympathisers. For a time, he was able to maintain his position as a disinterested outsider; but the nature of the situation meant that this could not last for long. By early October, four of the younger masters had left for England to volunteer for war service. Two of the sixth-form boys who had passed their eighteenth birthdays had also gone. Each time a master or a boy left to volunteer, and was publicly applauded for doing so by Mr Crosby, the headmaster, it had the effect of creating tension and exerting pressure on those of the minority opinion. For the 'patriots', it seemed like a return to the good times. For once, they were caught up in something that was larger than they were, larger than Ireland and its brooding parochial bigotries; something that once again allowed them to be part of the mainstream of events. Suddenly they felt that they had the moral high ground, and it was those of the minority opinion who needed to be on the defensive.

For the out and out republicans, nothing had changed, and they were more than capable of holding their own. John, as an Englishman, was not, but as an Englishman, he was inevitably a focus of attention from both sides.

He had still not decided how to respond when the first questions came. Being so isolated meant that he had very little room for manoeuvre – he either told the truth, told a lie, or told the questioner to mind his own business. He dismissed the idea of telling a lie, because in the end, the lie would become unsustainable. Faced with the choice of the other two options, he found to his dismay, that at first he did not have the courage to tell the truth. But it became increasingly difficult, as time went on, to ignore the fact that he was being talked about behind his back. As long as he maintained his silence, however, he would have to accept this brittle, mute hostility on their terms. This persisted for a surprisingly long time. It could not last, however, and nor would John have tolerated the situation indefinitely. The confrontation, when it did come, was most unsatisfactory, in that it resolved nothing, yet nor did it clear the air.

The headmaster, Mr Crosby, having called John to his office for what seemed at first a minor administrative matter, which was presumably a pretext for what followed, waited until John was leaving the room before coming to the point.

"Oh, by the way, I should have mentioned this before – I should be most grateful if you could let me know, as soon as you can, what your plans are."

"My plans? I'm sorry, I don't follow, sir."

"I should have thought that my meaning was clear enough. As you will know, several members of staff have already left to serve our country in her hour of need. Naturally, their places will be kept open for them, for to serve one's country is the highest call of duty. As headmaster, however, I have to make temporary arrangements to cover for them in their absence.

That was the purpose of my question. I would be grateful if you could give me as much notice of your departure as you can."

"I was not aware that my departure was imminent, sir."

"I take it that you will be doing your duty. You're fit and of military age – I can see no reason for delay." Crosby's tone became very frosty.

"My duty, sir?"

"Dammit man, you know perfectly well what I mean. The country's at war."

"I was not aware of that, sir."

"Not aware … ? Are you trying to be funny?"

"No sir. I thought that Mr De Valera's statement was perfectly clear – Ireland would be remaining neutral in the European war. I was not aware that anything had changed."

"Damn your insolence! How dare you mention that man's name in my presence? I wasn't referring to that traitor, or his traitorous Free State. I was referring to our country – England. England is at war, and it's the duty of every able-bodied subject of His Majesty to serve our country in her hour of need."

"I may be your subordinate, sir, but my private loyalties are my concern and mine alone. You have no business to make judgements or assumptions about them. If you regard England as your country, sir, then that is your business. I may be English-born, but I've chosen to come and live and work here. Ireland is my home, and as far as I'm concerned, Ireland is now my country. I no longer have any connection with England, so if the British Government chooses to get involved in a war, that's nothing to do with me."

"By God, you're either a coward or a traitor, and, I suspect, the former. If you think that just because you've come to Ireland, you can ignore what's happening in your own country, ignore the fact that your country is now at war, and that it's your duty to put yourself at your country's service, then you're mistaken. And if you think that you can use St Mungo's as a refuge for your cowardice, then you are also mistaken. If you will not return to England to do your duty, then you are certainly not staying at St Mungo's."

"You have the gall to threaten me with dismissal because you accuse me of doing something which you yourself have been doing these last twenty years, if not for the whole of your life."

"What do you mean?"

"You accuse me of ignoring what's happening in England, which you keep asserting is my country, even though I've told you otherwise; you, who refuse to accept what's happening in Ireland, the country of your birth, the country where you grew up, the country where you still live. ."

"Of course I refuse to accept it. The country's been taken over by a rabble of traitors. If they get their way, then in time we'll all be running around barefoot in rags and ignorance, kissing the robes of papist priests, submerged in the great unwashed mass of Catholic peasantry – it's not the same thing at all, as you know very well."

"On the contrary, it's precisely the same thing. Your class war against the majority of your fellow countrymen – and I use the term advisedly – may be none of my business; but at least I don't try to ram my opinions of that down your throat. By the same token, if I have a disagreement with England, and the British Government, then I have as much right to dissent as you do."

"I can't overlook avoidance of obligation of that sort. It's not the same thing."

"If that means you intend to dismiss me from my post, then the same standard would have to apply here in that case. I'm talking about the obligations that you and this school have been avoiding under the laws of this country, Ireland. I think you know what I'm talking about."

Mr Crosby stared at him for several seconds in silence, his face now livid with anger.

"That is not done. You should know that we keep our disagreements private in here. We don't involve the ... Free State authorities."

"I'm surprised you've been able to get away with it for so long. I suppose that what you agree to in here is up to you; but if I was no longer here, then I could hardly be expected to continue to be a party to that."

Crosby did not reply. He stared at John, as if unable to decide what to say. A weakness had been touched upon, and he had no defences – like the player at L'Attaque, whose flag is threatened by his opponent's scout, if only the opponent knew... John could only speculate as to what was going through Crosby's mind. In any event, he felt he did not need to say any more.

"If I might leave the matter in your hands, sir ..."

"Yes, yes ... I'll ... need to reflect upon this. You may go now."

In a way, it was most unsatisfactory. He would have no greater protection from the hostility of the 'patriots', and yet it seemed as if Crosby did not have the stomach, or the authority in his own school to dismiss him.

As he had expected, Crosby did not dismiss him following the interview, and he heard no more about the matter from him. The position of St Mungo's remained anomalous, and the time was probably overdue when the school would warrant closer inspection by the authorities. Mr Crosby, for all his jingoism, was surely only too well aware of this. In a calmer atmosphere, John might have felt sorry for him. As a headmaster, Crosby cut a forlorn figure – how the matter might have ended, John could not have guessed. Given, as seemed increasingly likely, that eventually he would be forced to leave St Mungo's by the pressure that was being applied to him, he had already started to make discreet enquiries about alternative employment. The news about Helen's illness, and then about her pregnancy, unexpectedly and inexplicably changed attitudes towards him at St Mungo's markedly. It was not so much that he was rehabilitated, but rather that the pressure of hostility towards him eased, as if the evidence of a domestic life which they could understand and sympathise with made him less of a demon in their eyes. Perhaps much of the violence of the world, even that which pursues its victims to the point of destruction, is casual and inconsequential on the part of the persecutors, a fact which, if anything, makes it all the worse. John, while grateful for the respite, was not deceived by it.

Helen came back to the cottage after just under a month in the hospital in Dublin. Her return was carefully prepared for. On the day, an ambulance drove her all the way from the hospital to the cottage. It was a Saturday morning, which meant that she would have John's attention for the whole weekend, before he had to return to work. Thereafter, the local district nurse would visit her at the cottage every day, to monitor the course of Helen's recovery, as well as the course of her pregnancy, which seemed to have been unaffected by her illness. From the beginning, things seemed to go smoothly. After such a long stay in hospital, Helen seemed glad to be back at the cottage again. It was a return home, to her husband, to the luxury of personal privacy once again, to a new beginning for both of them.

8

Shortly before Christmas, John received news he had been waiting for. He was invited for interview for a teaching post at a state school. His initial impression had been that all such posts would be closed to him because he was not a Catholic, and while this had as much to do with prejudice as anything else, it was, nevertheless, largely true. However, in this particular case, the post was at a south Dublin secondary school which was experiencing staff shortages due to staff leaving to go to England to join the war. The interview was held at the school in the headmaster's study on a Wednesday morning. John had taken a day's leave from St Mungo's without saying what he intended to do. Even if he was doing what might have been expected of him, he did not want to leave hostages to fortune. On the whole, the interview did not go well. It was conducted by the headmaster of the school, assisted by two assessors from the Board of Education. It was evident from the start that they were having great difficulty in overcoming their prejudices. John was English; he was teaching at St Mungo's, that notorious remnant of the colonial power; and he was a Protestant – or, at least, he wasn't a Catholic. They seemed concerned that, if he was appointed, he might be a corrupting influence on the children.

"You realise that the kind of colonial claptrap you doubtless peddle at St Mungo's would not be acceptable here," one of the assessors put to him.

"Colonial claptrap?"

"You've nominated history as one of the subjects you're offering. In state schools, we now teach the children the history of their own country – Irish history. We don't teach the history of England, with Ireland as an English province, which is what I presume you teach at St Mungo's."

"Well, only up to a point ..." John wondered again how long it had been since St Mungo's had received the attention of the Board of Education inspectors. It was not that Irish history wasn't taught at St Mungo's so much as the slant that was put on it; but he judged it inappropriate to go too much into that at this juncture.

"If you're offering history as a subject," said the headmaster, "you would need to demonstrate not only a knowledge of Irish history, but a sympathy with the subject matter, which might mean taking a point of view critical of England and the English Government."

"I can assure you that that would present me with no difficulty." John had found it hard to suppress a smile. The smile was not returned, however.

"I would have thought that might be difficult for an Englishman at a time like this," the headmaster observed. "Speaking of which, as you may be aware, this post became vacant when the incumbent decided, for reasons of his own, to cross the water to England to join the British army. Quite apart from the fact that I take a dim view of such things anyway, we are hardly likely to view your application favourably if there was a likelihood that you would be following your predecessor across the water for the same reason."

"I can give you a categorical assurance that I have no intention of doing any such thing."

The headmaster raised his eyebrows in surprise.

"That seems a rather remarkable assertion. From what I've heard, you won't have much choice in the matter – you'll be called up for military service."

John shrugged his shoulders.

"I have gone into that matter. As long as I remain in the Free State – Eire – they have no powers to take me from Ireland."

The surprise on the face of the headmaster turned to astonishment on the faces of all three. It was a moment which gave John an immense feeling of gratification and pleasure. What followed did not disappoint him.

"Perhaps you could explain that," said the headmaster. "Are you saying you would refuse to fight for England?"

"I came to Ireland, with my wife, only in August. We came to stay – to settle in Ireland. We knew perfectly well that there was going to be a war. One of the reasons why we came – why I came – was to avoid having to take part in the war."

"Do you mean to say that you're a pacifist?"

"No, that's not what I mean."

"Well, what then? The usual expectation is that if you're called up to fight, it's your patriotic duty to go."

"Patriotism in this case seems to mean blind obedience to a gang of disreputable politicians. I reject any claim such people assert they have on me. My life belongs to me, not to them, and if I'm to put it at such a risk, there has to be a valid reason for doing so. The fact that Neville Chamberlain wants to have another war with Germany is not a valid reason as far as I'm concerned."

"But," persisted the headmaster, "if you're not a pacifist, surely you could not expect to get away with such a point of view."

"You still haven't really understood what I'm talking about, have you? What I mean is that governments, the state, if you will, claim powers over individuals on grounds which are spurious, and which amount to a form of terrorism. Just because I happen to have been born in England, the British Government claims the right to force me to leave my home, my wife, my family, and to risk injury or death fighting for it whenever it chooses to get involved in a war with another state."

"But surely, whether you like it or not, that is the basis of modern civil society. Society could not carry on otherwise."

"I'm surprised you should advance such an argument, especially here in Ireland. My point is that when it's done without genuine consent, it is, at bottom, no more than a form of gangsterism on a large scale. When it's based on coercion and fear, as it almost invariably is, the state is no more than a version of the Chicago mob writ large. Have you already forgotten that that is precisely why you seized your freedom here in Ireland? The British Government ruled here without consent, and used that rule to impose, by force and coercion, a form of exploitation which reduced thousands to starvation and destitution. Subsequently, they attempted to enforce conscription for the criminal war they were pursuing in Flanders. What was surprising was not that you took up arms against this, but that it took you so long to do so."

"You're a kind of political dissenter," said one of the assessors.

The headmaster shook his head. "A dissenter is properly one who stays and remains defiant in the face of coercion -you would have stayed in England and gone to prison for your views."

"Which would have been a completely pointless thing to do. I'm not part of a political movement or any wider dissent. I'm just an isolated individual, and I would simply have been punishing myself."

"You're an exile," said the other assessor.

"Well, you should know about exile here in Ireland. I had no desire to try and change people's views in England – there's no point in trying to reform the unreformable. As far as I was concerned, I was in the position of being the only person left sane that I knew of, when everyone else around me had gone mad. I had no choice but to get out as quickly as I could, before I was swallowed up by the madness."

"You're an exile," said the other again.

"I'm an exile," agreed John simply.

In the end, he didn't know whether they were testing him or merely talking him out. He felt genuinely surprised that they seemed to have no sympathy whatsoever for the point of view he had expressed. If he could find no sympathy in the mainstream of Irish society, then where would his sanctuary be?

He did not get the post he was interviewed for, and for John this was a considerable blow. The situation at St Mungo's was continuing to deteriorate, and he was still far from certain of Helen. He endured a period of mental depression following the interview, and for a time saw a return to the vision of despair which had haunted him at the time of crisis with Helen.

9

It was during this time that John ran into Vincent Fitzgerald again. It was a chance encounter in the street, but they agreed to meet in the evening for a drink. John needed a sympathetic ear, or at least, an independent one, and judged from his impression of the man from their previous meeting, that Fitzgerald would be able to provide that.

"I suppose what I'm looking for," said John, "is to be reassured in some way about Ireland."

They were back in the lounge bar of the Queen's Hotel in Bray, seated once again in the two armchairs on either side of the glowing peat fire in the fireplace.

"That sounds ominous," said Fitzgerald. "I mean, it's a common experience when one moves to a new country, whether in pursuit of opportunity or for any other reason, to suffer a certain disillusionment with regard to the hopes one may have entertained of the place previously. The bright façade seen from afar off generally becomes a little tarnished on closer inspection."

"No, it's more specific than that -more to do with the fact that this is Ireland in particular, and that I am English. Was English, or English born ..."

"Now look, if I'm buying the drinks, you'll have to have a better story than last time. This time you're going to have to come clean." He set John's drink down beside him, and then sat down in the other armchair.

Fitzgerald was an attentive listener. He had an ear for detail, and was quick to sense when John was slipping over important details which he was reluctant to talk about. He was thoughtful for a while after John had finished, sipping his drink and staring into the fire in the grate.

"You know, you're a strange fellow and no mistake. I mean, for most mortals, the burdens of everyday living would be more than enough to bear. Trying to anticipate political events and their worst consequences would seem to many like seeking out troubles rather than trying to avoid them, as if you hadn't enough to contend with already."

John shook his head.

"Despite all that I've had to contend with since I came here, I've avoided far worse by quitting England."

"Oh, don't misunderstand me. I'm not disputing that point. Insofar as I have an opinion in the matter, I would probably share your point of view. But the fact that you worried about such things to the extent that you acted on them in advance sets you aside from the majority of ordinary mortals. But what really sets you aside is the way you've run up against the consequences of it."

He took another sip from his drink.

"You said at the start that you wanted reassurance about Ireland. Well, you should understand that Ireland, the Irish dimension, is at best a peripheral matter as far as you are concerned. It may be that part of your problem is being able to see past that; but once you've been able to get away from this school, St Mungo's, that should be easier. Don't let this setback about the job at the state school discourage you. Have another go – I think you'll get a posting if you try again, and that should put the matter more into perspective. No – I think you've run up against something much more basic."

He was reflective for a moment.

"I don't suppose you've ever been to Galway? Ah, well," he continued, when John indicated that he hadn't, "perhaps as an outsider you could never see it with the eyes of a native of the place. I'm well aware that most outsiders – perhaps especially English outsiders – regard Galway as one of the most God-forsaken spots on Earth, and I can understand why they might. But can you understand what it means to have such a place in your blood? To have been a child there, so that the landscape, the shape of the mountains, the darkness of midwinter, the violence, the terrifying violence of the wind and the sea, the cold purity of the light after a storm, the endless light of midsummer, the sea, always the sea, all this becomes part of those memories of childhood that are etched most sharply on the mind; the place you return to as an innocent in the shelter of your dreams, as a child returns to its mother's breast; the place you think of as home wherever you are on Earth – can you understand that? I can't help feeling that a city child could never have the same intensity of identity with place and landscape, because cities change in a way that landscape doesn't – that from your Manchester you could only half comprehend my Connemara. And perhaps even stranger to you would be the community there – about as far removed from an industrial manufacturing city as you could imagine. But that was my community: a small community which I had been part of – I had known nothing else – right up to the time when I had to leave it. Imagine then if you can, what it is not merely to be an exile from such a place, but to be an exile because you were forced to leave in circumstances which mean that it's impossible for you to return."

John experienced a quickening of interest as he began to understand. He nodded, but kept silent, waiting for Vincent Fitzgerald to continue speaking.

"I think I told you that I was a schoolmaster. I was an assistant master in the school in the village where I had spent all my life – a little township called Kilkirrin. It's on the coast, on the shore of an inlet of Galway Bay which is full of wide low-lying islands. The islands give the landscape a very confused appearance – you're never sure which is mainland and which is island. As a boy, it was a great adventure for me to cross over to one of the islands in a boat or on a homemade raft – something I had been forbidden to do because it was dangerous with the strength of the tides there. I was always slightly unusual in ways which, I suppose, set me apart from most of the rest of the community. I enjoyed school very much, and I did well there – when I was sixteen I became a pupil-teacher, and when I was seventeen I was considered bright enough for higher education. My father was the village cobbler, and he couldn't afford to send me to university; but I won a scholarship to the college in Galway City as a day student. This was during the troubles that led to the founding of the Free State in 1922, and it was an exciting time to be a student, even in Galway. But I was too earnest a young man to do anything so romantic as going off to fight for the Volunteers. I persevered at the college, took my teaching diploma, and came back to the village as a fully-fledged teacher, which is what had been expected of me at the start. I didn't have any regrets. I was doing the thing that I wanted to do – had always wanted to do – and I considered myself very fortunate. I was born to be a teacher, and the years I spent teaching at Kilkirrin school will have been the happiest of my life, I've no doubt of that. At the time, I would have considered my position to have been beyond question or reproach. It was only when an event occurred that caused my status to be questioned that I found out how insecure and marginal I was, despite my years as an apparently solid member of the community. What shocked me about it as much as anything, I suppose, was how completely attitudes towards me changed in the people around me. I was thirty-one years old, and I'd been a teacher for ten years. I was still unmarried, even though I was in quite a respectable situation in what was a relatively poor community. However, I'd been courting for a number of years, and I suppose at the back of my mind I had a vague expectation that this would lead to marriage. Her name was Rebecca ..."

Memories returned to him, and he was silent for a minute before he went on.

"She was the daughter of a farmer from just outside the village. Although we'd been seeing each other for some time, she never seemed quite ready to take the plunge and get married, and I was too much in love to question her. It was the sort of relationship that city folk, such as yourself, would probably consider naïve or old-fashioned; but it was not uncommon in country communities where transgressions of social norms could not be hidden behind the protection of anonymity. I concealed any dissatisfaction I may have felt, convinced that she would come round in due course; and otherwise I was happy enough.

"Then suddenly, out of the blue, she was to go to America. She announced it one day as a decision which had already been made. She hadn't discussed it with me, even though I might reasonably have expected her to have done so. It was just as if I was a casual acquaintance, for whom it would only be a matter of casual interest, which could be communicated in such a way.

"Not unnaturally, I was devastated. I was in love, and I had thought that she also loved me. I mean, what was I to think – that it had all been feigned; that it was a charade? But when I asked her about it, she just said that she had discussed it with her family and she agreed with them that it was time for her to go away. She said she realised I would be disappointed, but she hoped I would understand.

"I should explain, perhaps, about the significance of what was meant by 'going away', since it's not something I imagine you'll be familiar with. You see, in Ireland, we have the Emigration. I suppose it's partly a consequence of always having been a colonial territory. People have always had to leave Ireland for England or the continent to find work or opportunity, and since we've traditionally been met with hostility in England, we've often had to go a long way on our travels to find opportunity. Half of the wars of independence in South America early last century were won by Irish exiles; and in nearly every war the English have fought since Cromwell's time, they've been faced by independent Irish battalions fighting under a French or Spanish or American flag. After the great famine, the Emigration became a flood. Whole communities left because Ireland offered only slavery and starvation. And even seventy years later, after Ireland had won independence and it was no longer necessary to leave, at least for political reasons, people still left because by then it had become a way of life, as well as it still being an economic necessity, especially in the west. It's something which, in my view, has become the curse of Ireland; but it's a curse which seems to have become embedded in the Irish psyche. People go because it's what's expected of them – they go because everyone goes. Some will go for ten years or so, and return when they've made good in London or New York, and they can afford to buy some land. Others come back to the place of their birth to retire after a lifetime away, and all those they left behind are gone or dead. Most never return at all. But it's an expectation which is still general, at least in the west of Ireland, where there is still such poverty as you would not find in England, and emigration is still part of the culture. In the west at least, the majority of young people, from the age of about seventeen, start to prepare for going away. In some villages, including Kilkirrin, when the time comes for a young emigrant to make the journey, there is a ceilidh held in the house for all the friends and relatives, with singing and dancing. In our

103

village, farewells were always made the night before the night of the ceilidh, so that there were no last minute tears, and the young emigrant could slip away at dawn to Galway City, and then the road to Dublin or Cork. In the west of Ireland, 'going away' has become one of the rites of passage from childhood to adulthood. You cannot be counted a man until you have known the pain of separation from parents and family and the place of your childhood; and you can only reach manhood in England or America or Canada or Australia, or wherever the Irish have gone to the ends of the Earth as exiles. Not to go away is seen as strange, an aberration; not to go away by choice is childish, infantile; an attempt, as it were, to cling to one's mother's apron strings in order to avoid the test of initiation into manhood. Perhaps because I was different in other ways too, I wasn't aware of how the way I had acted had made me the object of a certain – if not contempt, then a lack of respect. If I'd wanted to go to college, there were colleges in Boston and New York that had become established routes to success for young and talented Irish migrants. At the very least, I could have gone to London. But Galway! I should say that there's nothing wrong with the university college in Galway City – it's a fine college – but for me to have gone there, and as a day student as well, was, I think, seen as an act of childish immaturity. For me to have then taken employment in the village, even as a schoolmaster, confirmed the view which I now realise was taken of me in private."

Vincent paused to sip from his drink before he continued.

"None of this might have been of any consequence, even after a lifetime if I had stayed – and after all, I was there for ten years, and perfectly happy – none of this might have been of any consequence, as I said, if I had not fallen in love as I did. I did not understand then, as I did later, that Rebecca was only taking the general view that, when it came to marriage, considerations of eligibility would inevitably become important. When she left for America, although I felt it as a great blow, I didn't at that point regard it as being the end of our relationship. She said that she would write, and for a time we exchanged letters, even if they were of a fairly innocent nature.

"Her first employment on arrival in New York was as a domestic servant in the household of a wealthy lawyer. It wasn't a happy time for her and she was glad enough to write letters home and tell of her troubles and anxieties. After a while she decided to take a secretarial course at night school, and in consequence of that she got a job as secretary to a businessman. This man himself had been an immigrant from Ireland ten or fifteen years previously. He'd originally come from County Wexford. He was one of the lucky few who made good, and by the time he took Rebecca on as his secretary he was running his own company in the construction business. Perhaps in any event someone like that would be a more attractive proposition to a young woman than the likes of me; but part of what made the difference was that he had made good not in Ireland, but in America. He was, if you like, a proof or justification of the myth of emigration, and to someone like Rebecca, that in itself would have made him more attractive.

"Not unnaturally, he took an interest in such a handsome young woman from the old country, and in due course it seems, they became engaged. At the time, I knew nothing of this. She wrote telling me of her new post as secretary at a building firm. Not long after that, her letters became shorter and more infrequent, and then she stopped writing to me altogether. My letters to her were unanswered, and I had no means of knowing what had happened.

"My first intimation of what was to come was when I went to visit Rebecca's family to see if they had any news of her. I assumed that even if she'd stopped writing to me, she would still be writing to her mother. My relations with Rebecca's family had hitherto been based on... toleration, I suppose you might say. I think that even to begin with, they regarded me privately with a degree of contempt, and if it hadn't been for Rebecca, they wouldn't have given me the time of day. Apart from the fact that they were farmers, and had the rather crude and uncultured outlook of such people, I don't think they saw me as a very good catch for their daughter. They regarded teaching as an effeminate occupation for a man – for them, a man's work had to be physical labour. I was never likely to be wealthy, or to own land, because I would not leave to seek success abroad, as was the custom. But as long as Rebecca treated me as a friend, they tolerated me. But now, when I went to see them, the change in their attitude was startling. I was told that if Rebecca no longer wished to communicate with me, then that was her business. They had nothing else to say to me, and I was told to clear off. As if to make the point, they threatened to set their dogs on me if I didn't clear off at once.

"It was the beginning of a nightmare. Something was obviously badly wrong, but I could only make wild guesses about what it was. In a way, the worst thing about it was that I didn't know. If they had told me the truth when I went to see them, what followed would probably not have happened. I was still in love, however foolish that may appear now, and I wanted to hear from her, and to know how I stood with her. If I had known, then I think maybe my pride would have saved me from what followed.

"After a period of waiting under these circumstances, I suddenly heard that she was back – she was home from America. I waited, but she didn't ask to see me; so I sent to the farm asking her if she would see me, if only to let me know where I stood. I sent several times to the farm, but there was never any reply. I had not even seen her, even at the place where I might have expected to see her in public – at the church at Sunday mass. At length, I heard the truth, or something approximating to it, from one of the women of the village – one of the village gossips.

"According to this woman, Rebecca had returned to Ireland with her employer in New York, the boss of the building firm, a man by the name of Joseph Murphy, in order to be married in her home village. The wedding was to take place the weekend of the following week. The banns had already been posted at the church, something which I hadn't noticed, but quickly confirmed. Joseph Murphy had not yet arrived in Kilkirrin. He was visiting his family in County Wexford, where he'd originally come from; but he was expected to be in Kilkirrin the following week, a day or two before the wedding, bringing members of his family with him. Rebecca was remaining in almost complete seclusion at the farm, partly to prepare for the wedding, but partly also, according to the village woman, because she wanted to avoid meeting me. The village woman gave me the first intimation of what was to follow, and of the idea that I was no longer welcome in the village – but by then it was too late.

"The woman told me that the view of the village, or at least of the majority who were subordinate to Rebecca's family, was that I should leave Kilkirrin before the wedding – indeed, I should leave before Joseph Murphy was due to arrive the following week. When I first heard this, I dismissed it as preposterous nonsense. The village was my home. I was a part of the local community, or so I thought: I was a teacher at the local school.

"My conversation with the woman took place on the Friday. The following day I went into Galway City, so I wasn't aware of what was brewing in the village. The following day, Sunday, I went to morning mass as I usually did. However, this was no ordinary Sunday. Almost from the moment I set foot outside the door of my house, I was aware that something was up – something was going on, and it involved me. As I walked to the church I saw people talking among themselves and looking at me – I was obviously the subject of their conversation. No-one spoke to me, even to return a 'good morning'. People looked away if I spoke to them, or looked as if I might speak to them. My feelings of apprehension increased. At the church, the tension in the air was almost tangible. The first thing I was aware of was that Rebecca was there. That in itself was enough to put me into a state of confusion and turmoil. It was the first time I had seen her in nearly three years. She was already seated near the front of the church. I think she was probably aware of the moment when I arrived in the church, but she didn't look round. What I found almost as startling was that her male relatives were sitting with her. In many village churches, certainly at that time, the women sat on one side, and the men on the other, a custom which was never broken. But now I saw Rebecca surrounded by a phalanx of her male relatives – her brothers, father, male cousins; and in the aisle, still standing, some acquaintances of the family evidently intending to bar my way if I should attempt to approach Rebecca. Apart from them, I was completely ignored – no-one spoke to me, acknowledged me, or even looked at me. When I came to sit down, I found my usual place occupied, and when I requested room to sit down, I was ignored – no-one even turned to look at me. I had to find a folding chair in one of the side aisles and sit by myself at the back.

"For such things to happen in a church, supposedly a place of Christian fellowship, was truly bizarre. The priest who was taking the service was fully aware of what was happening, and he knew it was wrong; but he could not face such a show of united hostility.

"There was a malevolence in that mass of people – I

wouldn't call them a congregation, not on that day – in their singleness of purpose, in their united hostility, which was both unnerving and unnatural. When the time for taking communion came, I was physically prevented from going forward until communion had finished. When I asked to be let through, I was ignored. I could have shouted out a protest, but by then I knew that the matter was serious – I was confused, and unsure of what to do. At the end of the service, the crowd again acted as if with a common purpose. Although I was sitting at the back of the church, when I rose to leave, I found my way blocked by a mass of men who kept me well away from the church door. It was clearly their intention to keep me as far away from the door as possible to prevent any chance of my speaking to Rebecca as she left the church. When most of the people had left, the men who had been barring my exit then started to push me out of the church. They were now just as determined that I should not be allowed to remain in the church. None of them would speak to me, so I was hardly able to protest. Also, I didn't realise that it wasn't yet all over. Outside, I started to walk up the village street towards my house. I noticed that quite a lot of people were just standing around instead of making their way home as they usually did, as if they were waiting to see something. About halfway up the village street, I was confronted by the men folk of Rebecca's family – her father, uncles, brothers, male cousins, and also some of the friends and acquaintances of these people, some of whom had acted as a human blockade in the church. They were standing in a line across the street, blocking my way, and I came to a stop facing them. I didn't see Rebecca at first, but after a few moments I noticed her standing about a hundred yards behind them, with some of the other women of the family, looking on impassively. It was Rebecca's father who spoke first. 'You don't seem to be very good at taking hints, Fitzgerald,' he said. I told him I didn't know what he was talking about, although by this time it wasn't hard to guess. He ignored me and went on: 'You were told that Rebecca doesn't want to see you any more, doesn't want any more to do with you; but you didn't take the hint, and kept trying to contact her.' I said that I hadn't heard that from Rebecca herself, and that I hadn't seen her for three years. That seemed to trigger his anger, and that of the others as well. I saw them stir with anger when I said that – I heard the rustle of it in the crowd. I was suddenly aware that there were men behind me, and I was afraid; but by then it was too late. Rebecca's father went on: 'You won't be speaking to Rebecca, Fitzgerald – she has nothing to say to you. You were told to quit this village, but it seems you haven't taken the hint yet.' I replied that the village was my home and always had been. I had been born there, and my work was there as a teacher in the school. It was as if he hadn't heard me. He went on: 'You aren't wanted in this village, Fitzgerald. You aren't wanted by Rebecca, or by any of us. Now that Rebecca has found someone worthy of her to marry, we don't want there to be any possibility of a risk to her chances from the likes of you.' I started to say again, with more bravado than I really had, that my livelihood was in the village, and I didn't need his permission to live in the village of my birth. But they were no longer listening – they had done with words, and even as I was speaking, I was struck from behind with force enough to send me staggering forward. Another of them kicked me in the groin, which bent me double with agony, then kicked me again in the face, which sent me sprawling to the ground. I was then given a beating as savage as any given in rough justice to any criminal. They all set on me, kicking me or wounding me with sticks or clubs. My head and face were kicked without mercy; my stomach and my back. I felt my ribs crack, then my left arm. I lost the ability even to attempt to defend myself and I just became literally a punch bag. There were at least eight or ten of them. Then I heard a shout, and for a moment they all stopped. Someone yanked my head up by the hair, and I was confronted by Rebecca's father, his face just a foot from mine. I could hardly see him because my face was covered in blood from my nose and my eyes; my hearing was affected from the number of blows to the side of my head. But there was still no mistaking the hate in the man's voice as he shouted at me. 'You'll clear out of this village Fitzgerald, and you'll never come back. This is just a warning. Next time – if you're ever seen in this village again – next time, we'll kill you.' He then kicked me in the face, which knocked my head back and to the ground, and then they all set on me with renewed force, kicking and kicking and striking me with sticks. My body was just limp like a dead animal, and at length I lost consciousness under the rain of blows.

"I suppose someone must eventually have called them off, otherwise I would have been killed. As I learned afterwards, someone sent for the priest, and I was carried up to the presbytery. There was no doctor in Kilkirrin, and Father Thomas, the priest, could see that I was badly injured, so he sent into Galway City for help. A motor ambulance was sent, and I was carried to the hospital in Galway City. When I returned to consciousness, I found myself lying in a hospital bed. I was in the hospital for more than two months. I had four broken ribs, a broken collar bone, a broken arm, broken fingers and a fractured skull. I also had internal injuries which I have still not fully recovered from.

"While I was in the hospital, I had the time to start trying to take stock of the implications of what had happened to me. I was asked at the hospital how I had come by such injuries, and when I told them, the police were called for me to make a statement to them. But when they went to the village, Rebecca's father and the others denied all knowledge of any assault, and it seemed that no-one in the village remembered being a witness to any such assault. That was hard enough to come to terms with. For ten years I'd been a respected member of the community, or so I had thought. For ten years, I'd taught these people's children, and I suppose I'd deceived myself into thinking that these things were of importance in the community as well as in my own life. I discovered on that morning that it was a deceit, a veneer of superficiality and manners; and that underneath the veneer was a very different set of values, which first of all distinguished between people who matter and people who don't, and which was concerned with protecting the interests of the people who matter, whether defined by power, wealth, influence, or simply by the ability to use brute force, as in this case. The first shock was the discovery, the understanding, that this was the reality, not the superficial veneer. If I'd been beaten up by a gang of thugs in the back streets of Dublin, although the physical hurt would have been the same, it wouldn't have threatened my confidence in my view of the world and my place in it – my belief in the veneer, if you like. But these people were my neighbours, people I'd grown up with and had known as part of my community all my life. To be attacked in such a way by these people was truly devastating. They didn't just break my body – they broke my entire world on that Sunday morning. That in itself would have been hard enough to come to terms with; but from that moment there was the beginning of a doubt, a doubt which, once created, grew and was hardened into certainty in the light of experience seen with altered eyes.

"In those few moments, while they were beating me, when they stopped and my head was pulled up for Rebecca's father to deliver his final threat, in that moment I caught sight of Rebecca herself. It was only a momentary view, and the blood from my face was in my eyes; but I saw her. I saw the expression on her face, and her face was impassive. She stood there, and it seemed to me that she watched with perfect equanimity as I was being beaten. I could recall times when she had expressed her affection for me; when she had told me how fond she was of me; when we had kissed as though we were lovers: and now this woman stood and watched as I was beaten, with no more concern than if she was watching a fairground spectacle.

"This is the darkness I've had to live with since that day. The violence, the hostility of the community was, in the end, only an adjunct to it. It was because of her that it happened – it was because it was important to her. I had become someone who no longer mattered – who stood in the way, as she and they saw it, of what did matter. Because of the way it happened, I could have seen it as an aberration, as unusual callousness on the part of one particular individual. But what made it difficult was that I knew that that was not the case. I knew Rebecca. I knew her well enough to know that she could not be considered unusually callous or vicious. Her temperament was perfectly normal for a young woman of her class and background. I began to doubt myself, not her. The suspicion was created that, setting aside the violence and savagery of the particular incident, what had happened was, in a curious way, essentially normal."

"How can violence, particularly of that kind, be regarded as normal, let alone acceptable?" John asked.

"Not the violence, but the motives behind it."

"But, you would not distinguish between the two …"

"Setting aside the violence, I said …"

"Callousness is a kind of violence, if you will. You said you saw her standing impassively watching you being beaten."

Vincent Fitzgerald smiled gently.

"I'm sorry to have been so long-winded. Because it's my story, my life, I attach greater importance to detail than perhaps is necessary, and I've said a great deal more than I needed to in consequence. I hope it hasn't been entirely without interest, but – in any event, I take it that you have understood the point of the story."

John was reflective for a minute before answering.

"Are you making a comparison between my Helen and

your Rebecca, or … are you making a more general observation?"

Fitzgerald shook his head. "Not my Rebecca, alas, not now. Nor was she ever, I'm afraid. And no, I'm not simply comparing her with Helen. I meant them both to be illustrations of the same point. You said in your own story just now that what you found most incomprehensible was Helen's apparent inability to accept you unless you went away to risk death or injury in the war. She would rather face the possibility of losing you if that nevertheless meant that you had, as it were, proved yourself according to her conventions. What you could not understand is why she couldn't accept you for what you are, as you are. The point of all this is to suggest, not that she and Rebecca shared a motive as two individuals, but rather that they were driven by a common motive. It seems to me that the presence of such a motive means that there's a gap in understanding between men and women – and even in the possibility of an understanding. No man should forget that he is valued by women in this light, because it must in the end affect the way a man relates to women. It means at its ultimate that in the secret places of a man's heart, in his feelings towards the woman of his love, at the very heart of that love, where there should be light, there is instead a shadow of darkness. The darkness is a gulf in understanding."

"Do you think that the darkness is reciprocal?" John was disturbed to find his own thoughts echoed so closely.

"Reciprocal how?"

"Reciprocal in the sense that women often complain that men only value them for their physical appearance – that men only want young and pretty women, and that places a great deal of stress on many women because they constantly have to make themselves as young and attractive-looking as possible."

"I don't think so. That's only because women are all chasing the same kind of man, and they're competing with each other all the time. If only they could unhook themselves from this competitive thing, I'm sure that life would be so much more civilised for all people, men and women."

"Have you found anyone else since?"

Vincent Fitzgerald shook his head. "I tried a number of times, but without success. In any event, it was Rebecca I wanted, and if I had been able to have her, she would have been the love of my life."

"And even despite what happened, what you saw, you still love her?"

"It may be hard to understand, but, yes, I still love her. When you experience love of that kind, it's beyond your power to change the way you feel, in spite of almost anything that happens. I know it sounds irrational, but unless you've experienced it yourself, you can't really understand."

Vincent had taken a photograph, now faded with age, from his wallet: it was a portrait of a young woman. From the glimpse he had, John saw that she was undoubtably pretty, with a distinctive face, if rather solemn in the moment when the camera had caught her.

"I'm sorry. But then, you don't seem to be offering me much comfort either."

Fitzgerald shrugged. "It wasn't my intention to dishearten you. After all, I don't think I'm telling you anything you didn't know, or suspect, already. Your experience seems to corroborate mine in suggesting that there is a fundamental gap in understanding between the sexes. At the same time, one would despair of life altogether if there were no grounds for hope, and the hope must be that if the gap in understanding is general, it isn't universal. Somewhere, perhaps, there is a woman who is different – who isn't touched by the shadow. In your case, of course, you also have a baby on the way, and I think that will make a difference." He smiled. "Most women value their children more than their husbands."

"That's a hope I set more store by than I dare admit, almost."

"And I envy you that, too."

"Have you ever been back – to Kilkirrin?"

"No." The wry smile again. "It isn't just cowardice, although there's a good measure of that, too. I'm also concerned for my parents, who still live in the village. When I go to see them, I have to meet them in Galway City, and as they are now very old and find it difficult to travel, I'm able to see them less and less. And when I do see them, it's almost as if they're being used against me, since it's through them that I get news about Rebecca, which I suspect is quite intentional. She's been happily married for nearly ten years now, and has four children. It's a bitter harvest."

"Because they might have been your children?"

"Because of that; although I'm now enough of a fatalist to think that, even if that day had never been, I still would never have had Rebecca. The darkness would still have stood between us. To be a fatalist is to be a pessimist, because fate is generally a bad master."

John nodded in agreement. "And I have served fate for long enough," he said.

10

The storm had subsided, leaving only the storms of winter. John and Helen celebrated their first Christmas at the cottage in the tranquillity of this understanding. It was a Christmas of candlelight and oil lamps and roaring peat fires. There was jolly music on the wireless, which John ensured was tuned to Irish radio as much as possible. The so-called 'PhoneyWar' meant that there was not much war news anyway, but John wanted the war excluded from their little world in the cottage as much as possible. On Irish radio, Irish domestic news took precedence once again, and as Ireland was not preoccupied with blackouts, wartime restrictions and spy scares, it had a blessed sound of normality about it.

Helen remained tranquil in herself. They had still not spoken about the night of the storm. The need to establish a *modus vivendi* between them had taken precedence, and it was as if Helen understood that the destructiveness and the cost of pursuing her prejudice would be too great. To despise the man whose child she was carrying would mean that she would have to despise the child, and even herself; and however strong the prejudice, she evidently no longer contemplated such self-destructiveness. The baby to be was the *raisond'etre* of life, and she needed no other justification for herself or her pride. Only a certain reserve, an awareness of the existence of a taboo subject between them prevented the feeling of a return to complete normality. Even the fact that Helen would not be seeing her parents for the first Christmas since she left home did not come between them – the association with the taboo subject was still too strong, as was Helen's memory of the journey to and from England as having been little short of a nightmare under wartime conditions. Long letters were exchanged, and on New Year's Eve, Helen spoke on the telephone from the Queen's Hotel in Bray to her parents, who were at an hotel in Nantwich. John, who had arranged the telephone call, was immensely pleased with its success, as Helen's spirits were lifted considerably by it.

During the holiday period, John began to fit out a nursery, and to discuss with Helen other preparations for the unborn child, even though she was then only four months into her pregnancy. They were signs that the darkness was in abeyance at least. Such was the apparent improvement, that John was sufficiently buoyed up by it to feel a sense of concern for Vincent Fitzgerald, whom he continued to meet from time to time at the Queen's in Bray. He had been considerably disturbed by Fitzgerald's narrative. Now that perhaps he had reason to think that the implications of the narrative might not relate so closely to himself, he was concerned lest he should appear self-satisfied with his apparent turn of fortune. However, Fitzgerald did not seem in any way put out. If he had perceived an essential truth, he said, it was hardly likely to be altered by the fortunes of one individual. He was undoubtedly pleased that John had found some respite; but in keeping with his temperament, he warned John against complacency.

"If the shadow is there, it will always be there, only waiting for the opportunity to re-assert itself. Do not forget it."

John was to remember his words.

Early in January, John received a letter from England. It was from the solicitor, a Mr Rutherford, whom John had engaged to oversee the winding up of his affairs in England,

and to attend to or refer any residual matters that might arise after his departure. Such a residual matter had now arisen: John's call-up to the army had come through, and since he was no longer living at the address he was registered at in England, the documents had been forwarded to his solicitor. Mr Rutherford, in his letter, said that these had been forwarded to him as a routine matter, in the expectation that they would be sent on to John himself, which Mr Rutherford had done. However, since Mr Rutherford had some idea of the nature of the situation, he felt constrained to make comment in his letter.

"I have to advise," he wrote, "that failure to comply with the order would be a serious matter. The laws relating to military service are among the most rigorously enforced, and under the present circumstances it is unlikely that any leniency would be shown by the authorities. If you do not report for duty at the time and place shown on the order, you will be deemed thereafter to be a fugitive from military service, and liable to be arrested and brought before a court by the British authorities if they apprehended you. I understand that they do not have the power to extradite you from Eire, but you would no longer be able to visit the United Kingdom, including Northern Ireland, or any British dominion, in safety, and this would be the case, legally at least, for the rest of your life. While I understand your position, I feel that since you have engaged my services in this matter, it is incumbent on me to advise you of the consequences of it. I would be grateful if you could advise me if you wish me to convey any specific response to the authorities if they should approach me asking for your whereabouts, as they are likely to do."

The order was still in its original envelope, which bore a London postmark. It was headed with the War Office crest. "By order of His Majesty," it began, and after a preamble in the most intimidating legal language, referring to various Acts of Parliament relating to military service, it came to the point. Having failed to submit a report from a civilian medical practitioner in response to an earlier communication (why hadn't Rutherford sent him that?), he was now required to report at the time and place stated. Rutherford's letter was somewhat superfluous. The form made it abundantly clear what the penalties would be if he failed to attend: arrest and prosecution for failing to obey call-up for military service, with the liability to suffer imprisonment or forced labour. Typed in the space provided, he was informed that he was to report to Fulwood Barracks in Preston at 0700 hours on Monday 15th January 1940.

Seeing the document in his hand brought everything into focus. Hitherto, the threat that had governed all his motives had been, in a sense, theoretical, a threat in the abstract, an assumption based on common sense. In an odd way, it was almost reassuring to have the threat confirmed, to know that all that had happened since the first exploratory journey to Dublin in the spring of 1939 once he had decided what he was going to do, had not been in vain. The threat had now materialised.

Seeing the document also rekindled his anger. That such a document could be issued to a supposedly free citizen of a democratic and civilised country made a mockery of all such notions. In his view, this was coercion and terror. As he stood gazing down into the flames of the sitting room fire, he allowed his imagination to construct what it would be like to obey the order, had he remained in England. To begin with, he would be parted from Helen, having witnessed her eagerness to see him go. That would be the memory of her that he would have to take away with him. The time quoted on the order would cause the maximum inconvenience and unpleasantness for the new recruit. In order to meet the time, he would have to stay overnight in Preston, probably for two nights, given the uncertainty of Sunday train services in wartime. Thus, the last day of freedom would be spent wandering aimlessly round Preston, trying to fill the cold and empty hours. He probably wouldn't be able to eat much, if at all. On the Sunday night, there would be a few hours pretence of sleep before having to rise in the middle of the night in order to be at the gates of the barracks before dawn on a freezing January morning, cold, demoralised and fearful. The nightmare would then begin.

He looked at the order again. Today was Thursday the eleventh of January. In theory, he would still just have time to travel to England to obey the requirements of the order. He experienced a moment of revulsion at the very feel of the paper in his hand. He was a free man in a free country, and so he would remain. As far as he was concerned, a state that sought to humiliate and degrade those on whom it relied to work and fight for it deserved nothing but disloyalty. He leaned forward towards the fire and thrust the document into the flames and watched with satisfaction as it flared and shrivelled to ash.

On the Monday morning, he awoke shortly after seven, and lay awake in the darkness for a few minutes without stirring. Helen, beside him, was still asleep. He could see the time from the luminous dial of the bedside clock. This was his moment, and he savoured it with intense pleasure. Whatever the other consequences, this moment was worth much. It was as well that Helen could not discern his thoughts just then.

A couple of days later, a note arrived in the post just before he left for work. It was from Vincent Fitzgerald, who requested that John meet him that evening to discuss 'a private matter of importance'. It was unusual for John to receive any communication from Vincent Fitzgerald, so he knew it would not be about a trivial matter. As before, they met at the

Queen's in Bray. It was a wet night, and John was grateful for the chance to shelter from the rain before cycling home. Vincent expressed his appreciation that John was able to meet him at such short notice.

"It's a wild night, and no mistake," said John, shaking his raincoat before draping it over the back of a chair.

"Well, at least it suits my mood."

John looked at him expectantly.

"I've had bad news."

"Oh?"

"I've just heard that my father has died."

"Oh, I am sorry."

"Well, it was about that that I wanted to talk to you. You see, you know some of the background to the situation, so you'll understand the position more easily than someone who doesn't."

"Was your father still living in the village?"

"He was."

"And are you still being threatened, even at a time like this, and so many years afterwards?"

"Well, it's not as simple as you might think. Firstly, these vendettas or feuds don't fade away over time. If anything, they become more institutionalised and bitter, even to the point where the original cause is forgotten, although that isn't so in this case. But my main concern is for my mother. Because the vendetta has persisted, she's now very vulnerable where she is, and what I want is to move her away from Kilkirrin, if not to this area, then at least to Galway City. However, while she's still in Kilkirrin, I'm restricted in what I can do, and I need the assistance of someone who isn't known in the village, but whom I can rely on as being competent on the spot. My circle of acquaintances is not as large as you might think, and I … had the temerity to think of asking you."

John laughed. "I'm flattered. What would it involve?"

122

"Well, first of all, to help bring my mother out of the village. I'm arranging for my father to be buried in Galway City. It's against the usual practice, but I've threatened to make a stink about how the church has turned a blind eye to what's been going on in Kilkirrin, if they don't allow this at least, and so it's been agreed. Once my mother is in Galway City, I can either find somewhere for her to live there, or bring her to live with me for a while until we can decide what's best for her. I would then need someone to help pack up the house in Kilkirrin so that our family possessions can be recovered."

"Presumably you want all this to happen fairly soon."

"Well, my father's funeral will be this weekend, on Saturday, in Galway City. That's already been arranged, so I'll be in Galway City on Saturday. Could you make it on Saturday?"

"I'm sure I can."

"The rest of the business won't have the same urgency, so if you're able to help me with that, it can be whenever it's convenient for you."

"A weekend would be best, of course."

"A weekend it shall be, then. What ... will you say to Helen?"

"I think," said John reflectively, "I shall bring Helen with me, if she'll come. We still haven't seen much of Ireland beyond the Dublin area, so I'm sure she will come. She can stay in Galway City while I go on to the village."

"I shall look forward to seeing you there."

11

It was not, as Vincent Fitzgerald had remarked, the best time to see Ireland. The wide meadows of County Kildare, so lush and green in the summer, looked uninteresting and drab in the dull light of January as they slid past the train windows. For John and Helen it nevertheless had the interest of a country never seen before. Helen had readily agreed to come on the journey to Galway. Now that she had come to terms with the idea that she would be staying in Ireland, at least for the time being, the idea of a journey right across Ireland to the west coast was something to look forward to with interest, even in January. The specific objective of the journey gave it, for Helen, something of the feel of an adventure. John had told her the main facts of Vincent Fitzgerald's story without going into any detail about the motives involved. Even if she understood them, he was not sure if she would sympathise. It was not, in any case, John's intention that Helen should become involved in the events in Kilkirrin. Apart from the fact that she was pregnant, he did not want matters to be complicated by events which, in truth, he did not entirely understand himself. He was even, if he would admit it to himself, a little bit afraid: he certainly did not want her to see that. For Helen, it would remain a little adventure, and the journey would go no farther than Galway City.

For the first part of the journey, the countryside, for all its drabness, had a familiar look to it. As far as Mullingar, the railway followed the Royal Canal, which they could see glimpses of from time to time. At one point they caught sight of a narrow boat negotiating a lock basin, a sight which, for Helen in particular, conjured up a mixture of homesickness and reassuring familiarity – they might have been in Cheshire watching a boat on the Shropshire Union Canal. Beyond Athlone, however, there was a different country – great peat bogs, barren moorland and poor hill country, often looking almost grey rather than green through the driving rain which now ran in rivulets down the train windows. It was a country which, for long stretches, seemed almost completely devoid of inhabitants, or even any sign of a human presence, save the occasional ruin of a cottage or a farm on a barren hillside. The people had given up the struggle, not just against the elements, but against seven hundred years of despotism, and they had gone – on the emigrant ships to America and Canada and to the ends of the earth, or to starvation and death on these bleak moors. The despots were gone now, but it was too late – the land was returned to the elements that had fashioned it, and to their solitude. Only the burnt and tumbled ruins remained as evidence of the bitterness of the struggle, and the numbers of its victims. For all that, this great emptiness was still unquiet with the ghosts of ten thousand summers, impervious to rain or time, whose voices echoed in the sea wind on the slopes of these green valleys, for those who had ears to hear.

Suddenly, there was the sea. It was almost a shock to see it again, the slate-grey expanse of Galway Bay flecked with white. Even as they arrived, the rain stopped, and the headlands of the bay and the sea itself sharpened into clear grey and black silhouettes under a sombre sky. They had come right across Ireland, and here at last was the sea – the Atlantic Ocean. It was John's first sight of it. He pointed to the horizon beyond the low shapes of the Aran Islands at the mouth of the bay.

"Beyond those islands, there's nothing but ocean for three thousand miles until America."

"America," Helen said, half to herself. "I should like to go there one day."

John was taken aback, but said nothing more. The train rolled on at a steady pace along the north side of the narrow inlet of the bay, slowly revealing the confusion of headlands and islands which made up the farther shore, dark fingers of land reaching out into the grey sea. Although the bay was narrow, there was a sense of immense space, of the land opening out at the edge of the world, of the nearness and farness of infinity. John remembered Vincent Fitzgerald's story. To see the landscape with his own eyes gave the story a drama and a force which even Fitzgerald's eloquence could not bring to it in the quiet of the lounge bar of the Queen's Hotel in Bray.

Vincent Fitzgerald was waiting to meet them on the platform at Galway City station. He looked very weary, and in his long raincoat, even more raffish than usual. He seemed a little shy on being introduced to Helen – he was certainly uncharacteristically short of words. He seemed, in an indefinable way, diminished, as though his spirit, if not his stature, was withered by the hostility or indifference of his native soil. There was a sense of something universal in it, as though it was larger than one man, or all men who were isolated as Fitzgerald was.

Vincent walked with them to the hotel they had booked on his recommendation. He briefly pointed out some of the landmarks of the town centre, including the college building where he had been a student, years before, and also a church at the end of a side street. At the hotel, there was a moment of awkwardness while it was decided what was to be done. John took Helen up to their room, saying he would meet Vincent downstairs in the lobby in five minutes or so. As they were looking round their room and stowing their suitcases, Helen expressed a petulant dissatisfaction.

"It's rather mean of you not to let me come with you."

"To be honest, I wasn't sure if you'd want to come on this trip at all. I mean, Vincent Fitzgerald's a stranger to you, and I couldn't presume you'd have any interest in the matter. If things had been different, then I'm sure it would have been perfectly alright for you to come to the village, but on this occasion it wouldn't be appropriate. We're going there for a particular purpose, and it may not be pleasant. There's the possibility of violence, and I don't want you involved in anything like that, especially in your condition."

"Violence? What sort of violence? Why didn't you tell me about this before?"

"I honestly don't know what will happen. I'm not saying there will be violence, but it's a possibility in view of the circumstances. It's a difficult and complicated business involving a family feud, and there is a dark side to it. I'd be very unhappy about the idea of you coming along."

"You should have told me before now. Why are you involved in this? What is this man Fitzgerald to you?"

John gazed out of the window, which looked out over the roofs of the town and out over the bay to the distant hills of County Clare. He had not faced the question so bluntly. It seemed to him now that he had been guided by an instinct, natural enough for him not to have questioned it, or even to have given it a name. But he did not like to question it, for to do so was to look again into the darkness. What set Fitzgerald apart from other men was hardly to be comprehended. It was a spirit which had haunted mankind since the beginning, a spirit hardly ever seen, and when it was, it assumed the form of a great divide, a difference as between the immortal and the mundane, the few and the many, between the future and oblivion; and because he was afraid that he was also marked with this fate, and because he only half understood what it meant, it had been easy not to think too deeply about it. The instinct had been one of solidarity; the fear was of something scarcely understood, and too large for one individual, or two, to grapple with. Now, as before, he turned away from it.

"I suppose," he replied, "that he's a friend of sorts, and I agreed to help him in a time of trouble."

"He looks a bit … unconventional."

She meant something else, but refrained from saying it. She could not, however, entirely keep the disapproval out of her voice.

"Yes, I suppose he does. But remember, this is Ireland, and you see things in Ireland which you would not see in England. People are judged by different standards here."

"But they are judged."

He turned to look at her, and she was not smiling.

"Yes, they are judged, and sometimes the judgement can be very hard, which is why I really don't think it would be right for you to come with me."

"Well, if there is a possibility of violence, I don't think you should be risking yourself for this Fitzgerald. After all, how long have you known him?"

"Not long." Not long, and perhaps all his life. "Don't worry," he went on, "I won't do anything silly, I promise. In any case, I think the risk of violence against me will be slight because I'm a stranger who hasn't been involved in this. I'll be back this afternoon, you'll see." He kissed her lightly. "Don't forget to get those things I told you about."

"No, I won't forget." She forced a smile for him as he left.

Downstairs, Vincent Fitzgerald was waiting for John in the hotel lobby.

"Alright?" he asked, looking an unspoken question. He had sensed Helen's misgivings.

John nodded slowly. "Alright," he said.

Vincent led the way out into the street. After a short wait in the town centre, they caught the afternoon bus to Clifden. On leaving the town, the bus followed the coast road along the north side of Galway Bay, the grey sea widening as they passed the mouth of the bay, travelling westward.

"It's a pity you're only going as far as Kilkirrin today," said Vincent. "If you were to go all the way to Clifden, you'd be going through the heart of Connemara, which is the most beautiful country in the world, even if I say so myself."

"I shall remember for if I come back here another time."

"Another time – yes." He was silent for a minute before speaking again. "I've written a letter to my mother to expect you, and to explain what is to happen today. She's sent me a reply to say that she understands – but you'll have to be patient with her. She's very old, and she'll be grieving the death of my father, with not much thought for anything else."

"But she will do what is expected of her?"

Vincent was pensive for a moment before saying merely: "She is grieving for him."

John felt baffled. Vincent had become increasingly taciturn as they approached Kilkirrin, apparently affected by memories of familiar places.

"Do you expect these people to interfere in any way?"

"I don't expect them to interfere, no. But if something does happen, you'll have to use your judgement and do what you think best." He stood up as the bus began to slow down. "Remember, whatever happens, we are both in your hands. I will be waiting for you here." His face was set and unsmiling, and with no more than a curt nod he turned away. John suddenly understood that he was ashamed of what he was doing and could hardly bear to face it. Had he thought perhaps that with a relative stranger, the humiliation would be lessened, and found out, too late, that it was not so?

The bus came to a stop at a lane end apparently in the middle of nowhere. Vincent stepped down onto the road and stood back watching as the bus slowly got under way again. At the last moment, as he caught sight of John, he raised his hand briefly. It was a formal gesture, as if done out of politeness, his face remaining impassive. John felt a wave of irritation come over him. He was going on this journey for Fitzgerald's sake – surely the man could at least be more demonstrative. He felt momentarily detached, even ridiculous, and thought of Helen's words again. What was he doing here? Why was he on a bus going to a place he had never been to before, on an errand which had nothing to do with him?

Such musings were short-lived. Fitzgerald had got off the bus at a point about two miles short of Kilkirrin. A few minutes later, the bus was entering the village. John had to focus his thoughts on the problem in hand. The bus came to a stop. John, who had been looking for something he might recognise from Vincent's description, looked questioningly at the driver.

"Kilkirrin?"

The driver nodded in reply. "Kilkirrin."

John stepped down, and watched the bus with misgivings as it moved away slowly down the road. Kilkirrin didn't look much like his idea of a village; but he had to remind himself that this was not rural Cheshire. From where he stood, the main road, along which the bus had disappeared, curved away inland. The coast road continued westward as a mere cart track. Another track wandered inland in a different direction. In front of him, about a hundred yards of windswept machair sloped down to a shingle beach. In England, such a meeting of the ways would have been celebrated by a village green surrounded by houses, a church and a village pub. Here, there was nothing, or almost nothing. Three cottages, widely spaced, faced the coast road from the landward side, and one of those looked as if it was derelict. The ruins of two more cottages could be seen down on the machair. John's first impression of Kilkirrin was of a scatter of cottages which hardly seemed to constitute a settlement at all. Almost all the buildings were in what was apparently the traditional style for the west of Ireland: long, single-storey cottages roofed with turf or thatch, some with a byre at one end, some with shuttered windows. They looked smaller and meaner than their own cottage near Bray, as if to emphasise the poverty of the west, a poverty which drove its people away. John found it difficult to imagine becoming sentimental about such a place. There was only one house that he could see which would be described as such in England – two storeys, built of brick, with a slate roof. Vincent had given him directions from the church, but he could see nothing that looked like a church. There seemed to be no-one about, apart from some boys kicking a ball around further up the village street. When he approached them to ask the way to the village church, they appeared not to understand, or not to listen. They were shouting among themselves – one shouted something at John in a derisory tone of voice, and the others laughed at him. One of them kicked the football at him, intending to hit him with it, and although it missed, the hostility was clear enough. John felt a touch of fear – not so much a physical fear as a fear of humiliation, of losing one's dignity, that a lone adult faces in such a situation. He shouted back at them, but they were already running away, yelling derisively back at him. He could not make out what they were saying. Perhaps they were speaking Irish – the thought increased his sense of isolation.

If he could not find the church, he was not going to be able to identify which of these little cottages was the one he was looking for. Most of the ones he could see looked inhabited, with chimneys smoking, even if there were few other signs of life. Still shaken from his first hostile reception, he felt disinclined to knock on any of the cottage doors. Instead, after a little hesitation, he approached the two-storey house, hoping that perhaps someone more civilised lived there – someone he could be sure would speak English. The wind coming off the sea was bitter, and he was already shivering involuntarily with the cold. The house had its own garden, guarded by a low wall – a neat lawn surrounded by borders which in summer would surely be bright with flowers. He pulled the bell-pull, waited, pulled it again, and was on the point of turning away when the door opened suddenly. The man who stood there wore a black soutane – a priest. This must be the presbytery – and this must be …

"Yes?"

Impassive brown eyes regarded him through gold-rimmed spectacles – a middle-aged man, rather heavy in the face, hair a little unruly and starting to go grey. The priest? He remembered Fitzgerald's story of what had happened in the church on that Sunday, and what had happened afterwards. But that had been ten years ago – fifteen years ago – he wasn't sure. Would this be the same priest? He tried to remember the name.

"Yes? Can I help you?"

A soft, west-of-Ireland accent, which reminded him of Fitzgerald's.

"I'm … looking for the church."

There was a pause while the brown eyes continued to regard him impassively.

"The church … I'm afraid the next service will not be until mass tomorrow morning."

"No, I didn't mean I wanted to go to church. I just wanted to know where it was. I didn't realise that this was the priest's house."

"I see." He was regarding John very thoughtfully. "Well, the church is just opposite, there." He pointed to a building nearly opposite the presbytery on the other side of the street – a small, extremely nondescript building which John at first glance had taken to be a village hall or something of the sort. He had vaguely been expecting a substantial stone structure with a tower or steeple, or at least a belfry. The poverty of the west manifested itself here also.

"Oh … right, thank you. Look, I'm sorry to have troubled you. It's just that, being a stranger here, I didn't know my way about."

The priest didn't reply for a moment, continuing to gaze at him speculatively.

"Would it be old Mrs Fitzgerald you're looking for?" he asked at length.

John was taken aback. Perhaps in such a small village it would not be so hard to make such a guess; but the shrewdness of the priest's question caught him off guard.

"I'm … sorry, but I can't discuss the reason for my visit. I'm acting on behalf of a friend whose business is confidential." He was sounding pompous and stupid, but he hadn't been expecting this. "I'm sorry to have troubled you," he said again, and turned to walk away.

"Well, if your friend is Vincent Fitzgerald, I would suggest that you're wasting your time."

John stopped and looked back reluctantly. He didn't want to involve the priest in any further conversation, but it was difficult just to walk away without seeming rude. He had promised Vincent not to discuss his errand with anyone in the village; but he could not at the same time avoid a certain curiosity.

"I'm afraid I don't understand what you mean."

"If you're here on behalf of Vincent Fitzgerald, then you're on a fool's errand. The man's a wastrel good-for-nothing. You'll do yourself no good becoming involved with him."

"What makes you say that?"

"When he used to live in this village, he was a troublemaker. He was a nobody who didn't know his place, and because of that he caused many people here a great deal of aggravation."

"Indeed?"

"Indeed. Villages like this are not the most tolerant of places, as you might imagine, and even if he'd kept himself to himself, he might not have avoided trouble. After all, he was a schoolmaster."

"A schoolmaster – what's wrong with that?"

"Nothing in itself, for one of his standing; but it isn't generally acceptable for a man of his ... inclinations to be in charge of innocent children."

"What do you mean – his inclinations?"

"He had unnatural inclinations which were an abomination to decent Christian folk. It was unacceptable that he should be in charge of young children."

"So what happened?"

"He was forced to leave in the end. It was for the best."

"Just because he was a schoolmaster?"

"No. There was also ... an unfortunate incident. He tried to ruin a young woman from this village out of pure malice. He tried to besmirch her reputation when she was hoping to make a marriage with a very eligible young man who'd made good in America. Fortunately he was stopped in time and chastised for his malicious intentions."

"Chastised?"

"He was given a beating by the men of the village, whose patience had finally run out, and he was then required to leave the village for good. It was unfortunate, but necessary."

"A beating – it's hardly Christian to approve of that, surely, whatever he might have done."

"It was a punishment which he deserved, given what he was, and what he had tried to do. Besides, I suspect that, because of his, ah, vice, he rather enjoyed being beaten."

John was unable to keep the anger out of his face and his voice.

"And what makes you think you know so much about it, then?"

"I was here at the time. I knew the man. Do you know him? You seem over-concerned about a man you claim not to know – or was it just a secret?" He smirked conspiratorially.

John was mortified at being so easily outwitted. He turned away abruptly with a muttered parting, feeling that he would be unable to restrain himself from hitting the priest otherwise. A quarter of an hour earlier he was wondering what on earth he was doing there on such an errand – now it seemed as if he had been part of this business all along, even before he knew it.

He walked across to the church, to calm down and get his bearings. Close to, he could see that it was a church, if a very nondescript one. 'St Joseph and Our Lady' it said on the board. He pushed the door open and looked inside. The interior was very plain, with whitewashed walls, and clear glass in all the windows except at the east end, where the crucified Christ was portrayed in stained glass. Apart from the two candles on the altar table, and the carved figure of Christ on the crucifix, it might have been a Methodist chapel. From his description, Vincent would have been sitting just to the right of where John now stood, on that Sunday morning. Rebecca would have been sitting on the far side, on the left. Did he really know what this was about? He thought about what the priest had said. Suppose it was true? Suppose Vincent had not told the full truth, and there was another side to the story? How would that affect his motives for being there? He could not avoid the feeling that the unspoken sense of common identity would be destroyed. It would then simply be a matter of degrees of prejudice and private tolerance. And he had undertaken to carry out this errand. And yet, if Vincent's story was true – and even the priest had confirmed part of it – then such allegations were scarcely credible. It was a story not of perversion, but of obsessive love, of a kind he felt he could well understand. He decided that the priest's insinuations were malicious, calculated simply to deter his presence. It was more believable that the perversion was in this village rather than in Vincent's mind. The malice, however, was given effect by the fact that, once the seed of doubt had been sown, it was hard to destroy.

He stepped out of the church and faced the village street again. As he looked across at the presbytery, a figure caught his eye, walking hurriedly away from the village across the field which lay behind the presbytery. It was the priest. John watched him go, and he knew instinctively where he was going – to warn Rebecca's family of his presence. His anger went cold, and he experienced the first twinge of alarm. He was undoubtedly now in danger, and he had nothing to defend himself with. But in that coldness he derived a certain comfort. The priest in his lair was an indomitable presence, mocking him with a malice which was unanswerable, potent against his impotence, a chill of doubt which sapped his resolve, as the bitter January wind sapped his warmth and strength. But out of his lair, scurrying away on such an errand as he knew the priest to be on, the power of his malice was diminished, as his figure dwindled as he hurried out of sight. Where then, was the perversion – in this village and its priest, or in the mind of Vincent Fitzgerald?

The cottage, when he found it, was a little way off the village street to the west, halfway up a gentle bank and with a commanding view of the sea. It was visibly dilapidated, with the traditional whitewash which adorned most of these cottages patchy and weathered, revealing the rough cobbles underneath, the turf roof sagging and in need of renewal. Only the solidity of its traditional architecture allowed the cottage to weather such neglect. It did not look as if the outside, at least, had had any attention for the best part of twenty years, which it probably hadn't. There was no garden – a rough track ran through the windblown grass up to the front door. A scatter of stones in front of the cottage might or might not have represented a property boundary.

The door was opened, in answer to his knocking, by an old woman. At first, only her head was visible as she held the door ajar, either from suspicion or against the cold.

"Mrs Fitzgerald? I am sent by your son Vincent. He told me you would be expecting me."

John held out the talisman that Vincent had given him to give to his mother. It was a curiously shaped piece of stone about an inch and a half across, stained or painted in various colours, with red predominating. He had no idea what it was. The old lady took it from him, and when she looked up at him again, her face was transformed. From being closed with suspicion, her face became transparent, her eyes wide with apprehension, fearful of he knew not what.

"Who are you?" she asked.

He gave his name, again saying he had been sent by her son Vincent. Her eyes were still wide as she continued to gaze up at him.

"Is it time? Is it time then? Oh, no, no, no."

She looked down again at the talisman, pressed between aged misshapen fingers, then turned suddenly back into the cottage, leaving the door open. Taking this as an invitation to enter, and also mindful of what might be behind him, John followed her in and closed the door.

The old lady stood facing him. Her white hair, tied back loosely, was full and copious, and gave her an immediate presence of dignity, despite her age and frailty. She wore an old-fashioned traditional black skirt which reached almost to the ground, and she clutched a dark woollen shawl around her shoulders. She had a long face which was dominated by large pale blue eyes now faded with age. Her old hands shook as she clutched at her shawl, but she said nothing. She stood silently regarding him with eyes still wide with apprehension, whether of him or his errand, he wasn't sure. She looked terribly vulnerable in her frailty. John felt more than ever like an intruder, uncomfortably conscious of the fact that it was perhaps of him that she was afraid, as a man and a stranger. He took his hat off, and held it between his hands.

"Mrs Fitzgerald, do you know why I'm here?"

"Vincent … Vincent cannot come here, because they would kill him." She seemed to be speaking to herself as much as to him. He was disturbed by the reference to violence which was still such a threat even after so many years.

"Vincent has asked me to come here in his place. We are to go to Galway City together. Vincent's waiting for us. Has he not told you?"

She said nothing, but only continued to stare at him with wide eyes.

"Mrs Fitzgerald?"

"He said I was to go to Galway. But I had forgotten the day." She turned away from him in agitation, then turned to face him again. "Am I to go to Galway today – now? That's what you want?"

"That's what Vincent wants."

"I know. But I had forgotten the day. And then I thought, perhaps .." Her hand went up to her mouth. Her voice was almost a whisper now. "Must it be now? Is there no more time? Oh, Patrick, Patrick."

John did not know what to do. He knew that Patrick was the name of Vincent's father, and he realised that the old lady was greatly distressed. His instinct was to reach out and comfort her with an arm around her shoulders; but his English reserve reminded him that he was a stranger in her house – a stranger, moreover, whose errand was the cause of her distress. She remained still, her eyes bright with tears. John wished that the earth would swallow him up, or that he could simply leave – but then the distress he had caused would be to no purpose. He could not turn away from the reason for his errand.

He glanced around him, and for the first time took in some of the details of the room. Almost the whole cottage was taken up by a single large room, which evidently served as living room, dining room, kitchen and workplace. It was dominated by a large hearth and chimney breast against the end wall. A peat fire glowed and smouldered in the hearth. A plain wooden kitchen table stood in front of the hearth, and a spinning wheel to one side of it. Against the wall and underneath one of the small deeply recessed windows which looked out from the front of the cottage over Galway bay, was a workbench. Seeing it, John remembered that Vincent's father had been the village cobbler, even up to the time of his death. The bench was covered in a scatter of curved-bladed knives, hammers, lasts and offcuts of leather. More tools were in a rack above the bench, and there were several pairs of boots on the floor underneath it. The bench was evidently just as it had been left by the old man on the day he had died. How slow he had been in understanding the old lady's distress. This room, this cottage, was her life. She would have come here first, perhaps, as a young woman, the bride of the young Fitzgerald, thirty years, maybe forty years before. She may never have laid her head to rest under any other roof since that day, and because it was now almost unimaginable that she should live anywhere else, this was also part of her bereavement. These walls, the furnishings of this room, which had the worn appearance of things long familiar, were part of her very consciousness. John might understand these things, but he could hardly share them. He could remember his grandparents' house, and as a child, how keenly he had sensed the presence of the past in the tall rooms, the garden with its orchard, the polished wood furniture in the dining room, the great mirrored dressing tables in the bedrooms, and the old-fashioned beds decently covered in Victorian frills and lace, the china ornaments on windowsills behind leaded glass windows which opened onto the garden. It was a place apart, a place, not simply of changelessness, but of continuity from an earlier time, for what was preserved was both age and youth. It remained unchanged because his grandparents had largely furnished the house when they were still young, and in keeping it as it was they were preserving a part of their youth; they also preserved a way of life which did not change because it did not need changing. They had found their equilibrium: if it seemed old-fashioned to the outside world, that did not matter to them. And to the young boy who walked through the quiet rooms, there was something almost mystical in such changelessness.

This low, thick-walled Irish cottage was a world away from his grandparents' house, and yet in it he recognised the same changelessness, the same sense of security in the past preserved; and seeing old Mrs Fitzgerald thus in what had been Patrick Fitzgerald's and her sanctuary, and seeing how easily it was shaken and brought down, its security made specious by death and the inexorable flow of events beyond the power of the individual, was disturbingly unsettling. He could not share her distress, but he could understand it. Was he not, after all, in a curious way, in a similar position himself?

Vincent had said that he would come back – in a day or two, in a week or two. It didn't matter if Mrs Fitzgerald brought little or nothing with her: but John understood in that moment that it would be impossible to say so in such blunt terms. She knew in her heart that once she left the cottage she would not be coming back, and now that the moment had come, she could not face it. For a moment, as she looked up at him, he saw her as she once was, her thick white hair as the gloriously full, soft tresses of a young woman, blue eyes bright with youth and not with tears, and charged with the strength and confidence of youth. The young woman would have laughed at him and his earnestness, and told him to be about his business. She had a husband, the strength of her own body, the expectation that her personality would fill the space created by the strength of her youth in its effect on those around her. What was distressing, what was shocking, was how demeaning was the frailty of age: that because her strength was gone, so also was her confidence, her expectation that others would respect her dignity as a person. She could only stand and weep in her helplessness.

John could not go on with this any longer. He could not force her to go. It was enough that he should be the agent of her distress, reminding her of the reality of her frailty. He could not bring himself to do any more. He reached out and touched her arm very gently.

"Mrs Fitzgerald, I cannot stay any longer. I must leave now. Vincent is waiting, and I have to meet him as arranged. If you're coming with me, please come now. If you've forgotten something to bring, we can have it collected later."

He put his hat on and pulled his coat closer about his shoulders in anticipation of the wind outside. Mrs Fitzgerald stood still with head bent, looking down at the curious talisman held between hands which still shook with infirmity. John was now acutely conscious of time, of the minutes ticking away. It would not be good to be stranded in Kilkirrin. He knew that the pressure he was applying to the old lady was brutal, but he was also conscious of other imperatives, not least his own safety. For endless seconds longer, she stood there. What made it so difficult was the awareness that, however hard it was for her, she would be forced through her infirmity to give in. She had nothing left – not even the dignity of freedom. She turned away from him suddenly, without looking at him, quickly like a child, and disappeared through an open doorway on the far side of the room. She emerged a minute later with a shapeless black cloth bag with draw-string closures, full of he knew not what. She took a coat and scarf from a peg on the wall, and took what seemed an inordinately long time putting these on, while John's impatience mounted. But still she was not ready to leave. She stood indecisively in the middle of the room, not looking at John, or at anything in particular, as if unable to make up her mind about something. John's impatience almost moved him to speak. Suddenly, however, to his surprise, the old lady dropped to her knees and began tugging at the edge of one of the flagstones that covered the floor of the cottage. Instinctively John knew what she was about, and when it became clear that she did not have the strength to move the stone, he went over to help, pulling the flagstone up onto its edge. Mrs Fitzgerald did not look at him, as if she took his assistance for granted; or perhaps she resented that he should be privy to such a secret. When the stone was raised, she pulled an oilcloth bag from a hollow in the earth beneath, and from this she took a small japanned metal box which she quickly slipped into the bag she was carrying. Only when the flagstone was replaced did she glance up at him, primly, as if to admonish him against betraying what he should not know. He could only guess at the contents of the box. What would remain precious at the end of one's life? Jewellery? Money? Legal documents? Letters? How desperately sad that it should be so little – but then, she was a widow, and it was all the rest that she grieved over. The little japanned box had to represent the future as well as the past.

She did not look back – it would perhaps have been too much to bear. The key was turned in the lock, and they set off slowly down the grassy slope towards the road. John heard the bus coming well before they reached the road, and he had to run on ahead to stop it. He was never so glad to see a bus in his life. Apart from the bitter cold, he did not relish the idea of being stranded in Kilkirrin. His encounter with the village priest had done nothing to dispel the impression of the place left by Vincent's story. Mrs Fitzgerald was quite calm and docile now that she had begun the journey away from her past. It was a journey which had in fact begun when Patrick Fitzgerald had died – this was the inevitable consequence. She climbed into the bus and went to sit down while John paid the fares. Everything was inevitable, and she either faced it calmly, or simply let it pass uncomprehended over her head – John did not know which.

He had hardly sat down himself when he suddenly caught sight of the priest again. The bus was winding its way slowly through the straggle of cottages which made up Kilkirrin, and as it turned a corner, John suddenly saw the priest in the road ahead of them. He was with two other men, and they stood aside as the bus passed them. As it did so, the priest caught sight of John and Mrs Fitzgerald. He drew the attention of the two other men, pointing and gesticulating. All three of them then shouted, and ran after the bus. The driver, thinking he had a fare, stopped the bus. One of the two men with the priest climbed aboard and, ignoring the driver, walked along to where John and Mrs Fitzgerald were sitting. He was not a particularly big man, but he had a coarse, uncouth appearance which was intimidating enough. John had no idea who he was, beyond surmising that he might be one of Rebecca's family – perhaps one of her brothers or cousins. As the man approached, John stood up so as to meet him on equal terms, and to block his access to Mrs Fitzgerald, as he was obviously heading for them. In doing so he was tacitly admitting that he was expecting trouble; but he sensed that, here on the bus, the other was at something of a disadvantage, out of his element.

"Where are you going with the old woman? Where are you taking her?" the man asked truculently.

"What's that to do with you?"

"I'm asking the questions. Where are you taking her?"

"Mind your own business." John experienced a sudden surge of anger at the man's insolence. If the man decided to start anything, he would find that John would hit him back very hard indeed. John's anger was reaching boiling point, and he found he wanted to hit the man, to smash his fist into him. At that moment he would have welcomed a fight. Perhaps the man sensed that too, and he hesitated.

John pressed his advantage.

"You haven't paid your fare mister." He nodded at the driver, who was looking back at them.

"I'm not riding."

"Well get off the bus, then – you're holding us all up." He raised his voice suddenly.

"Driver, drive on. Drive on."

After a moment's hesitation, the driver put the bus into gear, and it started off, quickly gathering pace.

"If you can't pay the fare at the other end, then you'll probably do a spell in the police cells until someone bails you out," John said with grim satisfaction. It worked – the man, after a moment's horrible indecision, during which he glared at John and mouthed incoherent obscenities, turned and scuttled back to the front of the bus. He shouted at the driver, and jumped off as soon as the driver had brought the bus to a halt. As the vehicle gathered pace again, the man looked up until he caught sight of John through the bus windows. He pointed angrily and shouted unheard threats or obscenities. All the raw violence of this place seemed to be embodied in the blotched, distorted face and the pointing arm.

Mrs Fitzgerald was not looking at the man. She sat looking down at her lap, where her hands were folded and still holding the curious talisman.

"Who was that man?" John asked her.

After a moment she looked up, looking straight ahead of her, not at John.

"Oh, he's one of Declan Brady's sons. Kevin, I think they call him. Such a great lout he's turned out to be. Even when he came back from England he was no different. I remember him when he was just a wee lad, and he was always in trouble then – although I think he needs to be in company before he's really bad. On his own he's not up to much."

"What was the priest doing in the company of such a man?"

She remained silent, continuing to gaze ahead of her. John thought she wasn't going to answer, but after a minute she said: "He's made his bed, and so he must lie on it. I don't think he finds it such a great imposition. It's hard for me to say that about a man of the cloth, but in Kilkirrin, even the church is not above that sort of thing."

"And the man, Kevin – is he ... Rebecca's brother?"

"One of her brothers. They're a whole brood of them – and as vile a brood as you're likely to find," she added softly.

John wondered if she included Rebecca in that judgement, and suspected that she probably did.

The bus was slowing again, and came to a halt. A moment later, Vincent Fitzgerald was standing beside the driver, and looking cautiously along the bus. He showed no emotion when he saw his mother sitting beside John. He paid the driver, then came slowly along the aisle towards them. John stood up and moved to the seat across the aisle, as Vincent bent down and embraced his mother. Neither of them spoke – it was a passionless embrace, or one so full of passion that words were superfluous. When he stood up again, Vincent turned to John.

"Thank you. Thank you for this. I am in your debt, sir."

He seized John's hand, and John almost winced at the strength of the other's grip. Vincent looked pale, sickly pale, almost gaunt, bundled into a dark, worsted overcoat, his hair tousled from the wind; and John could only guess at his emotions.

"Was there any trouble?"

John grimaced.

"You should have warned me about the priest. I was foolish enough to go to the priest's house to ask for directions when I got lost."

"The priest – Father Thomas?"

"Was he the same priest who was there when … when …?"

Vincent nodded for him to go on.

"He remembered you. He mentioned you by name and spoke of you in the vilest terms." John remembered with unease the priest's sly hints about Vincent. Objectively, they seemed even less credible now than they had been when the priest had made them.

Vincent, in a curious echo of his mother, said merely: "He would have had to come to terms with the Bradys if he was going to stay in the village as priest. He'll be well in with them now, I imagine."

"They were going to stop us – the priest and two other men, both of whom, I take it, were from this Brady family." John described what had happened. Vincent, listening, watched John's face intently, and when he had finished, looked down at the floor. They had both sat down to avoid the lurching motion of the bus, Vincent beside his mother, John in a seat across the aisle.

"That means it will be harder to go back," he said, apparently more to himself than to John. He looked up and smiled wanly, the first time John had seen him smile that day. He reached out and gripped John's arm briefly.

"You were not to know," he said. "We shall have to see what might be done."

146

12

Helen had not been impressed by Galway City. It had a parochial, small-town atmosphere in comparison with Dublin, which she visited fairly regularly with John. Her brief visit to England had not given her any impression of the wartime rationing which since then had started to produce increasing austerity there, beside which even the limited range in the emporiums of Galway City was a relative abundance. Such as they were, however, they had engaged her interest for barely an hour. She drifted down towards the harbour, drawn by the salt scent of the sea, the pungency of dried seaweed and the shore's corruption, of tar and oil and ships, and the skittering cries of seabirds scavenging the harbour basin. The sea was a stranger to her, she, from the solid certainties of Manchester brick and asphalt, of terraced streets and factory sirens, rattling trams, and genteel, china Sundays. The sea was a mere novelty on the sands of Blackpool or Formby, part of the general excitement of that special week in August, the unheeded boundary of the western edge of consciousness, there and not there. Now, how strange it was to be standing on the western edge of another country, looking out over another sea, unseen and unknown before, and yet to feel it was so familiar. The mewing calls of seagulls awoke a sense of the sea's boundlessness, of its freedom from the constraints of the land, of the idea of escape. Even a rusty coaster alongside in the main dock became the object of sudden curiosity.

Perhaps even this ship . . She was unsettled by thoughts she had not known for many weeks; thoughts she had put behind her, or assumed she had. It was in this state that the bitter January wind finally cut through her daydreams and drove her, unwillingly, back to the shelter of the town.

By three o'clock it had begun to rain again. The wind had shifted into the north-west, raw and blustery, driving the rain raggedly before it through the failing January light. Even in the short walk from the hotel, John and Helen got unpleasantly wet. Helen's unsettled mood had not been improved by John's incommunicativeness about what had happened in Kilkirrin that afternoon. Helen had embarked on the journey to Galway as an adventure, and despite her mood it was still an adventure, albeit one whose final stage she had been excluded from, or so it seemed. So when John would say little about what he had done that afternoon, her irritation only increased. She did not appreciate that perhaps John did not have the words to describe what he had experienced, and she merely allowed his reticence to add to her moodiness.

Vincent had asked John if he and Helen would attend the service for his father's funeral. John's initial assumption was that this was a matter of courtesy on Vincent's part, and so he did not think it appropriate to refuse, and said that he and Helen would attend.

The church turned out to be simply the chapel of rest for the main public cemetery in the city. On entering, John hesitated. He had intended that he and Helen would sit unobtrusively at the back of the church, behind the congregation; but the church was empty, or almost empty. A coffin stood on trestles before the altar, and standing in front of the altar and facing them stood a priest – a young man with a high, slightly balding forehead, and wearing a full white surplice with a stole of rich purple, the whiteness of the surplice and the colour of the stole picked out startlingly by

148

the pale light which flooded through the side windows. Standing behind the coffin in the first row of pews were two people – Vincent and his mother. The rest of the church was empty, save for three dark-suited men standing respectfully right at the back, who were obviously the undertaker's pall-bearers.

For a moment, John thought that perhaps they had arrived early – it was a minute or two before he understood the significance of what he saw. Vincent, hearing their arrival, turned and signalled them to come forward to the front. It was only when he and Helen had taken their places in the front row of pews that John understood that there would be no-one else. For the moment, there was only time for surprise. The priest took his place in the pulpit and opened the missal on the lectern. For a minute, there was a stillness: all stood motionless, looking down, hearing only their own thoughts; the muted gusting of the wind outside against the tall windows, a slight creak of the roof timbers deepening the silence. It suddenly seemed to John that perhaps this brief stillness was the true rite of passage for the man, whom he had never met, whose coffin now lay before the altar in an almost empty church. The old man might have expected ceremony; but ceremony was for the living: only in that long minute of inner unquiet might it be possible to discern the spirit of the departed man, the colour of the life which the spirit had animated, from the infant to the old man, and which, perhaps, in that stillness, it now grieved for.

The priest's voice was quiet in the emptiness of the church as he began to speak. He read aloud from the missal, reading the funeral service. The prayers were spoken as responses, murmured automatically with the ease of long familiarity. John and Helen, lapsed C of E both, kept their heads bowed in mild embarrassment at their inability to follow. There was no music, no sermon – it was the barest minimum the church

149

could offer. Could so long a life be dismissed in so spartan a ceremony: four mourners, two of whom did not even know the dead man?

At the end, there was another brief silence, and then the pall-bearers came forward, walking slowly in line down the aisle. Each took his place at one corner of the coffin: the fourth corner, at the front, was taken by Vincent. John found this strangely primitive. Was it done for effect, or out of necessity? He could not tell; but somehow it underlined the bareness of the ceremony.

Outside, the light was failing fast. Even the lingering light of the west was darkened by an oppressive sky from which the rain now fell in a steady downpour. The wind was now stronger, and gusting, so that the umbrella which Helen had brought proved useless. It would have been a dramatic setting for the last act, almost Wagnerian in its theatricality, if it had not been for the almost complete absence of ceremony. This was desperately near the edge: but then this was also Ireland, and when the old man had been a boy, during the time of the evictions, death had been very much less ceremonious even than this. This was what came to the poor, and even if it had been the balmiest of summer days, it would have been quickly over. As it was, the wind and rain and gathering darkness seemed to blunt the sharpness of grief. Mrs Fitzgerald walked slowly between Helen and John with head bowed, both in grief and against the elements. Vincent walked with head up, facing the wind, the burden of his father on his shoulder. His face was expressionless, and if he cried, his tears were washed away by the rain which streamed down his face and plastered his hair to his head. After the coffin had been lowered to the ground at the graveside, he continued to stand ramrod straight, bareheaded and oblivious to the rain as the priest read the burial service while attempting to shield the missal from the wind, which tore at the flimsy pages.

As soon as they decently could, they retired to the shelter of the church to wait until the rain had at least abated. Mrs Fitzgerald went into the church and sat down in one of the pews. Helen went to her to see if she could do anything for her – a tissue to dry her face, perhaps? But her offer was politely declined. The old lady wished to be alone, and Helen left her, sitting upright in the pew, her white hair straying a little from its fastenings and starting to come down in a cascade which hinted at its former glory, blue eyes steady and unseeing as she gazed into the past.

Helen joined John in the porch, and they stood for a minute, undecided as to what to do. Helen was feeling very unsettled and fatigued, and she wanted to return to the hotel at once. John had also had enough for one day; but there was no sign of Vincent. He had not returned with them to the church.

"Surely he's not still out there in this? What in God's name is he doing?" Helen was exasperated and wanted to leave, but felt that they could not leave Mrs Fitzgerald alone. After a few minutes they heard footsteps outside and Vincent suddenly appeared. He looked wilder than ever, his face and hair running with water, his coat soaking wet. Mud was caked on his shoes and smeared on the hem of his coat. They both looked at him in some astonishment. When John finally asked him where he had been, he didn't at first answer, seeming to need a few moments to gather his thoughts, while at the same time attempting to dab the rainwater from his face with a handkerchief which was already soaking wet.

"Where … where's my mother?" he asked at length.

"She's inside the church," Helen answered. "I think she'd like to be left alone for a few minutes." She could not keep a note of sharpness out of her voice, and Vincent seemed to notice this, glancing at her quickly before looking away again. He looked down at the mud on his shoes and coat, appearing to notice this for the first time.

"The gravediggers won't return until the morning. I had to loosely fill the grave in again, otherwise it would have been flooded by morning. They might have left it open until it drained."

Even then, John was about to ask if someone else would not do that, before he realised that it was pointless. If it had not been for the starkness of the situation he might have been as exasperated as Helen. As it was, he merely nodded. He looked meaningfully out at the steadily falling rain.

"I'm afraid it doesn't look as if this weather is going to abate, so if you will excuse us, I'd like to get Helen back to our hotel where she can get warm and dry again as soon as possible."

"Yes, of course." Vincent glanced at Helen again. In England, this would have been the signal for a polite parting of the ways, with a vague promise to keep in touch. But this was Ireland, as John at least understood.

"Will you be staying in Galway until tomorrow?" Vincent asked. When John indicated that they would be, he went on: "I wonder if you could spare me a couple of hours or so of your time tomorrow morning, before you return to Dublin. I'd be very grateful if you could."

Again, John merely nodded.

"If you'll give our regards to Mrs Fitzgerald for us. We really will have to be going."

"Of course. Goodbye. Until tomorrow."

An unpleasant ten minute walk brought John and Helen back to their hotel. As they were drying off in the hotel bedroom, Helen commented tartly.

"That man doesn't have any sense of propriety, does he? I mean, you don't just keep presuming on people, do you, especially if you don't offer anything in return? What could he offer, anyway? He should associate with people of his own level instead of imposing himself on people like us. What more does he want?"

"I don't know, Helen," John said uneasily. The whole business left him feeling uncomfortable, especially in Helen's presence.

She went on: "And as for that business of him staying outside in the pouring rain and filling in the grave himself, well, it was just bizarre. I can't help thinking that he must be more than a little mad." She started combing her hair out after drying it with a towel. "I still can't understand why you maintain an association with the fellow. It does you no credit to do so. Surely, if you're going to make friends here, they should at least be more on our social level. Are there none such, even at St Mungo's?"

"You can't always choose your friends, especially when you've settled in a new place. Those who might seem the most desirable to cultivate as friends are often the least accessible. If you're an outsider, and there are many strange and subtle ways in which one can be defined as an outsider, then one is usually kept on the outside. And in the end, I think, it doesn't matter. I don't think you're really talking about friendship – what you're talking about is connections, which is an entirely different matter. I'm not sure if I know what friendship is; but I feel that there are occasions when it's necessary to be able to respond to another human being, regardless of who they are, if the circumstances demand it. I suppose I feel that this is such an occasion, even if Vincent Fitzgerald is a little strange."

"Well, you may feel that the situation demands all this of you, but I hope you'll remember that it's demanding on me as well."

"I'm aware of that; but I would be equally prepared to accept the situation if our positions were reversed."

Helen sighed.

"You're always so full of words, John. But words are just words – they don't change anything. You should remember that too."

153

They dined in the hotel, since the weather continued foul, and then went to bed early. John eschewed further conversation about Fitzgerald in order to avoid further argument. He was also wondering what Fitzgerald might want on the morrow.

On a Sunday, the routine of the hotel was relaxed slightly. Breakfast was half an hour later than on weekdays so that guests could have a little longer in bed, while still allowing them time enough to dress for mid-morning mass at the parish church, five minutes' walk away. Guests could leave a little later than on weekdays, and morning coffee was served in the lounge for those guests returning from mass who had decided not to partake of something stronger in a public house. John and Helen, as non-churchgoers, were still packing in leisurely fashion in preparation for departure, therefore, when a chambermaid tapped at the door, bringing a message that there was a gentleman waiting in the lobby asking for John. Helen, guessing who it was, was immediately hostile.

"Can't you send him away, or at least make your excuses? I'm sure that would be perfectly in order."

John grimaced briefly.

"I did say I'd see him. I'll have to see what he wants at least. I shouldn't be long."

Downstairs, Vincent was waiting as before, sitting at one of the tables in the lobby. He gave John a somewhat rueful look, and then looked down at the table for a moment before speaking.

"I could have said goodbye yesterday at the church, even if the circumstances weren't the most propitious; so I suppose you can guess that I haven't come here just to say goodbye now."

"No." John was cautious.

"I know it's a cheek my coming here again to ask you for another favour, and perhaps a greater one even than yesterday. All I will say is that I will quite understand if the answer is 'no' on this occasion. I realise you have personal and family commitments, and I've already presumed on your generosity in a manner in which, at the moment, I have no means of repaying you for. However, I'm sure you'll realise that I haven't come with an idle request."

"No …"

"With your help, I managed to get my mother safely out of Kilkirrin. As long as she was there, I was very limited in what I could do. Now that she's safe, I can afford to be a little bolder. The cottage is now empty. What I intend to do today is to retrieve my mother's furniture and belongings before the place is broken into and looted."

"You're not serious?"

"About the cottage being broken into? I'm afraid I am. The Bradys are more than capable of it, now that the place is empty and apparently abandoned, and I doubt if the Factor will be very interested as long as the cottage isn't damaged. The longer I leave it, the more likely it is that the cottage will be broken into; so I've decided to do it today. I'll never have a more favourable opportunity. I've hired a motor lorry, and I'm going out to Kilkirrin this morning to empty the cottage. I'll have some help from the driver, of course, but I really need at least one other person, because speed will be of the essence. I was hoping that you would be the third person."

"Well," John was still cautious – "you understand that we will have to return home to Bray today, and we were intending to catch the lunchtime train. How long were you expecting this business to take?"

"Not more than three hours. An hour's drive to Kilkirrin, an hour at most to load up the lorry, probably less, then an hour back to Galway City. Is there an afternoon train to Dublin?"

"Yes, there is." John hesitated. "What about the Bradys? Are you expecting there to be trouble?"

"There could be trouble, yes. But we won't be hampered as we were yesterday by the presence of my mother, and in any case, I'll be prepared for trouble if it does happen. We won't be completely helpless. Also, if we stick to my timetable, I've timed it so that our arrival in Kilkirrin will be just after the start of Sunday morning mass, which most of the village normally attends – so if they're all in church, there's a good chance we'll get away unobserved."

John was thoughtful for a moment.

"I'll have to have a word with Helen. She's expecting to return home on the lunchtime train, and she won't be happy about any delay. Give me five minutes or so and I'll be able to let you know."

"Don't be any longer – I want to keep to my timetable."

Helen was furious, and it took all John's skill to prevent a serious row. As before, her invective was directed as much against Fitzgerald as against the inconvenience of a delay.

"And what am I supposed to do?" she demanded. "Just because this bloody Fitzgerald man wants to impose himself on us yet again, we're going to be late getting home, and I've got to hang around waiting while you go haring off on some futile errand on his behalf, which might well be dangerous. Supposing something happens to you? What will I do then? Have you even thought of that?"

"Of course I've thought of it, and I can assure you that I won't be taking any unnecessary risks. I'll leave that to Fitzgerald if it arises; but from what he's told me, I don't think it will."

But she was not yet pacified.

"And what about me? I had thought that we might spend this morning together. But once again, I have to take second place to this Fitzgerald. You're a selfish bastard and I'm sick of it." Her voice rose to a shout, and her face darkened with anger. John gritted his teeth. He did not want to leave her like this. He reached out and held her by the arms.

"Helen, listen to me. You do not take second place to Fitzgerald. That's simply not true. We're only in Galway because Fitzgerald asked me if I could help him out over this weekend, and that's all it is. I just thought you might like to come to Galway too, to see something of the west of Ireland. This is the first time I've been here as well. But I promise I won't take any unnecessary risks, and I've told Fitzgerald that we're going home today. If we don't catch the lunchtime train, then we'll have a nice lunch in the town somewhere, and catch the afternoon train. I know you don't like Fitzgerald, but I did promise the man I'd help him out this weekend, and this is what that amounts to. I can't imagine that it'll happen again, so please will you bear with me for about three hours?"

"How do you know it'll only be three hours?"

"Because we can only stay in the village for an hour at most. That's how long Sunday morning mass takes."

Her anger was turning to puzzlement.

"I can't go into explanations now. I'll tell you about it when I get back. Believe me, it won't be more than three hours."

Still sullen, she nevertheless allowed him to persuade her to wait for him in the hotel lounge taking morning coffee and reading a book. He left her finishing off their packing. Just as he was going out, he turned back for a moment.

"I'm curious. What is it about Fitzgerald that makes you dislike him so?"

Helen grimaced.

"I don't think that you'd understand, because you're not a woman. Personally, I think he's a creep, but I don't know if I can put it into words why. I suppose you might say that it's because, as a man, he lacks something."

157

13

The rain and wind of the previous day had cleared away to the east, leaving Sunday one of those mild, still January days which are the harbingers of spring. A layer of high cloud covered the sky which was now milky white, as if apologetic for the violence of the day before. The motor lorry lurched and bounced cautiously along a narrow lane which was no more than a dirt track, still covered in puddles from Saturday's rain. The lorry's cab was rather cramped, and John was squeezed in the middle, with Vincent on the left and the driver on the right. The lorry had been hired from a haulage company, of which the driver, a young man in his twenties, was an employee: it was doubtful if he would have hazarded his own vehicle on a trip of this sort. Vincent was giving directions on the basis of memories of the district of ten or fifteen years before. They had left the main road into Kilkirrin from Galway City for a back road which, after a circuitous route, ran into the village near the top end, avoiding the need to go through the main part of the village. Vincent's memory of this road had evidently exaggerated its suitability for a motor lorry. They bounced up and down in their seats as the lorry lurched over ruts and potholes, the driver cursing occasionally as the wheels skidded in patches of mud left soft by the rain.

"Are you sure you know where you're going?" he asked at length in some irritation.

Vincent assured him that he did. John noticed that his face was rather white and set, however – he was evidently feeling the strain. The stone dykes on either side of the lane eventually gave way, and they were then driving over open moorland in which the track was almost lost. Two or three times Vincent called a halt to get his bearings; but at length, he became more confident. A cottage appeared, then another – they had arrived. Slowly, the lorry advanced into the village. Here and there, a cottage chimney smoked, but there didn't seem to be anyone about. If their arrival had been noticed, it hadn't so far produced any interest. The Fitzgerald cottage was a little way off the main road to their right. John didn't recognise it, even from the previous day, until they had almost reached it. The lorry swung round on the wide grassy bank as, on Vincent's instructions, the driver backed the vehicle right up to the front door of the cottage. They were ten minutes late on Vincent's schedule, and Vincent impressed on the other two the need for haste. If he was feeling any fear at that moment, he was managing to conceal it under the demands of physical activity. Even the driver noticed the strain he was evidently under, however, while not yet understanding its cause.

The driver swung down the tailgate of the lorry while Vincent unfastened the cottage door. Notwithstanding his own injunction in favour of haste, Vincent was unable at first to do anything but walk slowly round the inside of the cottage gazing intently at everything he saw. He had not been in the cottage for more than ten years. It had changed very little in the intervening time, and the effect this had on him was sudden and severe. In all his haste and plans of the past few days, he could not have foreseen this – or rather, had not done so. He had been born in this cottage, and spent all his childhood and growing-up years there. For all the poverty of the time, and the humiliation of his eventual enforced departure, these years had been such as to give him, at the

159

time, a sense of security from the trust he had been able to put in his mother and father, because of the stability of their lives, however illusory such security was in reality. He might, if asked, have said that he had had a very happy childhood; but what he would have meant by that was that the memories of that time were a refuge in his mind – a refuge because they were locked in the past; and all the barrenness of the years since his departure, the shifting rootlessness of moving from rooming house to rooming house in a strange and indifferent city, had been made in part bearable because he had been able to return, in spirit, to this fortress in the mind, maintaining the hope that such things were not entirely lost. This was at the core of his sanity, even if sometimes it was below the surface of his consciousness. Its steadfastness was certain because it could not be taken away from him – the past is fixed forever, and the greatest power on earth cannot change it.

But now, he was faced with the physical remnants of that past, so nearly unchanged that merely to see them again, to one in such a state as he, was almost overwhelming. It was as if, without warning, the idea of return, that desire confined for so long to his dreams and the secret recesses of his mind, the longing for which could leave him physically shaken but which could never be spoken of aloud, even to himself, had for a brief moment been presented to him mockingly as a reality which he might reach out to take possession of. Mockingly, because not only were those memories separated from him by time as well as by place, but because of how those memories might be affected by the fact that he himself was about to dismantle these, their physical remnants. However forlorn they might seem now, they were imbued in his mind with a kind of sacredness because of what they once were. The things they had come to take away, the furniture, the moveable goods, were an integral part of the whole. Their sacredness was due in part to the fact that they were here, and had been here since the time of his earliest memories. His memories encompassed them as being part of their setting, as part of the cottage itself; and however long ago the events, he had no other memory of them than in this place. To take them away now, out of the cottage, would be an act of destruction that Vincent suddenly found he could not face.

John encountered him coming back into the main room of the cottage through the doorway at the far end of the room.

"Well?" It was obvious that something was amiss.

"I … I hadn't realised that seeing all this again, just as it was, would bring back such strong memories – that I'd feel like this about it. Taking all these things out of here will be like tearing apart my childhood. I'm … I'm not sure if I can go through with it after all."

"What?" John was dumbfounded. "Do you mean to say that you've brought us all the way out here for nothing? Well, let me tell you now, that I've got other ideas about that. We've come here to get this stuff, and we're bloody well going to take it. For God's sake, pull yourself together, man. You're supposed to be leading this trip. You can't remain in possession of the cottage. On your own admission, the cottage will be broken into by the Bradys. If you take the furniture and everything out, then at least they won't be able to violate that. This was your own plan. You told me it not two hours ago. Now, for God's sake, stop havering and let's get on with it."

John seized hold of a chair and carried it out through the front door of the cottage, handing it up to the young driver, who stood waiting on the back of the lorry. Another chair followed. Vincent stood watching, miserable with indecision. At length, John rounded on him.

"Are you going to make yourself look a complete idiot, or are you going to help?"

The man's resolve seemed to be crumbling; but the price was visible in his face. John's patience, however, was running out even faster.

161

"Here, help me with this table. Get hold of the other end."

Vincent, after a moment's hesitation, did as he was told. Thereafter, they worked in silence, broken only by an occasional query from John as to whether a particular item should go. Vincent's answer was always in the affirmative. It was as if, once he had decided to fall into line, he was determined that everything and anything which might be taken was taken. Even the rack above the workbench containing his father's tools was prised off the wall.

The allotted hour passed quickly. Given the delay at the start, its expiry found them still at work. John noted the time from his watch. By then, there was little pretence at order – they were simply throwing things into the back of the lorry so as to clear the remaining items from the cottage.

A shout and raised voices outside brought John to the cottage door. The lorry driver, still standing on the back of the lorry, had turned to face three men who had approached the cottage from the direction of the village. There seemed to be some sort of altercation going on. John stepped out of the cottage and walked round the back of the lorry. The driver looked down at him uncertainly.

"What seems to be the trouble?"

"Who the hell are you?" one of the strangers shouted at him before the driver could answer. He was an old man, with close-cropped hair, grey and grizzled, perhaps in his sixties, but perhaps much older. His face and bearing were coarse to the point of uncouthness, but at the same time he had about him the air of one who was used to being obeyed or deferred to. The other two were much younger, and after a moment, John recognised one of them as the man who had attempted to waylay him the previous day as he had been departing the village with Mrs Fitzgerald. Recognition was mutual, and the other shouted out to the old man.

"It's him – it's the fellow who took old Mrs Fitzgerald away yesterday."

The old man walked forward towards him.

"I asked you a question, mister. Now, either I get an answer, or we'll beat it out of you. Who the hell are you, and what are you doing here?"

John stood his ground, although inside, he felt his stomach knotting with fear.

"I'm Mrs Fitzgerald's legal agent. I've been appointed to supervise the transporting of all her effects and possessions from these premises to her new place of residence." He pulled a piece of paper from his inside breast pocket. "I have here a copy of the legal instrument which empowers me to take charge of Mrs Fitzgerald's affairs here at this place." The paper was actually a circular which he had absently stuffed into his pocket the previous morning. He waited tensely to see if the bluff would work. But the old man didn't seem to be interested.

"Where have you taken the old woman?" he shouted.

"That's none of your business," John replied crisply.

"I'll decide whether it's my business or not. And you can get this stuff back inside again. You're not taking it anywhere without my say-so. These Fitzgeralds were nothing but troublemakers. We put up with them here for long enough, and that gives us the right to claim what we want of their stuff, now that they've taken the hint and cleared out at last."

"I'm warning you that any attempt to interfere, and you'll be made the subject of a court injunction, and you'll be taken to Dublin to stand trial for contempt of court."

Most of what John knew about the law and legal processes had been gleaned from reading newspaper reports of trials. He wasn't sure how convincing it sounded now. The old man hesitated. The invocation of large and remote powers – the courts, Dublin – was unsettling, but only for a moment. This

163

was the wild west – the law had never troubled their lawlessness out here in the past, so why should it now?

The old man shouted something in Irish to his two companions.

"You've been given fair warning, mister," he said to John. "It's your problem if you're too stupid to take heed. Now you'll find out what happens to outsiders who ..."

He stopped suddenly. The two younger men, who had begun to advance on John with unmistakably violent intent, stopped in their tracks also. John was suddenly aware that Vincent was standing beside him. Long moments of silence followed before the old man spoke again.

"You! You, here! D'ye think I'd forgotten about you, Fitzgerald? You were told never to come back here. It looks like we didn't beat that into you hard enough."

"Never mind that, Brady. I haven't forgotten. There's an awful lot I haven't forgotten about you. Things that were done to me, and to my parents. I've had a long time to think about them, Brady. A long time to think about what your reward for all this might be. And it means bad news for you, Brady. Can you not feel it now? Do you not think you've overreached yourself this time, Brady? There's no-one else come up here. You haven't got your gang of thugs with you this time. There's just the three of you, and the news for you is bad. Can you not feel it, Brady?"

Vincent was speaking with a new voice, tense and charged with emotion – a voice that John had not heard before, and he was afraid. Even then, he could hardly concentrate on what Vincent was saying, since all his attention was drawn to the fact that in his right hand, Vincent held a revolver. The hammer was fully back, and it was levelled at the three men facing them. John saw Brady's expression change from confident arrogance to uncertainty as the old man suddenly understood the danger he was in. Even if John had had the quickness of mind to try to remonstrate with Vincent, he understood more quickly that it would have been a waste of time. Twenty years of loneliness and hate had suddenly come to the boil, faced with their cause and object. Brady had indeed overreached himself.

John almost leapt into the air as the gun went off. A second shot was followed by a third, the shots sounding appallingly loud in the confined space between the lorry and the cottage. For a moment, John thought that Vincent was not aiming to hit the men, or perhaps he was not a very good shot. At the first shot, the Bradys were also startled into activity – immediately they turned and started running down the slope back towards the village; but at the second shot, old man Brady pitched forward headlong to the ground. Whether the bullet had found its mark or the old man had only stumbled, John could not tell. The other two men ran back and hauled the old man to his feet, and with an arm around each shoulder, dragged him awkwardly away. It said a great deal for their courage, or for the hold old Brady had over his subordinates, that they had gone back for him under fire, and had not simply kept running.

Vincent remained motionless, the gun still held level, as if he could hardly take in what had happened. Whether he was overwhelmed with exultation or with shock, his emotions at that moment were beyond John's comprehension. John punched him on the arm.

"Are you mad? What the hell were you thinking of? The whole place will come down on us now like a hornet's nest."

Vincent slowly turned to look at him, seemingly without understanding.

"For God's sake, put that thing away, and make haste. If we don't get out now, we've had it."

It seemed an age before Vincent appeared to return to rationality, almost as if he were unable to comprehend what he had done. At length he nodded and, with a certain reluctance, put the revolver into his pocket. John was already shouting up at the driver, who jumped down from the back of the lorry and closed up the tailgate. John slammed the front door of the cottage shut as Vincent made to go back inside.

"We've no time to look for anything more. If we don't go now, we've had it."

When Vincent demurred, John shouted at him.

"Look, we're going now. We're not waiting till the mob turns up. If you want to stay, then we'll leave you to it; but if you want to get out of this alive, then you'd better come now."

Again, reluctantly, Vincent nodded.

"You'd better sit in the middle," John said as they climbed into the cab. "It's you they want most, especially after this little lot. You'll probably be safest there."

The driver folded down the front windscreen, the lorry being of antiquated design. He explained that it would reduce the risk of glass splinters if there was going to be shooting. John looked at him to see if he was being sarcastic – but he was only a young man, and he was clearly shaken by the events of the last few minutes. He had undoubtedly got more than he bargained for when he was detailed for this job, and he was evidently only too aware of the danger they were in. Much would depend on this young man being able to keep his nerve in the next few minutes. Before climbing into the cab, John swung the heavy starter handle, narrowly avoiding the 'kick' as the engine came to life. The lorry eased slowly down the slope towards the road.

"Which way?" the driver asked, as they approached the road. "They could easily catch us up on that little back lane, even if they were on foot. It's impossible to go fast on that road – it'd break the axles."

For a minute, there was indecision. Vincent contemplated driving at high speed through the village, even though the others objected that this would be suicidal. The delay almost proved fatal. As they hesitated, a large group of men, at least twenty strong, appeared over the rise on the far side of the road directly in front of them. As they streamed down the slope towards the lorry, another group could be seen on the road, coming from the direction of the village. The driver made up his own mind, and advanced forward onto the road just as the mob coming down the slope on the far side caught up with the lorry. There was a shower of stones – one hit Vincent on the face, immediately causing him to bleed profusely from the cheek. Others bounced off the bonnet, and a headlamp was smashed. Then the mob was upon them, banging on the sides of the lorry with fists and sticks. They tried to pull the doors open, but they were locked. John violently shoved one man off the running board who was attempting to reach into the cab.

"Drive, for God's sake, drive!" John shouted.

"I can't – they're blocking the way." The driver revved the engine, but the mob in front of the lorry was not intimidated. Some of them started to climb onto the lorry in an attempt to get at the cab from above.

Vincent suddenly reached forward with the revolver and fired over the bonnet, two measured shots. John saw at least one man hit – the bullet caught him in the shoulder, knocking him half round before he fell to the ground. The mob suddenly melted away from in front of the lorry. There was a crunching of gears and the lorry shot forward. The driver grimaced with fear in case the engine stalled; but it didn't, and they kept going, swinging wide at first, but back onto the road further down. The hangers-on fell off or jumped off as the lorry gathered speed. Almost immediately, those in the lorry heard the sound of a gunshot. The second group coming along the road from the village had caught up with the first group, and at least one of them had a gun, a shotgun. The lorry was still travelling relatively slowly and the gunman, running hard, was able to keep up with it for long enough to get a couple of shots away. He was firing wild, and his first shot went nowhere; but with his second shot he was luckier. John felt something strike his side of the lorry with a heavy blow, and at the same time the wing mirror just in front of him disintegrated into splinters. John felt a sudden stinging pain in his elbow, which was resting over the edge of the side window. Exclaiming with pain and alarm, he withdrew his arm to find his coat sleeve torn by the shot, and staining rapidly and heavily with blood at the elbow. Vincent leaned over to have a look, his own cheek still bleeding from the wound he had received.

"I think it was a shotgun. How bad is it? Does it hurt much?"

"Not much." John was too shocked to say very much.

Vincent looked at the wound critically for a minute.

"I don't think it's severed an artery or anything. Can you use the coat sleeve to stem the blood? There's nothing in the way of bandages we can use."

John nodded. "You don't look so good yourself."

Vincent grimaced suddenly with contrition.

"I'm sorry, John, truly I am. I almost fouled everything up, and now look. I suppose it's a bit late now to admit you were right. I don't know if there's any point in trying to explain it. All I can do is to apologise."

John nodded again. He was still too shocked to be very talkative.

"Well, with any luck, it won't be too bad. All the same, I'd like a doctor to look at it as soon as possible. Will that be alright?"

"Yes, of course. How do you mean, will that be alright?"

"Well, I meant ... the police – these guns. You hit at least one of them back there, and possibly old man Brady as well. If the police ..."

Vincent laughed. The relief at having escaped had made him lightheaded.

"The police certainly won't hear about any of this from the Bradys, and if they don't hear about it from us either, then there's an end of it."

"But supposing one of them dies, or is seriously injured?"

"This isn't staid respectable Cheshire – this is west Galway. It's not uncommon for a local disagreement here to involve an exchange of gunshots. The police normally stay well away. If they had to take official cognisance of an incident like this, they'd have to take official cognisance of all the illegal guns as well. I've heard that there's a small arsenal at the Brady farmhouse. It'd probably take a military operation to flush them out – so the police don't get involved if they can avoid it. Much of the countryside round here is run by people like the Bradys, and they make their own rules. But if they live outside the law, then they can't expect the protection of the law either – and it serves them bloody well right." He was remembering the last quarter of an hour again with evident relish.

"Why are there so many illegal guns?"

"Trust a bloody Englishman not to know that. They're mostly left over from the struggle for independence, and then the civil war between the Free State Government and the IRA. This is a British army revolver, taken from a British officer killed by an IRA man in 1920. The IRA man got killed in the civil war, and the revolver was passed to my brother, who gave it to me when he went out to Australia."

Vincent suddenly broke off and turned to the driver.

"Are you alright, mister? That was some piece of driving just now. There's many would have lost their nerve and panicked, especially with guns going off and everything, but I was impressed by the way you kept your head through it all. We're in your debt, young sir."

The young man nodded and grinned.

"I expect you heard it was rough out here, but I don't suppose you counted on it being quite as rough as that, eh?"

"I did not," agreed the young man with emphasis.

"Well, I'll see you right for any damage, and something besides as well. Now, if you're sure we've shaken off the pursuit, I think we'd better stop for a minute just to check that we've no unauthorised passengers aboard."

The driver brought the lorry to a halt, and Vincent leaned over and inspected the rear of the lorry through the wing mirror before climbing out after the driver, revolver at the ready. There were no unauthorised passengers, however. An inspection of the lorry revealed how the passenger-side door of the cab had been scored and dented by the shot from the shotgun, a number of small dents in the bonnet where stones had hit it, and the smashed glass in the left headlamp and wing mirror. The lorry was fairly old and battered to begin with, and the additional damage was only superficial. Vincent and the driver climbed back into the cab.

"Now, then, where are we going?" asked Vincent.

"This is the only way out," replied the young man. "We couldn't go through the village, and we couldn't use that back lane again, so this is the only other way. This runs into the main Galway City to Clifden road at Garroman. We can get back to Galway City that way."

"How long will it take?"

"It's about thirty miles all told, so maybe an hour and a half. Just hope I've got enough petrol ..." His voice tailed off as his attention was caught by something in the mirror. He leaned out of the window for a minute, looking back.

"What is it?"

The driver leaned back in again.

"Horses – it looks like they've sent riders out after us. I think we'd better go."

Without further ado, he put the lorry in gear and started

off. Vincent leaned over to look out of the left side window for a moment.

"The bastards don't give up so easily," he said grimly. "How fast will this thing go?"

"Not all that fast. It's only an old lorry. I might be able to get thirty-five out of her if I'm lucky."

"Can you keep that up?"

"Depends on the road. It doesn't look too bad."

"The horses will tire after a couple of miles at that pace. If they can't catch us up in the next few minutes, we should be alright."

"Suppose some of them are going across country to cut us off on the main road?"

Vincent was thoughtful, then leaned across to look out of the side window again. The riders appeared to be slowly gaining on the lorry; but for a moment, he said nothing.

"If they cut the road at Maam Cross, or between there and Galway City, is there any other way out?"

The driver pulled a face.

"We'd have to turn off the main road after Garroman, and then take the road that runs right round Lough Corrib and Lough Mask – but that'd be more than a hundred miles, and the trouble is, I haven't the petrol. I don't know if any of the cross-country farm tracks would take a lorry."

Vincent was thoughtful again for a minute.

"I'm trying to remember if there are any tracks or lanes they could use, but I don't think there are any. It's shorter across country to the main road, but if there are no tracks, it's all bogs and tussock grass, especially the farther north you go. They'll only be able to go slowly even on horseback. Do you reckon we'll be able to beat them to it, if we can shake this lot off?"

The driver was looking in his mirror.

"They're still catching us up," was his laconic reply.

171

Vincent looked out of the window again, and as he gazed at the slowly advancing horsemen, the full understanding came to him, like a cold weight in the pit of his stomach, that he was staring at the face of death. The riders were now much closer, the nearest only five or six hundred yards behind. There were at least half a dozen of them, but instead of forming a group as he had at first seen them, they were now strung out along the road as the pace began to tell on the weaker horses. The lead horsemen were now close enough for Vincent to see that each carried a gun – either a shotgun or a rifle. If they were able to draw level with the cab of the lorry so as to be able to fire into it from the side, it would be an easy shot from close range, even from on horseback. Vincent felt the revolver in his pocket He had one cartridge left; but his anger, and all his bravado, were gone now, and as he looked down at his boots, he was afraid. He felt nothing at that moment of remorse that John and the young driver would die also – the Bradys would make no distinction – but faced suddenly with death, his mind was filled with fear to the exclusion of all else. If it had been done in the extremity of hate or anger, perhaps it would have been possible to make some sense of it, to make it easier to face. But this was so cold-blooded – so horribly cold-blooded. Would he be able to look up and face it when the moment came? Those who die in fear die the worst, because the fear makes them lose their dignity, and to death is added humiliation. No-one chooses to die in such a way – those for whom fear comes are its victims, and they are as helpless before it as they are before death itself. All that would be seen if the fear possessed him would be the fear, the squealing terror, as he attempted to hide where there was no hiding place; the smell of urine as he soiled himself in his terror; and the gunman casually firing again and again until the squealing stopped, and the blood spattered with a stink of iron and red earth.

Did they know? In these last minutes while he still retained a semblance of self-control, did they yet know what was within, and despise him for it? When, with a great effort, he raised his eyes, it was to catch John looking quickly away. Were they also afraid? Did they even understand? But what did it matter? They knew now. They knew.

It was the driver who finally broke the silence.

"I think they're starting to fall behind. They're no longer gaining on us."

"You're sure?" Vincent wished he didn't have to ask.

The driver carefully studied the wing mirror for another minute.

"Aye, I'm sure. They're not even keeping pace with us now. The horses must be about finished."

John turned in his seat, with some difficulty due to his injured elbow, and looked back from out of the side window, to confirm the driver's words. The leading horsemen had dropped right back, unable at last to keep pace with the lorry. Even as he watched, he saw them pull up and wheel round, signifying that the chase was over.

"He's right, they've halted. They've given up," he announced cheerfully.

But Vincent remained sombre as he shook his head.

"They don't give up," he said quietly. "They neither forget, nor forgive, nor give quarter in the smallest degree. Nor will they ever give up."

The others remained silent.

14

The doctor, carefully holding a pair of surgical tweezers, dropped a third lead pellet onto a glass specimen dish on the surgery table.

"That's the lot, I think," he said, gently swabbing John's elbow with antiseptic. "It looks like a fourth pellet just creased the outside of your elbow and went right through. That's where most of the blood came from, and I've had to put a few stitches in there, to help the wound heal. A bandage should do for the rest, but you'll have to keep your arm in a sling until the stitches come out."

He wound a bandage round John's arm, cut it and secured it.

"I'll give you something for the pain – I'm afraid your arm will be quite sore for a while after the local anaesthetic wears off. It doesn't look as if it's been your lucky day."

He looked quizzically at John, and then at Vincent, who sat in a chair on the other side of the surgery, his face still streaked with blood.

Vincent's face remained impassive.

"No, I suppose that's right. I, ah, tripped and fell, and my gun went off accidentally. It's only fortunate that it wasn't much more serious."

"Fortunate indeed!" The doctor remained equally impassive. "It's extraordinary how some of these little country places out west are prone to accidents with guns. And if it isn't guns, it's knives, hatchets and cleavers. I've seen a lot worse than this. I'm sure it must be something in the country air that makes the people there so clumsy and accident-prone. I don't suppose," he went on cautiously after a pause, "that you know of any other, ah, accidents that may have occurred in this case?"

"Well, I can't say for sure; but it's possible that there may have been."

The doctor nodded slowly.

"It's as well to know, I suppose," he said.

Ten minutes later, Vincent walked with John as far as the square outside the hotel, but would come no further. He had not been able to shake off the effect of what had happened, and he was still sombre.

"I ... can't thank you enough for what you've done, or apologise enough for what happened. I can hardly find the words ... .do you understand?"

John nodded, not meeting Vincent's eye. The strain of the last two hours had been almost unbearable, not least because of what it had visibly done to Vincent. All the way along the road from Garroman, he had remained in the grip of the terror, expecting at any moment to be intercepted by further horsemen who had reached the road from across country. The other two, apart from their own apprehensions, had been silent witnesses to Vincent's private struggle with the darkness which rode with him; a struggle which, because it was visible, he could not win with honour, even if in the end, he did not lose with dishonour. When they had at last come within a few miles of Galway City and known that they were safe, Vincent had closed his eyes as the shadow departed. The struggle was over, and he was left only with shame. The reflection of that shame came between them now as they parted on the pavement in the square.

"I hope the rest of it works out alright," John said. He paused before speaking again. "What about the doctor? Will he talk, or inform the police?"

175

He was slightly concerned on his own account. But Vincent shook his head.

"Officially he doesn't know anything. It was an accident, remember? And in the unlikely event that the police do ask him any questions, well, he doesn't know much. In fact, the main reason why we went to him was because he's one of several doctors in Galway who can be relied on to be discreet in such matters. In any case, no blame can attach to you. I assure you, you need have no fears about that. And now, I must not detain you any longer. I'm sure I will see you again in Bray sometime."

They shook hands, and John's last sight of him was as he turned the corner of the street leading out of the square, his hands in his pockets as he hunched his shoulders against the January wind, his tousled hair half hidden by the turned-up collar of his greatcoat.

Helen was still sitting in the hotel lounge when John returned. She had a book with her that she had been pretending to read for the past two hours, during which time she had experienced growing anger and impatience at John's non-appearance. When John finally did arrive, however, she was not in the least mollified by his appearance. She stood up when she saw him approaching.

"Three hours, you said. No more than three hours. It's nearly half past two. I've been waiting here for more than five hours. Why did you do it? If I'd known you were going to treat me like a child, I'd have behaved like one and caught the early train back to Dublin by myself, and left you to it. Why did you do it?"

"I'm sorry love, truly I am. I had no intention of being as late as this. Could we go up to our room so I can explain. I don't want to talk about it here."

Helen had not moderated her voice, and her strident tones had shattered the semi-religious hush of the lounge. Several other guests looked at her pointedly or glared with annoyance. Helen remained oblivious of this, and continued in a voice now edged with derision.

"Of course not. If you'd come back when you said you would, that might have been possible. But I've just told you, it's half past two, and we have to be out of the room by twelve o'clock."

"For God's sake Helen, keep your voice down." John was mortified with embarrassment. "Where are the cases?" He found them near to where Helen had been sitting. There were two cases. Because of his injured arm he couldn't carry them both at once. He didn't want Helen to carry anything heavy because of her condition. He picked up one of the cases and took it outside to the street, setting it down on the pavement before returning for the other. Helen trailed after him each way, continuing to berate him in a loud voice. When he left the hotel with the second case, which happened to be hers, and started walking along the street carrying it, leaving the other case outside the hotel, she seemed to lose all self-control, punching and slapping him, and yelling at the top of her voice.

"What the hell are you doing? Where are you going with my case? Why aren't you bringing the other one? What the hell do you think you're doing?"

John stopped and stood still, his eyes closed, almost at the end of his tether. He had craved comfort from Helen, but instead she had become a demon. He cried out in pain suddenly as one of her blows struck his injured arm. His temper snapped, and setting the case down quickly, he slapped her in the face.

"Don't you dare do that again," he said, his voice thick with anger. Helen, momentarily silenced, sullenly rubbed her cheek, which was reddening where John had struck it. She regarded him resentfully.

"What's the matter with your arm?" she asked, appearing to notice it for the first time – his left arm, in its sling, was under his coat.

"It's injured, and it's quite sore – in case you hadn't noticed."

"Injured how?"

"Things didn't go according to plan this morning. There was trouble – shooting. I was hit in the arm. One of the reasons why I was late was that I had to go to a doctor to get my arm strapped up."

She stared at him critically.

"Trouble? Shooting? You said this morning that there would be no risk of that sort of thing. And what about Fitzgerald? Was he injured too?"

"Yes." John had not intended to tell Helen about the violence of that morning, but his anger and irritation had got the better of him, and briefly he recounted to her what had happened. Helen's face hardened as she listened, and when he had finished, she regarded him in contemptuous silence for a moment.

"You bloody fool. You selfish bloody fool. Suppose you had been seriously injured or killed? Did you think for a moment about what would happen to me? Or about the child?" She gestured at her own belly. "All you can think of is your own interests of the moment. It's bad enough as it is. Suppose you lose your job because of this – did you think of that?"

"Of course I won't lose my job. I told you, I didn't expect anything like this to happen. I honestly did not. And even as it was, there was no real danger of my being seriously injured." He had not said anything about the horsemen.

"With guns being fired? Don't talk such rot. You sound just like a little boy. You're pathetic, you really are."

She turned on her heel and walked away from him. He shouted after her, oblivious of everything but his own anger.

"That's rich coming from someone who was so keen for me to join the army and make her a widow in double quick time."

Helen stopped and turned back for a moment.

"At least you would have died with honour for your country, not uselessly for some worthless Irish vagrant."

John stood still and cursed himself in his chagrin. How could he have been so stupid? In his anger, his tongue had got the better of him; but how could he have been so stupid? He had hoped that that subject had been buried forever. For he himself to have raised it, and in such a way as this – how could he have been so stupid?

"Helen!" he called after her; but it was too late.

15

The tidings of war had fallen away to a low murmur, at least in the Irish press. The French and German armies eyed each other uneasily across the Rhine; but few shots were fired, and no-one seemed to know what to make of it. Snow lay deep on the Maginot Line, and the French at least, had no stomach to start anything on their side. Old soldiers might say that the generals were simply waiting for the start of the campaigning season with the first of the good weather in the spring; but to most other people it seemed increasingly likely that it was indeed a phoney war. At St Mungo's it was now several weeks since the last member of staff had left to cross the water to join up, and some of those who had already done so were confident, in their communications home, that they would be back before very much longer.

During this week in particular, the easing of the tension in the school was especially welcome to John. On the morning following their return from Galway, he had seriously doubted whether, in view of what had happened, he would have the mental energy to face a class of second years on a Monday morning, or on any of the mornings following, and he had considered sending in to say that he was ill. But to stay at home all day with Helen was out of the question, and where else would he go? In fact, he had no difficulty in coping with IIc that morning. It was not energy he lacked, but preoccupation. There were times when he might have forgotten the previous day's events entirely; but the boys all wanted to know what had happened to his arm, and he had made up some story about a fall. For a wild moment, he had toyed with the idea of telling them the truth, not so much to impress them, which would doubtless have been gratifying enough, but because he knew that the story would quickly filter back to certain members of staff, some of whom had never heard a gun fired in anger in their lives. He knew that it would do him no good, however. As it had been with Helen, he knew that no equivalence would be conceded between a private adventure which would be seen, here at least, as disreputable, if not discreditable, and the conventional and accepted tests of masculinity, of which military service in war was the highest. Indeed, as Helen had suggested, he would certainly be censured for deliberately impairing his ability to carry out his work, even though, since his right arm was unaffected, this was in fact minimal. His main difficulty in this respect was in riding his bicycle, an activity that had become precarious and interesting.

The unexpectedly absorbing preoccupation of work left him without the time he needed to think, however, and on that Monday evening, and on succeeding evenings he called in at the Queen's Hotel in Bray on his way home, to sit for an hour or so in front of the peat fire in the lounge, quietly gazing into the flames. He needed time to think about Helen, and about what he was going to do. He needed to talk his problems over with someone who was independent, but also able to understand his situation. Of all the people he knew in Ireland, Vincent Fitzgerald was the only one whom he could regard as both independent and sympathetic. However, there was no sign of Vincent that week, or in subsequent days, and while John looked forward to many conversations with Vincent, it was during that week that he particularly missed Vincent's intelligent and independent mind, especially in relation to his worries about Helen. Her preoccupations, and what she felt for him, were matters which he could not put out of his mind. Why should a relationship based on love be so fragile? Why should his desire for her, his need for her love and approbation, his need for her to satisfy his physical desires, be a weakness in him?

On the journey back from Galway, there had been a complete silence between them. Since their arrival back home, they had maintained a brittle truce. They had each continued their normal routine, but it had gone no further than that. Unless Helen relented, John could not see how it would end. If it went on like this, there would be nothing left for them. This was ground which was depressingly familiar, depressing because nothing had been resolved. The situation had remained unchanged; or rather, Helen had not eased the pressure on him which he saw as the cause of the problem. She would doubtless see it as being his problem, since, as far as she was concerned, she was only behaving in a normal way. In another way, the situation seemed to be resolving itself, bit by bit, into a choice between the sanctuary he had found here in Ireland, and his relationship with Helen. As these breakdowns in their relationship recurred, it looked more likely that at some point he would have to choose between them. But what choice was there? At least here in Ireland he was safe from that which he knew he could not face. If he returned to England, it would now be to face trial for refusing to obey the order for military service, followed by imprisonment or worse. He would probably never see Helen again. It had not occurred to him before to use this in his argument with Helen. He suspected that, in her present mood, even this would not move her.

This time at least, the break was not final. During the ensuing weeks, the effect of routine gradually eased the frostiness between them, so that something approaching normality returned. It was never entirely a return to normality, however. Each time the relationship broke down, a residue of the bitterness remained. It was only the demands of routine that allowed them to carry on without bringing matters to a head, or a resolution. Also of course, there was the child, as yet unborn, but whose arrival loomed ever larger. Neither of them, and certainly not John, wanted to break the *modus vivendi* which they managed to achieve during this period.

In early March, John received two letters from England. The first was from his mother. Her initial reason for writing was the fact that her brother Peter, John's uncle, whose wife had died young of tuberculosis, and who had gone to live with his sister when they were both becoming infirm with age, had been taken into hospital following an accident in the garden of their home, the house in Withington which had been John's childhood home. His uncle had fallen from a ladder he had been using while inspecting the roof of the house for wind damage following a storm. As a result of the fall he had suffered a broken arm and fractured ribs. In view of his age and frailty, his condition was considered to be serious, and he was receiving intensive care at the hospital. John's mother, now on her own, was in considerable distress, and it was in this vein that she had begun her letter. Further on, the letter was more measured and reflective, as if she had picked it up again after a break of some hours.

"I feel it would be a tragedy if he were never to see you again," she wrote. "Of course, I am hoping and praying that he will recover and be home again; but the suddenness of the shock has meant that I have had to reflect on these things, and at the moment I only have you to turn to.

"It has not been easy for us since you left to go to Ireland. We have both missed your visits to us and the help you gave us. Since the war began, there have been all kinds of complications that the war has brought. Apart from the day-to-day problems of rationing and wartime restrictions, we have experienced additional difficulties due to the fact that you have gone to Ireland at this time. Many of the other families in this neighbourhood have sons who have joined up, or are in the process of joining up with the forces. I have had to face coolness and even hostility from those who know that my son has not joined up but has gone to Ireland instead, and this has sometimes been hard to bear. To hear comments passed about one's own son in a shop or other public place, which one has no answer to, is a mortifying experience.

"I know you have reasons for doing what you have done, but that has not made things any easier for us. At the same time, however, I have to confess that I sometimes have a secret feeling of relief also. The war doesn't seem to be amounting to much at the moment, but if the fighting were to start in earnest in France, then a part of me at least would privately be glad that you were safe in Ireland.

"Is there any possibility that you could come and see us? Will they not allow you to visit your uncle on compassionate grounds? I have found this separation hard to bear, and now that your Uncle Peter is in hospital, it is many times worse. Please will you help me to bear this burden?"

John's reply to his mother reflected his dilemma.

"Perhaps it seems that I have made a mistake in coming here, especially if the war turns out to amount to nothing in the end, and some sort of peace is patched up to save face. But I didn't come to Ireland only to escape the war, but also to preserve my liberty. I will not accept that politicians have the right to compel me to leave my family and force me into military service so that they can acquire the means to wage war against other states, playing with the lives of millions like pawns in a game of chess. As long as ordinary people acquiesce in this, then so long will there be wars.

"Doubtless most people would find my attitude

incomprehensible. They would take the view that if they could accept such things, then people like me should be required to also. This has been the arrogance of majorities towards minorities down the ages. It is in large measure because of this that things have never changed, and probably never will change. If one's heart beats to a different drum, then to deny that difference in order to fall in with an arrogant majority is, in the end, to deny one's identity as an individual. If there is to be any hope for humanity in the long term, it can only come from that minority of people who have the clarity of mind to distinguish between justice and injustice, and the integrity of mind to be able to maintain their independence of thought and action in the face of a hostile majority and a hostile state.

"In my case, I have sought to avoid confrontation with the authorities, since the only people who would be harmed by such confrontation would be myself and my family. Instead, I have done the simplest and most effective thing I can do, which is merely to remove myself from their power. If the authorities cannot accept this and choose to make an issue of it, well that is their problem. However, having made my choice, I am now committed to what I have done. If I were to return to England now, it would not be conscription I would face, but, because I have purposely evaded conscription, arrest, trial, and imprisonment or worse. So for my own safety, in more ways than one, I must remain in Ireland. I have not forgotten about you, and you must not think for a moment that I have done. I haven't been without my share of troubles here in Ireland, and I long to see you both again. I pray that Uncle Peter will pull through, and that before too long he will be well enough to be able to travel. If I cannot come to England, then you must come to Ireland. I shall pay for all your expenses and make the arrangements. It's no further to here than it is to London, and you would be a lot safer here. If we are spared further misfortune, then soon we can all be reunited again, here in the peace of Ireland. I hope and pray for it."

The second letter he received was from the solicitor he had retained in England, Mr Rutherford. Mr Rutherford had written to advise him that the authorities, having now identified him as a fugitive from military service and therefore a fugitive from justice, had taken steps to proceed against him. Mr Rutherford had been informed that the authorities had visited John's house, and having effected an entry, had seized and confiscated all his property and assets, and declared all such property forfeit to the state. A warrant had been issued for John's arrest under the relevant section of law relating to military service. This having been done, John now had no rights at all, unless these decisions were reversed by the order of a court. Mr Rutherford wanted to be advised if John wished to make any formal response.

"Technically, it would be possible to challenge these decisions before a court," he wrote, "but practically speaking, your chances of successfully doing so would be remote, especially under present circumstances. You would have to appear before the court in person, and would therefore be liable to immediate arrest, as I advised you before. As far as I am aware, the authorities still do not know of your particular whereabouts. On your instructions, I have merely advised them that you have gone abroad. Please advise what you wish me to do about this matter."

At the moment of reading the letter, John did not feel the anger which he might have expected to feel – perhaps that would come later. At first, it only served to increase his sense of oppression. He had planned to have the remaining contents of the house moved to his mother's house when she was able to accept them, and before the lease ran out, or else sent for auction; but now he had been overtaken by events. It was

186

hardly surprising that the authorities would declare him a fugitive, and even take steps to confiscate his property; but somehow it alarmed him that it should be done in what seemed such a peremptory, even ruthless way. It occurred to him to wonder whether, if they took action against his property in such a way, they might also take action against his family. Would his uncle be refused further medical treatment, perhaps? What would he do if the authorities did victimise his uncle in such a way? It was a measure of the degree to which he was now separated from the generality of his society that such thoughts could occur to him at all – the thoughts of one who has lost all trust in authority, in society itself: the thoughts of a political exile. But he was committed to what he had done, and this meant that for much of the time he didn't need to think about it any further. It was on occasions when he was haunted by nostalgia that his doubts were at their worst. Nostalgia was not only about place and time, but above all about people; and this was his greatest loss – and the hardest to face, because it was of his own making.

In his letter of reply to Mr Rutherford, John asked if the solicitor could at least try to draw up an inventory of all the property which had been seized by the authorities.

"I feel that I should at least register my dissent from what the authorities have done," he wrote, "even if there is nothing I can do about it. It may seem unlikely now, but a time may come when there is a more just government which is prepared to review and where possible redress the injustices of this present period. If I or any of my heirs are alive to see such a time, I am sure it would help my case if I had registered a protest and had a list of property which was taken. I would be grateful, therefore, if you could make arrangements for this to be done on my behalf."

John did not expect any sympathy from Mr Rutherford for his point of view or his predicament; but one did not expect sympathy from lawyers at the best of times. Nor, realistically, did he expect there to be any change in the position of the British authorities, or a restoration of his property. Such a thing might be conceivable in France or some other continental country, or even here in Ireland, where change had happened once, and could happen again; but not in England, where an old reactionary establishment, entrenched against change, bore grudges across centuries of injustice. It would remain, he was sure, a forlorn protest.

16

The awakening of spring saw a quickening in the pace of events, both in the microcosm of life that was John's world, and on the wider stage which seemed to be its counterpoint. The extension of the war to Scandinavia with the German invasion and the fighting in Norway seemed to end any hopes there might have been that the war would fizzle out by the summer for want of any substantive reason to continue it. Norway seemed almost as remote as Poland, but the fighting there left no doubt that the war was far from being over. There was speculation in the press that if the Germans were prepared to go to the trouble of invading Norway in order to achieve a strategic outflanking of Britain, then there must be a danger that they might invade Ireland for the same reason, notwithstanding Ireland's studied neutrality. John privately dismissed such ideas as nonsense, but nevertheless found it unsettling that the war seemed to be looming ever larger despite his determination to turn his back on it. It was a feeling which, unknowingly, he shared with many people. For many months there had been no real fighting, and many people had somehow got used to the idea that this was all the war would amount to. The psychological preparedness for war which people had brought themselves to the previous summer had been blunted by anticlimax, and a new expectation of peace – privately held and unspoken for the most part, but genuine enough; so that when the real war finally erupted in May with the main German assault in the West, for many, the shock was greater than the declarations of war in September had been.

John was fortunate in that, for the time being at least, the great events of the wider world remained in the background, to be worried over only in odd minutes between classes at St Mungo's, or in that sleepless hour before dawn when the night magnifies the terrors of the day into spectres of ill omen. On the 25th of May, Helen went into the cottage hospital in Bray to begin her confinement. She had not yet gone into labour, but the doctor in Bray had advised it as a precaution given the isolation of where she and John were living, and the nearness of her time. The 25th was a Saturday, and this gave John the whole weekend to assist in settling Helen into the maternity ward in the hospital, ferrying clothes, personal effects, books for her to read, and other essentials, to Bray on his bicycle, as Helen thought of and demanded things she needed.

In spite of everything, John was completely caught up in the spirit of the great event with a sustained feeling of suppressed excitement, like a bottle of champagne vigorously shaken but with the cork still held firmly in place. For it was nothing less than a great event, the birth of his first child. It was this which was the reward of life. The struggle to win and maintain a living, to maintain a place in society, to keep oneself above the line in the face of the vicissitudes of chance, and the hostility of those who watch and wait for the smallest opportunity to push one below the line out of malice or greed; the endless, meaningless choreography of such ritual dances to the music of convention were all performed for the sake of this prize, the immortality of the common man. But for John, as for every man, this related to himself, and himself alone, since this was to be his child, his seed, his identity being carried forward, the issue of the woman whose cleaving to him was his reward for having danced the dance to its end. It was the manna for which alone one lived, and beside which everything else was ashes.

During those last few days in May, Dr Grey's routine visits to the local cottage hospital in Bray were given additional interest by the presence of one of his patients in the maternity ward there. He had become interested in the English couple who lived out along the lane to the west of the town the previous November, when he had been called to their cottage to attend the woman, who had been seriously ill with pneumonia. He had immediately sent her into hospital such was the seriousness of her condition, and although she had seemed to make a good recovery, he had continued to attend her regularly to monitor the progress of her pregnancy. His relationship with them had never extended much beyond the formal professional minimum. Although, in terms of class and education he presumably had more in common with them than with most of his patients, they had chosen to maintain a distance from him. From the little he had been able to glean from his own contacts with them, he had formed the impression that there was more to this distance than mere English reserve. He felt that there was a tension in their relationship, which he had sensed on that day in November when the woman had been delirious with pneumonia. Why had they been out in the storm the previous night? Had they quarrelled, and if so, about what? The husband's undoubtedly genuine concern for his wife's condition seemed to suggest against marital infidelity, and there had been nothing of that in anything he had heard about the couple elsewhere. They were certainly interesting, because of their aloofness, because they were English, because they were middle class.

The last week in May was to prove one of the most decisive weeks in Helen's life. It would not have occurred to her to doubt this even beforehand. This was the birth of her first

191

child, a child whose life she could expect to define the rest of her own life: for was this not the lot of women, their joy and their sorrow, their pride and their strength, beside which all the works of men were childish in comparison? The event had loomed disproportionately on her horizon, however, because in it she had increasingly expected to find a salvation from the growing sense of dislocation she felt about their life in Ireland. The physical isolation of living in a remote place in a strange country, cut off from her own people and unable to make any other human contact, was compounded by the isolation of being unable to discuss her predicament with John. The anger with which he responded to the very idea of a return to England had become a barrier between them. Because it was a subject that was 'off limits' it meant she was equally inhibited from talking about her sense of isolation, of being trapped in a place where she no longer wished to be. For John, Ireland was a sanctuary – he was glad to be here; he had a place here. For Helen, it was only a strange country. It was not enough for her simply to be with John. She had discovered that she needed a familiar society, and a position of status within such society; and to be cut off from that was to deny something essential within her. There was even a contrariness about it – to the extent that Ireland was a sanctuary for John from the society she felt cut off from, it thereby increased her sense of isolation.

But now there was the baby. Upon this still unborn mite she had already placed the burden of filling this void, as well as fulfilling her maternal desires. Perhaps the change in both their lives which the arrival of the baby would bring would become a more secure basis for their life together here in Ireland. She now doubted whether there could be any other.

For several days after Helen went into the cottage hospital, there were no immediate signs that she was about to go into labour. Since she was not ill, and, apart from the limitations on her movement due to her condition, otherwise fit, active and mentally alert, she found that time started to lie heavily on her. John would visit her for an hour or so each evening on his way home from work; but before then, there was the whole day to get through. The routine of the ward was undemanding to the point of boredom, and if anything was rather irritating. She could see no good reason why they had to be woken from whatever sleep they had managed to get at six in the morning, so as to be ready for the daily round by the midwife or the doctor at ten-thirty, or why 'lights out' was at eight-thirty in the evening, when there was still another two hours of daylight at this time of the year. They were fed at seven in the morning, at noon, and at four in the afternoon, times that Helen found quite barbaric. At home, she liked to 'nibble' between meals if she felt hungry. Here, there was strictly no food until the next mealtime, no matter how hungry you were. Ordinarily, she would have chafed under the restrictions of such a regime – indeed, it occurred to her more than once to ask John if she could return to the cottage, since she was in the mood to risk having the baby at home rather than endure more of the hospital. But this period of enforced idleness also gave her a lot of time to think about her situation, and what courses of action she might take, even if some of them seemed daunting and unrealistic at that stage. Also, even here, she was not immune from outside influences. Since she was not bedridden and was allowed to walk about in the ward areas, she had access to the newspapers which were left in the visitors' waiting room. As well as the *Irish Times* and the local press, usually there were one or two British newspapers as well. These were full of the unfolding military catastrophe that was befalling the Allies in France. At this stage, Helen had no clear response to the news of these events. She was only interested in her own personal life, and the lives of those in her immediate circle, and her only interest in the war at that stage, was in how it impinged on her and those in the small world around her. Now, of course, even the greatest events in the outside world were overshadowed by the imminence of her own great event, and news about the war was only of passing interest. Nevertheless, in the long, boring hours she spent perusing the newspapers in the visitors' waiting room, news about the war could hardly be overlooked, and even the casual reader could not fail to appreciate the immensity of these events. In a matter of days, the Germans had managed to achieve what they had failed to achieve in four years of the Great War. All the fears and expectations of another war of slaughter on the Western Front were finally unfounded. There would be no Western Front – France was defeated. In a few unbelievable days, the might of France had been broken, and what was left of the British Expeditionary Force was being unceremoniously evicted from the mainland of Europe.

Helen, who normally never took any interest in politics or foreign news, could only feel a general sense of unease and foreboding about these reports. Suggestions that the Germans might follow up their victory in France with an invasion of Britain were still muted, so that, as yet, Helen's feeling of disquiet at all this news lacked that which would give it a focus and a sense of urgency. Her memories of that week were of a curious mixture of happy expectation tinged with a little fear, boredom, and worries about the future of her relationship with John, all set against an almost surreal background of half-understood news reports that outside this sleepy rural backwater, the world was falling apart.

On the Friday morning of that week, Helen gave birth to a baby girl. The child was born in the early morning, just as the newborn sun first touched the windows of the little hospital that looked out over the sea with a blaze of clear summer light. Helen remembered a nurse pulling the curtains open and light flooding into the room, washing away the foetid semi-darkness and the terrors of the night. By then it was all

194

over, and it was remarkable how quickly it was possible for the memory of the hours of pain and sweat and the fear of being alone and helpless among strangers in a strange place, and the fear of a new, unknown world, and the harsh electric light in the hot darkness of the night, to recede into the background of thought, into the aftermath. Now there were just two things – the indescribable moment of first holding the baby, of first looking into her tiny face, pink and crinkled, eyes still closed tightly against the unaccustomed light, before she was whisked away by the midwife; and then sleep, calm and untroubled after the turmoil of the night, blessed in the knowledge that it was all over, that the great enterprise had been successfully accomplished, that she had not failed herself or John or the little new life she had brought into the world.

It was early afternoon before the news reached John, more than twelve hours after Helen had first gone into labour. Dr Grey telephoned St Mungo's from his surgery. He did not get to speak to John personally, which he found a little curious. He would have been much more interested had he been present some time later, when John was called to the headmaster's study. The headmaster had waited until the end of the lesson period before summoning John, and he kept the interview brief.

"I have received a telephone message from a Dr Grey at the cottage hospital in Bray, to the effect that your wife gave birth this morning to a girl child. She and the child are both well, according to the message." He was reading from a paper on which the message had been written, in the tone of voice of one who reads unfamiliar words.

"Oh." John was too overwhelmed by the news to speak for a moment, but then went on: "Was that it? Did they say when the birth happened, or ..."

"That was the message. There was nothing further. You may return to your duties."

"But, what …"

"I said you may return to your duties. I will not have you wasting the school's time with personal matters. I understand that you have a class to teach in the next hour. You will return to your duties immediately. That will be all."

Somehow, the news filtered round the school during the afternoon. John, still smarting from the interview with the headmaster, ran into Carter, the young science teacher, in the staff room after the last lesson of the day.

"Hello – I hear that congratulations are in order." Carter shook his hand and grinned.

John, affected by the unusual display of warmth, was moved to recount the interview with the headmaster.

"It was almost as if I were a criminal, with whom he could barely bring himself to speak."

Carter shrugged.

"Well, in truth, that's exactly how he does see you, in effect. In his view, you ought to have gone back to England and joined the army, so that by now you'd be in France dying for your country like a hero and a true Brit – instead of which, you're skulking here in Ireland, enjoying the soft life of a civilian, enjoying the pleasure of having a woman to your bed, and now a family as well."

"But that's simply a normal life – what any man might reasonably expect."

"I know, but in his view, you have no right to expect it, let alone to enjoy it. In fact, between you and me," Carter lowered his voice conspiratorially, "I think there's more than a little envy in it. I reckon it's a long time since His Nibs last had his bit of fun."

John was taken aback.

"But he's married, isn't he?"

"Oh, he's married, yes – someone who gets to his position could hardly avoid it – but I've heard that his wife quite openly boasts that he 'considers her' and doesn't impose himself on her."

"Considers her?"

"It means they sleep in separate rooms – no conjugal rights and all that. It's no wonder he's bitter, especially when he sees someone like you. I'd be careful about what you say and do if I were you."

John was too full of his own news to be unduly daunted by Carter, whom he had privately dismissed as a professional alarmist. For the time being, he filed Carter's words away in the back of his mind.

It was decided that the baby was to be named Laura, after Helen's mother. Dr Grey had pronounced her to be fit and healthy, so Helen was allowed to return home on the Sunday afternoon. Although this meant that Helen would immediately be faced with having to cope with the baby on her own during the day, Helen herself had whispered to John that she was tired of hospital food and hospital hours, and couldn't wait to get home. John had not been able to take the Monday off work as leave – leave had to be asked for at least a week in advance so that cover could be arranged, and even then it was at the discretion of the headmaster. After the interview on Friday, and what Carter had told him, John had little doubt as to the response to a request for leave for such a reason.

Of all the memories of that Friday, the one which, for John, remained the most precious, and stayed in his memory for the rest of his life, was the moment when he first saw his daughter, little Laura, first held her in his arms and gazed down into her eyes, now clear and fearlessly open, challenging the light of the world. What was there to say at such a moment? To think that this tiny mite represented all his hopes and aspirations, that she carried such a burden of expectation on the shoulders of her fragile little frame, even now, on the day of her birth. Truly, she was the light of his world.

17

The arrival of the new baby caused a little ripple of change which was noticed by all those with whom John and Helen came into contact. Vincent Fitzgerald was one who noticed the change. It was only occasionally now that John called in at the Queen's in Bray on his way home from work, so Vincent saw very little of him during this period. In the ordinary course of events, he would have expected that this would lead to the end of their acquaintance. He had seen it happen before. Newlyweds had time only for each other, and then, when the first baby came along, the baby became the centre of their lives, if only for the practical reason that the baby needed constant attention, and their opportunity to indulge in social life became, for the time being, almost non-existent. But underlying this, there was also an increasing divergence of interest. Married couples with young children tended to associate only with other married couples with young children. It was not only that children had become the centre of their lives, and that only in the company of other couples with young children could they talk endlessly about this new and all-absorbing interest; there was also a sense that, having achieved the status of marriage and parenthood, the time when they were single was an earlier and less mature stage in their lives which they had now left behind, and that those who remained single and childless were likewise somehow inferior beings, with whom one no longer associated in one's new status. It was something that Vincent had seen often enough for him to have become inured to it. It was part of the loneliness of being single; and it was part of his mental defences not to allow it to affect him too much. As he was dismissed by such acquaintances, so he in turn had to be able to dismiss them, in order to maintain his self-respect.

In any event, he also now had other things on his mind. In January, his mother had come to live with him in the rooms he rented in Bray. The rooms were not spacious, even for himself alone. Now that his mother was there too, they were distinctly cramped. It was never a good idea to live too close to one's mother, no matter how good the relationship, and the situation was unsatisfactory. For the time being, however, they had to make the best of it, at least until something else could be arranged. Even as it was, the old lady was finding it hard to come to terms with living in a strange place, even with her son. Kilkirrin had been her entire world, and the sudden relocation had caused her considerable shock, quite apart from the circumstances of it. Dublin and the east coast was virtually a foreign country to her, and Vincent doubted that she would be able to cope with living on her own there.

Vincent had not, however, entirely severed his connection with the west. Old O'Grady in Galway, who had been a friend of his father, might be able to fix up somewhere in Galway City for his mother to live, in due course. This had not been possible earlier due to the aftermath of the events in Kilkirrin in January, which had complicated matters. O'Grady had played a part in that too, fixing up the visit to the doctor for John, who had met him briefly. O'Grady had contacts in Kilkirrin itself, which were a valuable source of information for Vincent, as it proved on this occasion. The Galway police had apparently got wind of the incident, and although they had not been over-sedulous in their pursuit of the matter, given that it involved the Bradys, they had received, via their informant, a very one-sided version of events, favouring the Bradys, which had given rise to a rumour that they now had an interest in interviewing Vincent Fitzgerald. Vincent was actually in Galway City when he heard this. He and O'Grady were sitting in the lounge of the same hotel John and Helen had stayed at. O'Grady was a wizened little man in his seventies. He didn't particularly approve of Vincent Fitzgerald, but he maintained the connection for the sake of Vincent's father and for Mrs Fitzgerald. In O'Grady's view, Vincent had proved unworthy of his father, and had wasted the opportunities which had been given to him. Someone who had had the benefit of a college education should have made more of his life. He should have gone to England or America, which is what would have been expected of him. But O'Grady's disapproval of Vincent Fitzgerald also stemmed from the distance between them in terms of intellect and education: the resentment of the uneducated lower class of the educated elite; and a certain satisfaction at seeing one of them fall on hard times, even if he was old Fitzgerald's son. What separated them was unbridgeable. What brought them together were memories, for each significant in their own way, of the dead man.

"Obviously, the Bradys don't want you anywhere near Kilkirrin, let alone in the village, and this is their way of doing it."

"Well, I don't have any particular reason for being over here now, so I'm not going to be greatly inconvenienced by that. On the other hand, I wouldn't want to have any problems for the future. I think it's a bit much for them to try and force me out of the entire county. After all, if needs be, I could cite the doctor who took the shot out of my friend's arm, or the haulage company, or the garage that repaired their motor lorry."

O'Grady shook his head.

"You'd meet a wall of silence. The Bradys have influential friends here in Galway City, and people like that wouldn't want to get on the wrong side of them. You'll just have to accept it for the present. After all, you said yourself that you've no particular reason to be over here now."

O'Grady gave him a half-curious glance. Vincent shrugged his shoulders and shook his head, as if he didn't know what O'Grady meant.

"I suppose not. It just seems excessive, even after what happened in January. It's carrying the matter beyond what seems rational, even for a vendetta. It makes me wonder where it will end."

"You'd be well advised just to take the hint and stay clear."

"Not see Galway again? Not see the sea again? Not see the hills again? That would be hard indeed."

O'Grady said nothing. He sat looking impassively ahead of him, waiting for this outburst to end. It was as if his disapproval grew visibly with every word of it, until it revealed not only opprobrium, but an opprobrium that was rooted in an incapacity to understand or even to experience those emotions which to Vincent seemed inseparable from the human spirit. Was this the gulf that divided him from the greater part of mankind – that divided the educated from the majority? Were they so dull that they could regard things which might in him cause ecstasy or despair, with such bovine indifference? Who was it who had said that it was in these things alone that man was made in the image of God? An English heretic perhaps; but were this to be true, then how would he be left in the midst of humanity? But before he allowed this to soothe his pride, he had to remember that his father was also an uneducated man, in much the same mould as O'Grady, who now sat in private judgement of him, as he knew his father would have done. He was a wastrel, a dreamer, who deserved no more than he got. He needed O'Grady more than O'Grady needed him. This was his link with the past, and a world that was slipping out of his reach; and perhaps even O'Grady, for all his bovine taciturnity, was not entirely unaware of the undercurrents of his thoughts. He drew a deep breath, and looked at the old man.

"So, I'm to be a permanent exile, beside that muddy pond they call the Irish Sea."

"I'm telling you what you asked to know. What you choose to do is up to you. After all, the Bradys don't own Galway, but they do have a lot of influence here, even in Galway City. It's up to you to judge what the risk is. As for it being permanent, well … that might not be what it's about."

"Oh?"

The old man lit a cigarette and drew on it before speaking.

"I'm no friend of the Bradys. Never have been. None of us were in our part of the village. So we don't get to know the ins and outs of their private business. Even their hangers-on don't get to know, I doubt, if it's something big; and I reckon this must be something big."

"What is?"

O'Grady shrugged.

"Whatever it is that's making them so jumpy. I don't know what it is, but something's up, I can tell you that much. Something they don't want outsiders to know about. If you were to ask me, I'd say that either they're up to no good in a big way, or they've had some kind of bad news. If I find out what it is, I'll let you know, since they've taken against you particularly; but at the present, that's all I can tell you."

Why were they so concerned to keep him away just now? He had never had anything to do with their business, nefarious or otherwise. And if it was bad news, why should they want to keep him away in particular? Perhaps his overworked and solitary imagination saw too much significance in the matter. His thoughts seemed to be transparent to O'Grady, who puffed contemptuously at his cigarette, regarding Vincent through the smoke. The old man was no fool, after all.

18

As July slipped into August, the brilliant summer seemed to become almost oppressive in its unchanging glory, as if the abundance of life that grew in the bounty of its radiant warmth brought more sharply into focus the distinction between those for whom such blind fecundity also meant life, and those who, even in this torrid August, still stood in the depths of winter.

John hadn't seen Vincent Fitzgerald for several weeks, and when he ran into him again at the Queen's one Saturday evening in early August, they agreed to walk along the front together rather than endure the stuffiness of the lounge bar. Eventually they found a seat on high ground overlooking the sea, away from the crowds of holidaymakers who still thronged the seafront and the beach below.

"It's as if they didn't believe it was going to last, and are making the most of every last minute of it," said John, indicating the holidaymakers below.

"Well, and why shouldn't they make the most of it? After all, it isn't only the weather that won't last."

"That sounds a bit heavy."

"Perhaps I envy them the simplicity of being able to enjoy themselves in such a way – or the good fortune."

"Anyone can enjoy walking along the beach."
Vincent shook his head.

"It's a matter of states of mind, and how much emotional baggage you're carrying with you."

"Something's up?"

"I don't know for sure. I met old O'Grady again the other day. He was a friend of my father, from Kilkirrin." Vincent recounted the conversation to John. "I can't understand why they should make such an issue of the matter now, so long afterwards. Or rather, it seems to me that there could only be one possible reason why they might do so."

"Something to do with Rebecca?"

Vincent nodded without looking at him.

"Isn't that just some kind of wishful thinking?"

"Maybe. Maybe it's also true."

John was silent for a minute before replying.

"Why do you persist with this? Can't you see what stupidity it is? It's destroying you. Instead of giving yourself the opportunity to live, and perhaps achieving those things that are taken for granted by the majority, you expend your life carrying the torch for a woman who, if she remembers you at all, would have only contempt for you, and whom you will probably never see again. Can you not see this? You're wasting your life. All the years which have gone are more precious than you realise at the time, and as they slip away, you're left with less and less chance of life. You're behaving like a love-sick juvenile, and yet you can't seem to see it."

"For God's sake man, don't mock me with it. It isn't as if you haven't got troubles of your own in that department without presuming to judge me. Do you really think that I'm not aware of these things? Or what the consequences are? Do you think that because you're married, you know all there is to know about love? Perhaps what's happening to me is unwholesome and destructive; but what you fail to understand is that it doesn't happen without cause. Yes, I might have settled down with some pleasant, homely woman, if I could ever find one who would take me on, who would give me a chance of life, as you put it. Sometimes, indeed, the desire for life becomes overwhelming. It shakes me with fear, of death, of oblivion, and with rage against the time that slips by barren and unfruitful. Don't think I don't feel such things. But always, in the end, it isn't enough. Any other woman would be as a stranger whom I would be unable to relate to because she isn't the one I love. If you can't understand the imperative of that, then you won't understand anything about me. Even though I know that to wait without hope for such a one is nothingness, is death, I'm caught by something I have no power to resist.. The image of her has been seared into my brain, into my identity as a man, and for me, now, that image, her image, is life.

"You find it hard to accept that this is love. For you, the married man, love is possessing the woman you have, living with her in domesticity from day to day. What you don't seem to understand is that when this is denied to you, love doesn't necessarily die. For me, she has become what I would wish her to be, and this is the source of my love for her."

John shook his head.

"I can't even begin to understand that. And I can't accept it. It seems to me to be simply a cruel delusion. When you speak of Rebecca and say that she is life, she is life not because of the image of her that you hold in your memory, but because she's fertile and fruitful, and that is life. If she will not have you, then it will be with this other man that she will fulfil her promise of life. If you can't bear to face that, then your only salvation is to find a woman with whom you can live and have children."

Vincent shook his head.

"Part of my difficulty is that I accept the inevitability of what's happened, if that's what's intended for her. That doesn't mean that I've stopped wanting her, only that I'm conscious of the great chasm that lies between us, and the burden of facing how far I've fallen, and sometimes that's very hard to face without complete despair. Wherever she is in the world is the only place I want to be. Everywhere else is a wilderness. But if there's no place for me there, what then? I'm only too aware of the truth of what you say. But it means that somehow I have to find myself again, and reclaim my dignity."

"Have you not thought of going to America to try and find Rebecca, if you can't forget her?"

"I have, many times. But even apart from practical considerations – I don't know where in America she now is, and I could barely afford the fare to New York, let alone the cost of an extended search of the continent – even if I was able to find her, I would have to face the likelihood that she would still reject me, and I can't do that. Not now – not after all that's happened. In any event, things may have moved on from that."

"How do you mean?"

But that was all John could get out of him. He would not elaborate. For John, it was an unsatisfactory end to the conversation. He had hoped to discuss his own problems with Vincent, and had not expected it to end like this. They parted amicably enough. Vincent said that he would have to return home to attend to his mother, who would be fretting if he left her too long. They shook hands, and he left John sitting pensively on the bench, looking down at the beach as the tide ebbed, the sea gleaming silver in the soft light of the setting sun.

19

Helen folded the letter up carefully and put it into her pocket. The letters from home (as she thought instinctively of her parents' house in Cheshire – this primitive Irish cottage she regarded increasingly as a place of exile despite all that had happened there in the previous year), mostly written by her mother, were still the high point of the week for her. What a strange thing the imagination was. Home had always been a place of familiarity and certainty, a place of comforting predictability, even when it had been a four-roomed mid-terrace rabbit hutch of a house in the back streets of Stretford. The house in Nantwich, with its long garden at the back, the rooms as reassuringly solid as their wood-panelled walls and well-made, comfortable furniture, had remained 'home' for her even after she had married John. The rather transient squalor of their early married life, whilst happy in other respects, had an impermanent precariousness about it, which could not at that stage replace the solidity that the house in Nantwich represented. This was the substance of her imagination, which even the traumatic return of the previous autumn had not shaken. The letters from home told her of familiar things as well as the changes brought about by the war, and wound them together in such a way as to make the latter seem almost as familiar as the former. It was as if the war was something she could experience through the eyes and experiences of her mother, and through the house in

Nantwich, so that she could make of it a more familiar reality than that of this cottage on the road out of Bray.

Summer had come again, and in the cottage garden, where John had not turned the soil over for cultivation, the unruly Irish meadow was bright with the colour of wild flowers. Something in that very wildness seemed to jar with her spirit, held between reality and imagination, between exile and home. Now that baby Laura was occupying most of her time, what right did she have to allow this other to have even the possibility of disturbing the equilibrium of motherhood established by the baby's demands? But it was this which jarred. It was this which was at the centre of the picture she painted for herself in her imagination. Even baby Laura, insofar as she had a separate persona of her own, had a place in this picture: indeed, especially so, since she represented the continuity of the family. Already it was possible for Helen to think of Laura as her baby, rather than John's and her baby. And perhaps also it was attractive to think of her family in terms of continuity in the female line – a half-formed, half-worked-out idea based on an uncertain mixture of dependence and a desire for stability. Such thoughts were as yet sublimated within a general feeling of nostalgia for home, particularly when she received one of her mother's letters; but they moved ever closer to the surface.

20

Superintendent O'Neil of the Galway police turned the pages of the file slowly, reading each one carefully.

"Not a lot to go on at the moment. Is your man still in place?"

Inspector Franks, whose report the superintendent was reading, nodded.

"He is, but because he's not a member of the Brady family, he's not privy to the way decisions are taken – he can only report what's been decided after it's happened; and as you can see, not always that, even. Sometimes it's a matter of judging what's going on from what they're told to do. The Bradys have always run a pretty tight ship."

O'Neil was thoughtful. "The main concern is if it's political. Now there's a war in Europe, the last thing Dublin wants is a general resurgence of political violence, especially after the events of last year."

"There's no suggestion of anything like that here, and the last time I was able to speak to our man, there was no indication of it either."

"That should be encouraging. When there's political trouble brewing, there are usually rumours of it from several different sources."

"But there's definitely something going on, even if this incident isn't connected to it."

"You know, old man Brady's a sentimental old bastard

underneath, when you get to know him," O'Neil reflected. "I would have thought that he'd be reaching the stage by now when he'd be starting to turn his mind to the future, of his family, and his own private little empire."

"The succession."

O'Neil nodded.

"I'd have thought that whatever he's up to would more likely have to do with that – making sure of the future for his favourites. I can't see old man Brady getting involved in politics again now – he's been out of it for too long."

"And all this about this man Fitzgerald?"

"I'd be inclined to see it as part of the general picture. Your man mentions the family feud from years ago involving Fitzgerald, and we've nothing on Fitzgerald to link him with anything political; so it's just a matter of sitting on it until the detail emerges, as I've no doubt it will."

"Fitzgerald had a gun – a pistol."

O'Neil shrugged.

"That's a bit rich, coming from the Bradys."

"But one of their people received quite a serious injury. As you can see, he was named as Declan Brady, one of the old man's nephews. Gunshot wound to the shoulder."

"You're not saying that that was on the line?"

"No, no, that was on the grapevine – and our man confirmed it."

"Is he pushing us, or what? It's almost as if the old man wants us to mollycoddle him in his old age. He knows the score. If he formally notifies a crime, he gets the works."

"Perhaps they don't believe that any more."

O'Neil shook his head.

"No, it's not that. After all, they didn't report the incident when it happened, so they'll hardly do that now. As it happened a while ago, it may not be connected to this. And if they're thinking we've maybe gone soft under De Valera's

Government, well they should know that's not true either. Only last month there was that business down in Kerry."

"But that was political. As you say, we don't know yet what this is all about. Maybe if we pulled this Fitzgerald in, we might get a new line on it."

Again, O'Neil shook his head.

"Officially, nothing's been notified to us, so officially there's nothing to investigate. But whether it's political or not, old man Brady should know the score by now. What can you tell me about the character who was with Fitzgerald? Apparently, he was English."

"Mostly, just what's available from official sources, which isn't much more than you can see here. He arrived in Ireland in August last year, with his wife, apparently to settle here. He took up a post as a teacher at a private school in Dublin, and they live in Bray, just south of Dublin. No criminal record, and no other problems or incidents reported – until this one."

"Why would such a one get involved in something of this sort, or have any association with someone like Fitzgerald?"

"Fitzgerald also used to be a teacher, apparently."

"That's a bit thin. You might make any sort of connection on the basis of something as tenuous as that."

"Perhaps they knew each other already."

"Mmm, perhaps – although if the Englishman only arrived in Ireland for the first time last year, they can't have known each other for long. But he came here to settle, with his wife, in August last year. That's odd in itself. Why would he do that, at such a time? Everyone knew last year that a war was almost inevitable, and by August it was expected any day."

"A coincidence?"

"No. He came here because of the war – I don't think there can be any doubt about that. But it's anomalous – it doesn't fit any pattern. I see in your report that you have a contact who sounded out the émigré community about him

– I was impressed by that." O'Neil permitted himself a brief smile.

Inspector Franks nodded in acknowledgement. "But – he drew a blank," he said. "No-one had heard of our Englishman."

"Perhaps that isn't surprising. The émigrés are almost all from the British ruling class who came here shortly before the war started, to avoid being interned because they had connections with the new Germany, or were sympathisers with it. There's a peculiarly internecine quality about betrayal among the British elite. They've ruled for so long in England that they've become almost totally detached from the people they rule over, and yet, because they understand their subjects completely, they're also able to control them completely. Few ruling elites in the world have so little to fear from the people they rule over as the British elite do from the English. Betrayal from within is never forgiven, and there are special punishments for those who break that taboo. But betrayal from below they can deal with, not least because it's so rare. The English know their place, and their craving for respectability means they're easily led and very predictable. But not, apparently, in this case. This Englishman evidently has a mind of his own. At a time when almost all his compatriots were loyally preparing for a war that their ruling elite had chosen to get involved in, he left his country and came to Ireland, which most people expected to remain neutral in the event of a war. I would say that that makes him very unusual."

"A conscientious objector? There were quite a few of those in the Great War."

"No. A conscientious objector stays to face the music. It's a kind of political protest. This is something else."

"Maybe he's just a coward and couldn't face the war."

"Maybe. Although that wouldn't exactly square with him

getting involved in this business with Fitzgerald." He tapped the report. "You mention an unsubstantiated report that the Englishman was treated by a certain doctor in Galway for gunshot wounds."

"Well, it was unsubstantiated. As you know, that particular doctor is often resorted to by victims of the various turf wars between the local bandits, because he can be relied on to be discreet. So I can't confirm the source of that story, but I suspect it's probably true."

"It paints a strange picture of the man if it is."

"Aye, but no stranger than Fitzgerald, I would say."

"You know, I've just seen what those two have in common, and what probably brought them together. Each in his own way is an outcast from society – from the society that created him."

"Now, is that not a bit far-fetched?"

"No, I don't think so. The reasons are compelling in both cases. Fitzgerald we know about. The Englishman appears to have turned his back on his country by coming to Ireland on the eve of the war. Maybe he'll return to England in the near future; but the longer he remains in Ireland, the more likely it is that he's an exile from his own country, and one with no hope of return. So in his own way, he's also an outcast – a refugee. A man without a country."

"Do you think he could tell us any more about this business? I could go across and speak to him off the record."

"I would very much doubt that he knows anything. All the indications are that he was just helping Fitzgerald out. If your man doesn't yet know what's at the root of all this, it's highly unlikely that the Englishman does. But there's no harm in leaving him on your list just in case unexpected developments mean that you need to talk to him. Even if he can't tell us anything useful, I don't doubt it would be an interesting conversation."

21

It was proving to be a hot summer, an almost unbroken succession of long sunlit days which started with the clear breathlessness of a summer dawn, through the shimmering haze of the sun's zenith, to glorious evenings that lasted almost till midnight. From June, through July and into August, there was hardly a day when the warm green countryside did not call to the spirit to abandon the dust of towns and buildings. It had been hard to resist this call, but apart from occasional weekend cycle rides into the countryside around Bray, John had not been able to see much of the summer. Helen was unable to join him even for these, principally because of baby Laura; but the carefree joy of the previous August was gone, and Helen was content to use the commitment to the baby as an excuse to join him as little as possible. It was not that she wouldn't have appreciated a break from the constant commitment to the baby; but John was aware that she regarded it as his fault that she could not have such a break because they were, from her point of view, isolated in the middle of nowhere in Ireland. If they were back in England, Helen's mother would give her some relief. John felt the implied hostility towards him with a slow anger; but he kept his thoughts to himself and said nothing.

It was in the dusty town that he found some consolation. His eye was caught by a poster advertising performances in Dublin by a visiting theatre company. It was apparently an

English repertory company on tour. Dublin was their last port of call. They were playing every night that week, and on an impulse, John, who was on his way home on a Monday evening, made his way to the theatre and bought a ticket for the following night's performance. It was a temptation to go and see that evening's performance, but he didn't wish to provoke Helen's resentment needlessly, although in the event she seemed largely indifferent to the matter. In the past he would have been more concerned about that than he was now. Now, he was just relieved that there had not been an argument.

The play was Noël Coward's *Private Lives*, which John hadn't seen before. It was a new kind of theatre, with much greater realism than in any other play he had seen, and John's head was filled with images of the play on his homeward journey. The following day, at St Mungo's, he was still preoccupied with it, and as the day wore on, he realised that what he wanted above all else was to go and see the play again. He called in at the theatre and bought a ticket for the following night. The next day seemed to drag unbearably, until at last it was over, and it was time to make his way to the theatre again. Well before the performance was over, he understood the nature of his fascination. However good the play, and the acting, it was one of the actresses who had drawn him back. There was no denying that Susanna Ashton was lovely, with her long blonde hair, full thighs and shapely figure. But it was her ability to project herself in the character she was playing, the power of her personality as much as her physical beauty which had captivated him. She was exquisite, and it was no longer enough for him just to see her again. Drawn as a moth is to a candle flame, he wanted to speak with her, to hear her voice say his name, to know that she had been consciously aware of him as an individual, for however short a time. The idea grew, until it became an obsession which drove his waking consciousness to exclusion of almost all else. But even as it grew, so also did a contrary feeling of diffidence, the significance of which he understood too late. After the performance, he stood in the lobby as the audience poured out into a warm August night. There was a side door that gave onto a corridor leading towards the back of the building. At the farther end was another door marked 'Private – No Entry'. He stood uncertainly before this, as his courage failed him. One or two individuals passed in and out of the door without taking any notice of him. From what he could see of what was beyond the door, it probably did give onto the actors' dressing rooms. But he could not go any further. He didn't even have a programme, and he had no clear idea of what he would say. It would be better to leave it until the following night, even if that would bring other problems in its train. He made his way back to the lobby and out into the street. Still he could not make up his mind what to do. Perhaps he might see her coming out of the side door to the theatre, or she might come through the lobby if she had ordered a taxi. Perhaps ... But he could not wait any longer. It was going to be hard enough explaining to Helen that he would be home late for a third night in succession, without making things even more difficult for himself.

This time, Helen did have something to say.

"It would have been nice to at least have been asked. After all, I don't get a lot of respite from looking after Laura, and this would be the third night in a row you'll be coming home late."

Helen was feeding Laura, who was in an uncooperative mood, breaking off and complaining every other minute, so that Helen had to keep comforting her.

"I know ... I'm sorry. It's just that you don't often see theatre as good as that, and they're only here for a few days."

"A few days – does that mean you'll be home late even after this?"

216

"No ... . of course not."

The irritation in Helen's voice was communicating itself to Laura, who was becoming more fractious as a result.

"I mean, it's bad enough having to go all day with no-one to talk to without it extending into the evening as well. I still don't think you understand how isolated I feel stuck out here. You're a selfish bastard, John, you really are."

Was that first August, hot and fecund, August of freedom, still only a year ago? Knowing what he did, he could only hold his peace.

This time, he did not hesitate, but pushed through the swing doors at the end of the corridor. He turned a corner, to be faced by another set of swing doors. He went through, and almost bumped into someone going the other way.

"Do you know which is Miss Ashton's dressing room?"

The man hardly looked at him.

"Number seven," he said as he disappeared through the swing doors. John found himself looking down a corridor along which was a row of doors. Some of these were ajar, and the sounds of conversations came to him. He couldn't see any numbers on the doors. As he stood there, one of the doors opened and someone came out. It was one of the male actors. On an impulse, John asked the actor for his autograph, proffering his theatre programme. It was what he was supposed to be there for, although he felt more than a little sheepish in doing so. Again, he asked for Miss Ashton's room, and the other pointed to one of the doors as he walked away. The door was ajar, and voices could be heard from within. As John moved towards the door it opened wide and a man's figure appeared in the doorway, leaning back into the room as he continued to speak.

"...we'll just assume it'll be the same as last time, but if there's any problem, I'll let you know Suze, OK? Oh, it looks as if you have a visitor."

John had a momentary impression of a tall, lanky figure wearing dark slacks and a pale grey roll-necked sweater, a sallow-complexioned face prematurely lined, and a thick mane of hair, worn long, and a uniform iron-grey colour. John waved his programme vaguely at the man as he passed, then knocked on the open door.

"Yes, who is it?" he heard her call out.

She was sat at a dressing table engaged in cleaning off her make-up. She was still wearing the dress she had worn on stage, and her hair was loose, in a golden cascade down her back. She glanced at him as he advanced uncertainly into the room.

"I was wondering ..." he began diffidently.

She turned towards him and smiled at him, making him completely tongue-tied. She took the programme from him and quickly turned to the page which included stage photographs of all the cast.

"And what's your name?"

John told her his name, and as she wrote beside her photograph in a wide extrovert hand, he told her how much he had enjoyed the performance.

"Will you be taking the play on tour in Ireland?"

"No. I mean, we've no plans to. As far as I know this is the only venue in Ireland. Next week we're due to go back to London."

"What will you do then?"

"I'm not sure. Normally when your contract finishes, it means you're out of work until you can find another one. If you stay with the same director, something may turn up quite quickly, but you can never tell."

"I'm sorry you won't be staying in Ireland."

"Well, so am I, I suppose. I've enjoyed our visit here. But – other things intervene. One of the boys has received his call-up papers, and the other expects to at any time, so we don't really have any choice in the matter. I suppose it's quite likely that I'll be called to join the ATS or the Land Army or something like that. So even if I don't get work, I'll be doing something."

"Yes, I see. I suppose that in one way at least, that makes things a lot simpler. But we will miss you, all of you, and I in particular will miss you."

"You're very kind. You're English, aren't you?"

John shook his head.

"No. I was born in England, but I'm Irish. Ireland is my country. I live near Bray, just south of Dublin."

"Oh, I see. I suppose we don't always think of Ireland as being a separate country. A lot of Irish boys have come over to England to join the forces. My brother's in the navy, and I remember he mentioned recently that there are a lot of Irish lads among the new recruits."

"So I believe. It may not always be idealism that drives them, though. Some parts of Ireland are very poor, and for some of them, the attraction may be as much to do with regular meals and regular pay as anything else. To go and fight for another country out of idealism alone, as with those who went to fight in Spain, is a much rarer virtue, I think."

"But I'm sure that many who do come and join us are idealists. When I was in London a couple of weeks ago, you could see all the white smoke trails in the sky as our aircraft battled against the enemy aircraft. For us in London, it feels as if we're fighting for the whole of the free world against Hitler. There are soldiers of many nationalities there now, all fighting the same enemy."

There was nothing he could say in answer to this that would not diminish him in her eyes. It was enough that he had identified himself as Irish. He merely nodded and smiled.

"Well, whatever you end up doing when you return to England, I sincerely hope that you come through it safely, and you'll come back to Dublin one day."

She smiled at him again, and at the last, he was tongue-tied once more. Outside in the street, John did not immediately make for the railway station, but wandered aimlessly, subject only to the turmoil within. He could not yet order his thoughts. He had spoken with her. He had heard her voice speak his name. He was no longer a stranger to her, no longer merely another anonymous face in the auditorium. The seemingly impossible had happened. To have spoken with her … But in speaking with her, he had still had to be devious, on the defensive. The war would not go away, and it sullied the memory of even this moment. He would never see her again; but what was he going to do? Thrice he had gone back to see her, drawn by something beyond his will to control. He had allowed it to happen because of Helen; and the ghost that had maligned him had been victorious. The words came to him unbidden.

"Ah, Vincent, how I have misjudged you."

22

In early September, news reached John of the death of his cousin Henry. It was news which was to prove fateful for John also. Henry's ship, a corvette, had been sunk by German aircraft while it was escorting a convoy through the English Channel. There had apparently been no survivors. The news came in a letter to John from his mother. She was the only person in John's family who wrote to him in Ireland, which she did as much as her infirmity allowed, mostly with news about the slow recovery at home of her brother Peter, who had suffered a bad fall in the spring of that year. Helen maintained a regular correspondence not only with her parents, but with some of her friends as well, a correspondence that had become more voluminous as her thoughts were increasingly focused on her old home in England.

"What does your mother say?" Helen asked as he read the letter. He could hardly conceal it from her, as she had collected the letter from the post that morning. He handed it to her without comment.

"Oh, no!" She was immediately distressed, and tears filled her eyes. "He was such a nice man, too. Oh, why do the best always have to die first?"

She rounded on him.

"What are you going to do now? Are you not shamed, even by this? Your own cousin?"

"And what would you have me do?"

"Stop being a coward and do your duty like a man."

"As I remember it, you were encouraging me to follow Henry's advice and volunteer, so that I could be posted to the same ship as his. If I'd done that, I would now be dead. Is that what you want?"

"That's all you can do isn't it – make excuses while brave men like Henry are dying to save your skin."

"Henry's death has nothing to do with me. He chose to go to war. If I'd followed his advice, I'd be dead too. Is that what you want? Do you want me dead?"

She didn't reply.

"Answer me! What is it you want? You have a husband who loves you, even in spite of all this. You have a beautiful baby daughter, our daughter. We have a cottage to ourselves in beautiful countryside. We're secure here. Millions of people would give an arm and a leg to have what we have. What more do you want?"

"You know what I want. I'm sick of this God-forsaken place. I want to go home, and if you were a man, you'd come with me and do your duty."

"Why is this place God-forsaken? Is it because there's no war here? Is it because thousands of people are not being killed or maimed or brutalised by savagery, and are just leading peaceful ordinary lives instead? Do you think that God has a bloodlust like mankind, and likes to see mass slaughter in order to be appeased? Is that your idea of God?"

"God is on the side of freedom and democracy, which means he's on our side in this war. If you weren't such a coward, you'd see that yourself."

He stared at her.

"You're mad. You really believe that, don't you? Politicians' claptrap. They all claim that God is on their side in every war, to try and fool people into supporting them."

"You're just twisting what I say to try and cover your own

cowardice. You can't face the truth that God is on our side in this war because it's a war against tyranny and evil. He's on our side because we're fighting for freedom and justice and democracy. That's the truth, only you're too much of a coward to see it."

"Truth? Your truth. It was your truth that I should have volunteered so that I could be posted to the same ship as Henry. If I'd followed your truth, then I would now be dead. Is that what you want? Is that what you want? Answer me!"

He seized her by the arms and shook her violently.

"Answer me. Is that what you want?"

"Yes, if you're such a coward."

He struck her in the face, knocking her to the ground. She lay dazed for a few moments before getting to her feet. She screamed at him.

"You're a coward. That's a measure of your cowardice, that you'd hit a woman. You disgust me beyond words. You're a stinking coward, and I want you dead. Did you hear me? You've got your answer. I want you dead."

She ran from the room. John buried his face in his hands to hide his own pain. Somewhere, as if from a great distance, he could hear Laura crying.

That night he slept on the settee in the living room. It seemed as if the force of events had overtaken him and he no longer had the power or the will to resist. He was afraid, but he no longer knew what to do. He slept heavily, waking only once, to hear Helen with Laura. It seemed strange, as he lay there, that something so familiar and so close should already be beyond his reach. When he awoke again it was well past dawn. The house was quiet, and the fires in both the dining room and the kitchen were out. He did not delay to get anything to eat or drink, but went straight to get his bicycle, and set off for the station. It was the longest day he could remember. St

Mungo's had recently suffered its first casualties of the war, both at sea, and both, ironically, due to accidents rather than enemy action. In consequence, the mood among the staff was more sombre than it had been, with little of the war fever that had latterly made the atmosphere so tense. The conversation in the staff room was about the bombing of London, which had been going on without remission for several days. For the first time, doubts were raised about the war. Perhaps Britain had been too rash in taking on the might of the new Germany, as a successful German invasion seemed increasingly likely. Such talk made the burden of that day all the harder for John to carry. When at last, after what had seemed like years of waiting, the bell went at the end of the final lesson, he felt totally drained. He no longer had the spirit to prepare himself for what was to come.

At the end of the journey home, it seemed as if his reluctance to go on had transferred itself to the very air, which pushed against him as if it were a glutinous liquid, making his limbs heavy and weak. Perhaps this was a fantasy, a dream – but the time for such things was gone, and long gone. The back door of the cottage was locked, which it never was normally: a further sign that something was wrong. He searched for his key and opened the door. The air in the house was dead and empty, the fire in the kitchen grate cold ash. He called out her name once, gently, the knowledge of her desertion already breaking his voice. He went through the house, each room a false hope, until the last, and hope had no further refuge.

She had left a letter on the living room table. He knew what it was, and it was a long time before he was able to open it. Even then, he waited for some slight remission of hope – a word, or a sentiment through which he might be redeemed for her; but there was nothing. For hours he sat in the fireside chair in the kitchen by the cold ash of the last fire, or walked aimlessly through each room of the house, while the long light of a summer evening shone level through the deep windows and splashed the sun's colour on walls and beams. There was nothing. How could such a thing have destroyed them both? He could not see it in any other way. What alien need in her did such madness fulfil? Was human love so insubstantial that at the last it could so easily be brushed aside by something so crude and elemental? Surely he did not love her in such a way? She was not unattractive; but he loved her for what she was, and perhaps even more, for what they had been together. And now, seemingly, that was all gone.

He did not sleep that night. It seemed to him then that, however irrational it might be, he had to decide there and then what he was going to do. The matter would allow him no sleep otherwise. Should he capitulate to her blackmail, if those were the only terms she would now offer him? But to contemplate such a thing only made more obvious the extent of her malevolence. It was unlikely that he would ever see her. How many times had he followed through the logic of the matter in his own mind, even if she refused to listen to him? Unless he was able to give a false identity, he would probably get no farther than Liverpool, since there was presumably by now a warrant out for his arrest. He would go to prison, at least until a trial was arranged; and thereafter … She would never come to visit him in prison. She would not, in her own estimation, debase herself.

"My husband is in prison because he won't do his duty and fight – he's a coward. My husband is a coward… a coward… a coward…"

It would be his just punishment for causing her such shame. He had no other way out, as she must very well know. To return to England would mean death – probably a squalid suicide in a prison cell after almost unimaginable mental trauma. Even if he avoided arrest and managed to reach her as a fugitive, she would dismiss him out of hand. She might even report him to the authorities. This again stopped his train of thought abruptly. It would be inconceivable to do such a thing to someone one loved. But he could believe it of her now. The motive, the instinct at the root of such an action was surely something that was essentially evil. He kept coming back to that. It was something which, because it was evil, struck at the very basis of the relationship between a man and a woman, making of it a trial, a judgement, an unending judgement, with rejection as the punishment; and in this case, *in extremis*, prison, or worse. Could not this be a caricature, a gross caricature of reality? Perhaps for some, for the fortunate, it was; but perhaps even for them, it was not entirely so.

And baby Laura – darling little Laura – would he ever see her again?

23

Helen walked over to the window, still in her nightdress, and pulled aside the heavy curtains. She had slept late following her long journey from Ireland, and it was now nearly midday. She was greeted by bright sunlight and a view of the garden, with the apple tree already heavily laden with ripening fruit. The view lifted her spirits and she stood for several minutes taking it in, before a discreet knock at the door called away her attention. It was her mother, bringing her a tray of tea and toast.

"I wasn't sure if you were awake, but I thought this might be welcome anyway."

"Oh yes, it certainly is, thank you."

"Baby Laura's asleep now. She was awake twice in the night and again this morning, and I gave her a bottle feed each time. She's had a nappy change too, so she should be alright until this afternoon."

"Oh, I do appreciate that, Mum, really I do."

"Well, you were so tired when you arrived yesterday. You looked absolutely drained and exhausted, so I could see you were going to need a lot of sleep. And baby Laura has been no trouble. She's just lovely, and it's been such a pleasure to hold her and feed her. I may be a grandmother, but I'm not so old that I've forgotten how to cope with a baby."

"Bless you, Mum, you're a treasure. I know it's been rather sudden, but I do hope you don't mind – well, you know."

"You know I don't mind. It's lovely to see you again, and baby Laura. This is still your home, and you know you're always welcome here. Obviously I'm concerned if things have gone wrong and I want to do whatever I can to help; but I can help only as much as you'll let me."

"You're already doing as much as you can, and it's a tremendous help, Mum, really it is. I'll only need a day or two to get back onto an even keel again, and then, well ..." Helen looked at her mother. "Do you think that you'd be up to looking after Laura during the day – during the week, I mean?" she said quickly. She was confused for a moment.

"Well, yes, of course, if you need me to."

"What I mean is, I've come back to England for good, Mum. This is my country, and this is where I belong. I'm not going back to Ireland again. Nothing would ever induce me to go back there again. I'm back here for good. That means I'll need to find a job as soon as I can. I assume that, with all the men away to the war, that won't be too difficult. They'll have to make allowance for the fact that I'm a nursing mother, but I'm sure that, within reason, it shouldn't be very difficult to find something suitable."

"Only when you're ready, Helen. Give yourself time to recover from the journey first."

"Yes, of course. But I don't want you to think that it was my intention to live off you. Since I'm here on my own, I intend to find a job as soon as I can, so I can pay my way."

"Well, that's fine, love. But I don't want you to get all agitated about it unnecessarily when you still need to recover from the journey. In any case, I don't suppose you'll be able to do anything until you've got a National Identity Card and a ration book sorted out. I'll come with you into town to help you get those – they may need witnesses or something – but we can leave that for a day or two until you're properly recovered."

"Oh, yes. We'll have to bring Laura with us, then."

"Of course. Besides, for all I know, Laura may need documents of her own, baby though she is. It may be a bit more complicated because she wasn't born here – but we'll just have to wait and see." She paused before going on. "You say you've come back to England for good. Does that mean that there's no possibility of a reconciliation between you and John?"

"I can't see how there can be. After all, it was his decision to break up our marriage."

"His decision?"

"Yes, his decision. He expected me to stay in that hell-hole of a place just to pander to his cowardice. Because he refused to volunteer, or even go when he was called up, it meant that we were going to be stuck in that God-forsaken country for the rest of our lives. I know now that that was his intention all along. I was rather naïve and didn't realise it at first. It was only gradually that I came to understand what he was about. And it was so primitive – we didn't even have electric light. Compared with what we were used to even in Stretford, it was like going back to the Middle Ages, almost. We could have moved to a town, I suppose, but it would still have been a strange country, and I could never settle there. There was something alien about the place – but he just couldn't see that, let alone understand it. All he seemed to care about was the fact that, as long as he was there he was safe from being called up, or from being arrested if he didn't go. Apparently Ireland isn't ruled by England any more and it's almost as if it's a separate country, although I don't really understand why that should be. It was that which drew him to Ireland; but he didn't explain that to me of his own accord. I had to draw it out of him bit by bit, and I think that deep down, he was ashamed of it, which is as it should be, even if he would never admit it. But that was the main reason why I had to leave.

Surely you understand that, Mum: how impossible it is to live with a man who's a coward. I felt revolted inside by the very idea of living with and being intimate with a man who's a coward. I'm sure a real man would understand my feelings; but he seemed incapable of any such thing."

"Perhaps he objects to the war on moral grounds – a conscientious objector."

"Well, he may be entitled to his views, I don't know; but he isn't entitled to expect that as a woman I would put up with such views. I certainly won't, and I think that it was entirely unreasonable of him to think that I would. In fact, I don't think he is entitled to have such views. It's a man's duty to fight for his country when he's told to do so, and there shouldn't be any argument about that."

"Even after the Great War – the trenches?"

"That's nothing to do with it. It's a man's duty to fight, and that's all there is to it. All the real men have answered the call this time, the Great War notwithstanding, so I'm sure that's no argument. It's only the cowards who won't go. In fact, conscientious objectors are sent to prison aren't they, so obviously they're not entitled to hold such views. John's such a coward he can't even face prison. That's why he went to Ireland – that's clear enough now."

"Well, I suppose it's hardly surprising if he stays in Ireland if he faces arrest and prison here."

"But he's such a coward about it. That's what turns my stomach. If he'd done his duty in the first place, he wouldn't be facing prison now."

"No. I suppose if you feel as strongly as that, I can understand … What … financial arrangements have you made, if you don't mind my asking? Has John agreed to pay you maintenance or anything like that?"

"Well … no. We didn't discuss it. Don't you understand, I couldn't face him any more, Mum. I just had to get out. It was lucky I'd managed to save enough money for the journey. If I'd waited to talk to him it would have been far worse, and I just couldn't face it."

"So you left him without warning?"

"Only in the sense that he's so selfish and insensitive that he neither knew nor cared about my feelings."

Helen's mother sighed.

"Even so, I'm sure John would be prepared to pay some sort of maintenance."

"Maybe. Maybe he won't get the option to choose. I'm sure the court will be entirely sympathetic to my point of view once they know that he's a coward who won't fight for his country."

"What do you mean, the court?"

"When I divorce him, of course."

"Divorce? Helen, do you know what a shocking thing that is to say? John's the father of your child, of baby Laura."

"Haven't you understood what I've been telling you? I can't bear to live with him any longer. I can't even bear him to be near me. What else can there be except divorce?"

"It's not that I haven't understood you, Helen; it's just that divorce is such a terrible thing, especially for a woman. There's a stigma associated with divorce which you can't ever escape from. And apart from that, there's the awfulness of having to go to court. Court cases are always horribly complicated. I don't even know if you could get a hearing if your husband refused to attend."

"Mum, I need encouragement from you, not discouragement. I've had a long time to think about this, and I've made my mind up. I cannot remain married to a man who's a coward, especially now, when we're at war. I know that there's a stigma attached to divorce, but for me, there's an even greater feeling of shame about being married to a coward. There can be no possibility of a reconciliation, so I need to be rid of him. That may sound shocking, but it's the decision I've come to. I'm still a young woman, young enough to marry again, and to make a better choice this time, with the benefit of experience. If I petition for a divorce, I'm quite sure that, now that we're at war, the fact that John refuses to fight for his country due to cowardice will count very much in my favour in the view of the court. Believe me, Mum, I'm quite sure I'm right about this."

Helen's mother did not give further voice to her doubts. Perhaps she was old-fashioned, and the younger generation would be more tolerant of such things. The war itself already seemed to be overturning much of the staid respectability of peacetime, and against the larger events of the war, a divorce did not seem such a great matter. But her instinct was to doubt that old prejudices could be dispelled so easily, and to fear that her daughter would discover the reality of this at the cost of much suffering.

24

L iam Brady poured himself another drink from the opened bottle, draining the last drop of ale into the glass. He drank some of it before turning to old O'Grady again.

"So, what does he want to know for?"

"I've told you, he just wants to keep in touch. It's where he was born and raised, isn't it?"

"What is there for him to know? He took his old mother away back to Dublin, so there's nothing for him in Kilkirrin now."

The old man temporised.

"Most of his forebears are buried in the churchyard there."

"That's no reason for asking questions about what's going on in Kilkirrin now."

O'Grady remained silent. It had been several days since he had last visited Kilkirrin, and to be accosted here in Galway City by one of the Bradys was an unpleasant surprise. Since he no longer lived in Kilkirrin, he didn't regard himself as being subject to all the constraints suffered by those who lived in the village. Brady was clearly not of that opinion.

"You know what the score is. There's one law in Kilkirrin, and that's Brady law. That's the way it's always been. Everyone knows their place, and even if they don't like it, they know to keep their noses clean if they want to stay out of trouble. You know that well enough."

"That doesn't mean that people are going to stop being curious, about what's going on in the village."

"We decide what goes on in Kilkirrin. And what people get to know about it."

"Well, it's obvious something's going on, even if no-one knows what it is."

"Who said anything was going on?"

"Does anyone need to say anything, when there are armed men guarding all ways to the Brady farm and even walking through the village like gunslingers in a western at the picture house?"

"I've told you, we decide what goes on in Kilkirrin. And it would be best if people don't concern themselves about what's none of their business."

"That might be so for most people, but Fitzgerald mightn't see it like that, especially if it's something to do with Rebecca Brady. Is that what this is all about – is Rebecca Brady, or Rebecca Murphy, or whatever she calls herself now, back in Kilkirrin?"

Brady leaned over the table until his face was only a few inches from O'Grady's.

"Watch your mouth, you old goat, and mind your own fucking business. And that applies even more to Fitzgerald. He's been warned off coming anywhere near Kilkirrin, or he knows what'll happen. And I'm warning you now that from now on you tell Fitzgerald nothing about Kilkirrin, otherwise the same'll happen to you. The boss has plenty of friends around Galway, and they know where to find you. Understand?"

The old man made no sound, too frightened to speak.

25

D r Grey looked up as Dr Mahony came into the surgery without his jacket, and sporting rather striking red and black braces.

"My word, they look rather snazzy."

"Almost meretricious. But it's a glorious day, so why not?"

"Well, it may be a glorious day out there ..."

"Don't tell me. So what's wrong now?"

"Well, if you'd seen the way Dodds have been messing about with their prices. I mean, they want seven and six for their digitalis now."

"Seven and six? Ridiculous! What do they mean by it?"

"Their excuse is ..." Dr Grey perched a letter against the glass beaker in which he had been preparing a solution of digitalis. "Their excuse is that most of their stuff comes from a London supplier, and because of various 'difficulties' caused by the war, their prices, 'regrettably', have had to rise."

"Hah! Well, in that case, regrettably, we may have to consider getting our stock from another supplier."

"They might all have the same story."

"Well, if there are no honest men among them ... I mean, digitalis – why do they have to go to London, for Christ's sake, to get digitalis? What's wrong with our own native Irish foxglove? We could almost pick it from the hedgerows ourselves."

"If things go on like this, we may end up doing just that."

"As bad as that, eh? I must say, I've never really thought about how this business might affect us. Not in that kind of way, I mean. I suppose it's entirely conceivable that if even general medicines end up being in very short supply across the water because of the war, they'll become very expensive to buy over here."

"It's entirely conceivable – which is why the Government should have been planning for self-sufficiency here years ago. It's all very well them talking about an emergency now – what were they doing when they had the time to make preparations for it? But it's probably too late for that now."

"And so, we're stuck with Messrs. Dodds and Co., and all the other rascals of their ilk. I wonder what'd happen if the Brits lose the war?"

Dr Grey shrugged.

"I imagine it would mean that the supply of medicines from Britain would cease completely, at least for the time being. We'd probably have to try and come to some arrangement with a German supplier, and I don't imagine that'd be cheap."

"Do you think the Brits will lose?"

"It's not looking good for them at the moment. I have to admit, there's a part of me that would like to see them thrashed; but, as you can see, it's not as simple a matter as that." Dr Grey dropped the letter onto the table.

"What do you recommend? It's obviously something which is overdue for consideration."

"Well, Dodds and Co. don't inspire a great deal of confidence. I can just see them tamely passing on higher and higher prices from their London supplier until supplies suddenly dry up, and then they won't know what to do. I think we should start looking for alternative sources of supply, preferably local and Irish ones. Looking at the way these prices have changed even in the last two or three months, I think

236

there's a high probability that the supply of many of these items will dry up completely, or the prices will shoot through the roof. We need to start looking for alternative sources now, otherwise we'll end up in the same boat as Dodds and Co."

"Some items have to be imported. There's no way round that."

"Maybe so; but the sooner we start looking, the sooner we'll be ahead of everyone else."

"What about crossing the water ourselves, at least to Liverpool, and buying our own stuff?"

Dr Grey pulled a face.

"To be honest, I'd be inclined to see that as something of a last resort. It'd be essential to have a contact who was willing to show us some loyalty when times got tough, as they almost certainly will do, and at the moment, we don't have anything like that. There'd be the expense and difficulty of making the sea voyage, and the uncertainty of how long the trips would last if things got bad over there, or if the ferry services became unreliable. And if the Brits impose export restrictions on medicines, we might end up trying to smuggle the stuff out. No, I have to say, I wouldn't be happy with anything like that as a solution, for a variety of reasons."

It was Dr Mahony's turn to look doubtful.

"It looks as if whatever we end up doing, it's going to be very time-consuming. You're definitely pessimistic about staying with the likes of Dodds and Co.?"

"I'm afraid I have to be. Even if supplies don't actually fail, but end up becoming very expensive, we could find the practice being squeezed financially to the point where life becomes distinctly unpleasant. If we hadn't taken steps before then, we'd only have ourselves to blame. I'm convinced that most of our requirements could be met from Irish sources if we were prepared to spend the time finding them. And beyond that, it's not as if we're completely cut off from the outside world. I remember seeing an item in the paper about shipping services from Cork to Portugal, and even an aeroplane service, so I've no doubt that there are ways and means of finding a solution, if only we take the trouble to find them."

"Ah, so it's a trip to sunny Portugal you're after, and never mind dreary Liverpool."

Dr Grey smiled.

"Well, I wouldn't say no if we agreed it was necessary. But it shouldn't be necessary actually to go there. The point I'm making is that as long as normal trade and communications exist between Ireland and Portugal, and indeed, other neutral countries, to import a small parcel of medicines from Portugal from time to time shouldn't be a particularly extraordinary thing to do, or wildly beyond our ordinary means. We have to get out of the way of thinking that we must always be totally dependent on Britain."

"Well, I have no problems with that. I'm yours to command. We can split the task between us if you'll tell me what you want me to do."

"A perusal of trade directories would be a good place to start. It might give us an idea of who makes what. But I should say that I wasn't really joking just now, you know – about the digitalis. I'm quite sure we'll end up making some of the stuff ourselves, from the basic ingredients."

"It'll take me back to my student days. Not that we actually made the stuff ourselves, even then, apart from students who had come to medicine via chemistry."

"Well, it looks as if a refresher course in pharmacology will also be called for. I shall look up some details for that."

Dr Mahoney busied himself with some papers for a minute before speaking again.

"Talking of Brits, how are your particular Brits these days?"

Dr Grey had to think for a moment.

"Oh, you mean the young couple in the cottage just

outside the town? Now that you mention it, I've heard that all is not well with them."

"They've recently had a baby, haven't they? I don't know much more than that."

"Mmm. Sometimes you flatter yourself that you hear all the gossip; but perhaps I don't know as much as I should in this case. They arrived last summer, August time, I think. Apparently they're from Manchester, or somewhere round there. He's a teacher – teaches at that Protestant school in Dublin, whose name escapes me just now. The baby was born in May – I attended as her GP. Everything seemed fine then. The baby was healthy – a girl. But I remember Yvonne, the district nurse, telling me some time later that she sensed on more than one occasion when visiting the house that something wasn't quite right. She wasn't sure what it was, but there was definitely something. Now, I was called out to the house away back last autumn sometime – I can't just remember the exact date – to attend the woman, who had come down with acute pneumonia. It was so bad that I had to send her to hospital straight away."

"Yes, I remember that now. I remember we spoke about it at the time."

"Well, because of the stage the condition had reached, there must have been a delay of many hours at least before I was called out. It was the husband who called me out, and he was extremely concerned and worried about his wife when I was examining her. I remember noticing one or two things which may or may not have had any significance, but which somehow seemed to tell a story. Firstly, the man himself was exhausted. He was completely done in, as if he'd just finished a twelve-hour shift at a factory or something of that sort, although this was only early afternoon. There was also some of the woman's clothing in the kitchen, damp and steaming; and when I examined her, her hair was slightly damp, as if it had recently been dried from being wet. As far as I remember, there had been some sort of storm the night before – hours of heavy rain. There was a lot of flooding by the next day. It was a bad storm. I asked the husband what may have brought on the pneumonia, and he admitted that they had been caught by the storm; but it must have involved a prolonged exposure for the woman to have brought on acute pneumonia. I briefly examined his lungs as well, but they sounded alright, so he probably hadn't been exposed to the storm for as long as the woman. I didn't ask any further questions at the time – the woman had acute pneumonia, she needed treatment immediately, and at that moment, that was all there was to it. So, I could only conjecture as to what might have happened. Why would they have been out in the storm, presumably for hours? As far as I know, they had no horses or livestock, no children then; no obvious reason to go out at such a time. One is left wondering if they'd had an argument of some sort, or even a fight. And so, although I never found out what happened, I was left with the vague impression that all was not well."

"And Yvonne thinks that's still the case, you say."

"Well, it looks as if even that's been overtaken by events. Yvonne mentioned the other day that she doesn't think that the woman is living there any more, or the baby. She received a note from the husband cancelling any further visits. She said she called round a couple of times during the following week, but there was no-one there. The husband was presumably at work, but the woman and child weren't there either."

"She might just be visiting relatives in England for a while."

"Well, as you say, there might be a perfectly ordinary explanation for it, although it does seem to be rather a long time for her to be away from her husband just visiting relatives, especially with a war on over there."

"The war might have something to do with it; although,

240

thinking about the war, from that point of view, you might say that it's rather odd that it's she who has gone back to England and not he."

"Ah, you mean to join the army for war service?"

"Well, this is a very patriotic war across the water – England standing alone against Hitler, and all that sort of thing. You would have thought that virtually every Englishman would have returned to England to join up under the circumstances. Even some of our own lads have gone to join up, although I suspect that lack of employment prospects on this side of the water may have had a part to play in that. But I know that two of Jimmy Maguire's sons have joined up, and I gather he's none too pleased about that."

"And well he might be. But it is rather strange that our Englishman hasn't gone back to England. Even more so given that he teaches at that Protestant school. I gather they're pretty hot on patriotism for the old country there, or so I've heard."

"A last outpost of the empire."

"Something like that. It has that reputation. At the least, I wouldn't have thought he'd have to worry about them not keeping his job open for him whilst he was away."

"Well, for all we know, he may be planning to return soon, especially if his wife has already gone back."

"I suppose so – and yet as far as I know, he hasn't gone."

"I don't suppose it matters much exactly when he goes to join up."

"Ah, but I think perhaps it does in this particular case. It may already be too late. From what we hear in the news reports, it looks as if a German invasion of England is expected almost daily. It'd be pointless him waiting until the Germans actually invade, whatever the outcome of that might be. He'd be no use to the army – soldiers aren't trained up overnight. If he was going to go at all, he should have gone with his wife – long before then, even."

"I see what you mean. I suppose it's pointless trying to guess, if there's some particular reason why he hasn't gone."

"But I wonder what that could be. Not family reasons, surely. His wife's gone already, and he has no other family here, presumably. He only arrived in Ireland last year – he's still a stranger in a strange country. It's unlikely to have to do with his employment – if anything, I would have thought that at that place, he'd be encouraged to leave for England to join up."

"It must be that he's got another woman here. What else could it be? That might explain why his wife has returned to England, if she found out he was having an affair with another woman."

"I expect you're very likely right. I'll have to remember to ask Yvonne what she thinks. If it's not that, then he looks a rather isolated character, all things considered."

"If you're that curious, why don't you call on him to enquire after his health? He is your patient after all."

"I might just do that. Interesting idea."

"Well, if you do go, remember to pick some foxgloves while you're out that way."

26

Helen stopped to listen again. It was undoubtedly closer now, although still indistinct: a deep-noted droning which seemed to pulse and fade, as if carried to her intermittently on the south wind. She recognised it as aircraft noise, but no more than that. Whether the noise was from one aircraft or many, she could not tell; nor, therefore, how far away it might be. The streets were quiet now, and her footsteps echoed grittily in the stillness. The bleary glare of the street lights had been replaced by something akin to that ghostly half-light of country areas at night, reminding her of home; and also, incongruously, of the cottage at Bray. But here the half-light was often broken by blocks of total darkness in the shadows cast by the buildings along the street, and in the shadows, her steps faltered. What she had started with determination had become something of an ordeal.

She had been on her way home from work. In October, not long after she had arrived back from Ireland, having received her National Identity Card and having registered for work, she had been directed to work in the office of a factory in Trafford Park. This was not what she had expected to happen, and she felt that no allowance had been made for the fact that she was still a nursing mother, quite apart from the fact that it was obviously unsuitable for her. But, having admitted that her mother was able to look after Laura during the day, she had been given no choice by the authorities. She disliked the job intensely. She found being cooped up in an office all day filling in ledgers or doing meaningless and repetitive filing often unbearable. Almost equally unpleasant was the routine of the journey there and back – the alarm clock before dawn; the walk to the station after being parted from little Laura; the crowded, dirty trains; the jostling throng of people crowding through the factory gates; the same dreary office, where she had to be from a certain time every morning until a certain time every evening. Suddenly this dreariness was her whole life. Sometimes she was almost bewildered by the oppressiveness of it. She had not imagined, when she came back to England, that she would be coming back to anything like this. This was what her parents had escaped from in Stretford all those years ago. One scarcely needed to think about whether it still existed or not, for even if it did, it was only for other people – people who didn't matter. It was surely unjust that she should be expected to endure this. On returning to England, she had vaguely imagined that she would get a job in nursing or looking after children, or if something more glamorous, with the ambulance service. The grimness of industry was for men, or at least, for the lower orders. It was not for her. But she had committed herself to getting a job and not just living off her parents, so escaping from this grimness would not be quite as simple as just walking out on it. Almost from her first week at Trafford Park, she had desperately been looking for another job, preferably near Nantwich, and preferably looking after children. But there was no shortage of women looking for these more desirable female occupations, and so far, she had had no success. But escape she must – it was unacceptable that she should have to continue to endure this. What was almost as distressing as the day-to-day unpleasantness of the job was the fact that what for a long time in Ireland she had looked forward to as an escape had turned out to be a trap, equally or more unpleasant than the one she had fled from. Now, she did not know where to turn. Having left Ireland, she could not go back there, and still would not, for nothing had changed on that front. But if she could not find congenial employment, what was she going to do? Under normal circumstances there would be an easy way out – and indeed, the problem wouldn't even arise: she would get married, and then she wouldn't have to work. But she was already married, and even if she got a divorce, it was likely to be difficult to find a man who was prepared to take on another man's child. She would probably have to get rid of Laura …

Such thoughts caused her to weep with frustration. Why did John have to be so selfish? She would not be in this situation if he had joined up when he ought to have done. They would have returned to England, and while he went to his army posting, she would be living at home with Laura, as an army wife on his service pay. None of this unpleasantness would have happened. But this was wishful thinking, and she knew it. She knew now that John had gone to Ireland intending to stay there when the anticipated war started. As it turned out, he had only just made it in time. Without that specific intention, there would presumably not have been any reason for him ever to have left England. He would have joined up with the rest of them, and things would have been as she wanted. But given that he had gone to Ireland driven by such a purpose, there was no possibility of him ever returning to England. Privately, in her own mind, she had now understood and accepted the truth of that. And so now she was trapped. It was John who had trapped her, because he would not overcome his cowardice. There was nothing else that she could have done, and no reasonable person would have expected her to do anything else. Nor could she accept that she was in any way trapped by pride. It was up to John to contact her if he wanted to see her or Laura. Indeed, he ought to have contacted her before now, to ask how things were with her, and more particularly to make arrangements for paying maintenance to her. It was he who had brought about their separation, and the present situation, by his refusal to fulfil his duty to his country. Having forced her away, he ought at least to take up his responsibility to support her and his child. But since arriving back in England, she had heard nothing from John. She could only assume that it meant that he had lost all interest in her, and even in Laura. In one sense at least, it would simplify the issue if it were true, by confirming that she was in the right. But in truth, she did not like to think about how John thought about her or about Laura, and what he might be feeling now. Such thoughts were disturbing, because even now it was difficult to forget entirely how he had loved her, and the intensity of that love, and the joy he had had in little Laura.

What was she to do? It would be of considerable help if she could get maintenance from John. It would give her the breathing space she needed to look for a congenial job without having to work in the meantime. She could quit this job straight away. But if John wasn't going to volunteer payment, she would have to write to him and ask for it. At the moment, she wasn't sure if she could bring herself to do that. She shouldn't have to demand what was her right. But if she was forced to endure this job for much longer, she might have to swallow that amount of pride at least. And if he refused to pay, what then? It would mean having to resort to the courts, and lawyers and legal bills, which she knew she would not be able to afford. It was this that prevented her from petitioning for a divorce, which she would otherwise have done by now. She needed another man to support her, and for this she needed to be free of John. But she knew that John might contest her claims if it came to that. She could not cite adultery, cruelty or desertion, the usual reasons for divorce; and John would doubtless claim that it was she who had left him. She would be reliant on the court understanding and accepting that she could not be expected to live with a coward. Surely such things would be taken into account? But it would cost money... Damn him – damn him to hell!

She stumbled as her foot missed a kerbstone in the darkness. She was no longer sure of where she was, or how far she had come. She was making for Chester Road, in order to reach the city centre. When the air-raid sirens had gone off at the factory, the day shift had been stopped, and all those who were within walking or cycling distance of their homes and assigned air-raid shelters were sent home. Those who travelled from further afield by bus or train were told that they should go down into one of the site air-raid shelters near the factory. This Helen absolutely refused to do. The idea of having to spend the whole night in a gloomy concrete dungeon full of grimy sweaty factory workers was more than she could bear. By the end of the day, she couldn't wait to get away from the factory, and nothing was going to stop her, not even an air raid. She was determined that she was going to spend this night in her own bed at home, not in a place she regarded as little more than a prison. She had slipped out of the factory gates amongst all the local workers who were walking home, and started walking down the approach road into Trafford Park. There was no point in going to the station because the trains on this line had been stopped because of the air raid. However, she was hopeful that trains on the main line might still be running, and if she could reach the city centre she would surely have a good chance of getting home. Even if she could reach Chester Road, the main line to Altrincham ran alongside it, or there might be buses. Although it was dark, it was still only early evening, so there was plenty of time to get home that night. She hadn't gone far, however, when she was caught by the blackout, and all the street lights suddenly went out. She had been forced to stop for several minutes until the apparent pitch darkness was gradually infused with that ghostly glimmer which is the natural light of a night sky. It was some minutes longer before she felt able to trust this uncertain near-darkness, and had almost lost the confidence to go on. By this time she was completely alone. It was as if the rest of humanity had somehow vanished; and with the darkness came an almost equally disconcerting silence, in which her footsteps sounded unnaturally loud. Her progress was now much slower, not only because of the darkness, but also because of the stillness, which she somehow found intimidating here in the centre of the city. Even distant sounds seemed largely absent. Once, the silence was broken by the noise of a motorcycle, perhaps only a few blocks away, the sound echoing dismally through the empty streets; and once by the rather mournful hoot of a locomotive whistle from somewhere further off. It was this that gave her the courage to carry on. It surely proved that trains were still running, so if she could reach the main line, she should still be able to get home that night. But progress was now something of an ordeal in what little light remained. In the shadows cast by buildings along the street the darkness was almost absolute, and she had to feel her way along, step by cautious step. Again, she cursed John. If it wasn't for him she would never have been put into this predicament – struggling to get home from a job she hated in a city she had long since turned her back on. Did he have any idea what he had done to her?

She was no longer sure of where she was. Surely she should have reached Chester Road by now. She seemed to have been stumbling forward in this near-darkness for an interminable length of time without getting anywhere. Trafford Park Road joined Chester Road at quite a sharp angle, so it would be difficult to miss even in the dark; but so far, she had seen no sign of it. Even when she reached Chester Road, there would still be a further walk to the first railway station, to find out if trains were still running on the Altrincham line. But she had to keep going – it was too late to turn back now.

It was then that she first became aware of the noise – the sound of aircraft engines. It was still only faint – background noise heard intermittently. To begin with, she took no special notice of it. Since returning to England she had become used to the sound of military aircraft as part of the conditions of wartime. Even if one hadn't previously come across aircraft much, one quickly got used to the sight and sound of them in the skies above. Such things were of no interest to Helen; but living as she did, right out in the countryside, she was still slow to appreciate the significance of aircraft noise at night, especially in a city. At home, the 'blackout' meant making sure that the windows were all covered completely by the heavy curtains her mother had made specially for that purpose. With the curtains drawn, it was then safe to have the electric light on, so there was no particular inconvenience, at least, not during the winter. What it would be like at the height of summer, when one might want the windows open at night because of the heat, she didn't know. This was the first occasion she had had to contend with the effects of the blackout. Every previous night since starting work at the factory, she had boarded the train at the station near the factory and had been taken all the way to Nantwich station. There had been one occasion when the train had been caught in a blackout because of an air-raid warning. All the train's lights had gone out, despite the window blinds, which had made sitting in a crowded compartment rather awkward. All the stations they stopped at were also in complete darkness; but it was the memory of this journey that had given her the expectation that, even during an air-raid warning, the trains would still be running. This was the first time that the full significance of the blackout had impressed itself upon her. At home, one did not usually go wandering about outside at night; but this was her first experience of city streets in complete darkness.

Thus far, the alarm she felt was still incipient – a feeling of tension because of the difficulty of walking, of making any progress, because of the darkness. It was the guns that changed her alarm to fear. The first guns to fire were several miles away, south of the Mersey, but their firing broke the stillness of the night. Helen felt panic start to rise inside her. She did not know what the explosions were – when she turned to look in the direction of the noise, she could see anti-aircraft shells bursting in the sky to the south; but she had no knowledge of such things and had no idea what she was looking at. The shock was not just the noise of the guns, but also the realisation that this was not just another tedious exercise as other air-raid warnings had apparently been. It was also a fear of the unknown, as she did not yet know what an air raid was about. Panic clouded her thoughts. She could not focus her mind on what she should do. Perhaps she should look for an air-raid shelter to take refuge in. But she had no idea where such shelters were, and to try and find one would mean more stumbling through darkened streets not knowing where she was. She felt she had no alternative but to carry on. At least she would know where she was when she reached Chester Road.

The sound of aircraft was much louder now, and continuous, pulsing with the dissonance of many engines. She quickened her pace as her panic grew, even though she could no longer see where she was going. More than once she fell, the second time banging her cheek against an unseen kerbstone. There was a lot of blood, but she scarcely more than brushed at it with the back of her hand as she picked herself up to carry on. The noise suddenly increased in intensity as the anti-aircraft guns in Longford Park began firing. Helen did not know what it was, and for a moment she stopped, disconcerted by the suddenly increased noise of gunfire. Then, in the dim light, she recognised that she had reached the junction with Chester Road. So much had simply reaching this junction become an objective in her mind that for a moment she almost felt as if she had reached home, and for a minute she just stood there, not knowing what to do next. When she did move, she had lost her way, her mind clouded by disorientation from panic and the cacophony of noise. She walked without knowing that she moved, as her mind tried to shut out the noise and the terror of the night. When she fell again, she did not understand that she had not tripped – it was the ground concussion of exploding bombs hitting Trafford Park Road two hundred yards away. She only felt the aftershock – her hearing was destroyed in that moment – but she was no longer aware of it. How could she not have known that she was so close? It was lighter now, and she could see the house, where Mum and Dad were waiting for her, had been waiting anxiously for her return all through the long hours of darkness, the dreary train journey and the walk from Nantwich station in the last of the night. It was over now, and there was only the sweetness of homecoming and seeing little Laura again, asleep in her crib, her breathing quick and tiny as her life was fragile. And joy was hers as they greeted her homecoming from exile, and no longer would there be any strangeness or parting; and warm arms were around her as of old, and tender voices. I love you – I love you for ever and ever.

27

Mrs Fitzgerald walked over to the window and looked down into the street outside. It was a suburban street of no particular distinction; but to her it was incomprehensible that anyone should create such dreariness and ugliness as a place to live in, in preference to the sea and the sky and the country of the far west, where she had lived all her life. Dublin was a prison, a place of despair, where all who were refugees from the Ireland of the west, as she was, found themselves trapped without hope of escape. Cities were places of regimentation, where regimentation itself became a master, a mindless god which ground down those who did not conform to its rule. But at least, in this prison, she was kept at one remove from the worst effects of it by her son Vincent. They had moved to this first-floor flat in south Dublin not long after her arrival from Kilkirrin. It was more spacious than the rooms Vincent had been renting in Bray, which had proved to be completely inadequate to accommodate both of them. She understood that Vincent had done the best he could, given the constraints he was under. He had done nothing wrong with regard to Rebecca Brady, and he was not responsible for the hostility of the Brady family. But she could not see the matter in terms of a criticism of Kilkirrin, or the way of life represented by Kilkirrin. She could never have comprehended that in its narrow-minded backwardness, it was in its own way as much a prison for the human spirit and its creativity as suburban Dublin was for her. Vincent could move in both worlds because in him there was a need for something from each of them, even if neither of them gave him fulfilment. Vaguely, she was aware of this, but she could not see that, in this sense, Kilkirrin was also as much a jungle as Dublin. The Bradys had not always been what they were now. They had emerged as a force to be reckoned with along with the rise of the IRA during the period which led to the creation of the Free State, and the civil war that followed. Although their side had lost the war, the Bradys had remained powerful in Kilkirrin and that part of Galway. It was a power that the locals were resigned to. Before the Bradys, it had been someone else; and such a state of affairs would always be so. Mrs Fitzgerald had seen what happened to those who fell foul of such power. When it happened to someone else, one shrugged one's shoulders and looked the other way. One knew what might happen otherwise. But even now, when she herself had become a victim, she could not see that it was this, and only this, that made Dublin a jungle too.

She was afraid. The jungle of Dublin was more real now than any other could ever be. It was early morning, still before the world became busy with throngs of people on their way to work, and when milk carts and newspaper boys had the streets largely to themselves. To other eyes, it would be a scene of reassuring familiarity; but to Mrs Fitzgerald it was as if darkness had come, and not light. It was the start of the third day that Vincent had not returned home. In the blank light of an uncaring day, she could no longer pretend that nothing was wrong. There was a part of her which already knew the truth, from that unquiet voice of doubt within. On the morning Vincent had left the house, she had noticed one or two small changes from his normal routine, as if that day was to be different in some way that he had not spoken of. He had said nothing, however, perhaps so as not to alarm her. But now, after a second night and the start of a third day, she could no longer wait passively for his return. From that unquiet voice she guessed that Vincent had gone back to Kilkirrin. He must somehow have heard news of Rebecca Brady – there could be no other reason why he would risk going back there. She did not know what to do. The obvious course was to report the matter to the police. But in Kilkirrin, the police, the Garda, were seen as agents of the Free State, those who had betrayed republicanism to the British, the enemy in the civil war. Even though that was all long past, the habits of a generation were not so easily discarded. It was instinctive to turn to one's own kind in time of need; but here, there were none, or none that she knew. This was an alien place where she knew no-one. It was this which, in the end, was the most important thing. Trust might be sought in the strangest of places when necessity required it; and so it was now. Vincent's friend might be an Englishman, and therefore probably a Protestant; but he had Vincent's trust, and for Mrs Fitzgerald that now outweighed any other considerations. Of course, it was he who had brought her away from Kilkirrin on that fateful day in January, so he was not a complete stranger to her. The difficulty would be in finding him. She did not know where he lived. All she knew about him was that he worked as a teacher at a Protestant school in Dublin which was notoriously pro-British and anti-republican, although apparently these sentiments were not shared by Vincent's friend. She had heard the name of the school mentioned, but now, when she needed to, she could not for the life of her bring it to mind. She felt sure that she would recognise the name if she heard it. Perhaps the best thing would be to ask at a post office. Her first thought was that she could not face the ordeal of going into the centre of Dublin, to the main post office, and could avoid that by going to the local post office just around the corner; but of course, the school itself was likely to be in the centre of the city, or be reachable only by going through the city centre. It was an ordeal she would have to face. But it was a further half hour before she eventually put on her coat, fastened a scarf around her head, and made her way slowly down the stairs to the street door.

28

Dr Grey knocked again at the cottage door, and stood
still, listening for sounds from within. It was six-thirty
on a weekday evening, late enough for anyone with a nine-to-
five job to have arrived back home, but a little early for most
to have departed again for evening activities or entertainment.
But Dr Grey knew nothing about the Englishman's lifestyle
or routine, and so such generalisations could only relate to the
appropriateness of the time for making an evening call. It was
now well after nightfall, but no lights could be seen in any of
the cottage's windows, although the dim light from candles or
oil lamps might be hidden by drawn curtains. Perhaps the
Englishman had had to work late. Perhaps he had left early to
go into Bray, or back into Dublin, or was staying in town for
the evening to go to the cinema or the theatre. But even here,
there was evidence of a different story. A few steps from the
door, and still visible in the bright moonlight, was what
remained of a vegetable plot, once cultivated but now
overgrown with weeds; and the rest of the garden was as wild
and rank as a meadow. Right by the door there were a number
of uncollected milk bottles, now all pecked open by birds.
There was no-one at home. As if to confirm the fact, Dr Grey
tried the handle of the door. He exclaimed slightly in surprise
to find that the door was open. It swung inwards out of his
grasp, to reveal the dark interior of the cottage. Strictly
speaking, he had no business going any further; but such a

thing was only too easily justified. It was possible that someone was lying injured and helpless within – it would be reasonable to at least confirm that such was not the case.

Dr Grey struck a match and lit the kitchen lamp. Here were more indications that no-one was at home. A clothes horse stood in front of the kitchen fireplace. The clothes draped over it were dry, but the fire was cold ash. On the kitchen table was a cup of cold tea that looked as if it had been left for a couple of days at least. In the other rooms it was the same story. The house was empty. It was hard to judge how long it had been empty. The milk bottles indicated that it had been for more than a day at least. And yet the house did not have the air of having been abandoned. Wherever he was, the Englishman was coming back, or such was his intention.

It was now appropriate for him to leave – he had seen enough. But ordinary curiosity remained unsatisfied. He noticed a letter lying on the living room table, address-side up. It had already been opened, and so there was only a moment's resistance to the temptation to read it. On a first brief scan it was necessary to read through the names of people not immediately identifiable; but Dr Grey quickly remembered that the Englishman's wife was called Helen, and that the baby, whose gestation he himself had attended, was called Laura. And yet something seemed to remain unexplained, something which was peripheral to the letter, but central to what had happened. Perhaps one might guess; but it would remain a guess. A second reading made it clearer.

"The doctors have told us that Helen's injuries are so severe that she has no hope of life. She is being kept alive on a ventilator, but her head injuries are such that she will never regain consciousness, and they say that it is a matter of a few days only before her heart and other organs fail. We go to see her every day, although she is deeply unconscious and cannot hear us. No-one can know the agony we are going through as we are forced to watch our darling daughter die, being unable to do anything to save her. If you have any feeling for her left you will come to her while she still lives. And little Laura, who has lost her father through his indifference, will soon lose her mother also. Have you no feelings for her? In view of what has happened, I can now only agree with Helen's view that none of this would have happened if you had done your duty. She would not have been forced to take this job, and therefore would not have been where she was that night. You should consider this, and what your responsibility is to your wife and child."

Dr Grey read the letter again. This, surely, was the answer to the question of the Englishman's whereabouts. And yet, it was not so – could not be so. It was inconceivable that he had set out on a journey to England as if he had just gone down the street to the local shop to buy a newspaper. Even knowing what he did, Dr Grey was able to hazard more than a guess that if the Englishman returned to England under such circumstances as these, it would be for good. The tenuous link he had established with Ireland would be broken, and it would not call him back again. Even in the dim light of the oil lamp, it was possible to see that there had been no hurried departure, still less a permanent one. The scatter of personal belongings, clothes, unwashed cups left as if only five minutes ago – there could be no doubt that the man intended to come back. The letter bore a date of some ten days back, and even allowing for the uncertainty of postal services, Dr Grey judged that he could not have been gone for as long as that would suggest.

Why had he not gone back to England? Whatever held him here, the link was more than tenuous. Or, there was no link at all: it was that he could not go back, even to see his dying wife. It seemed to Dr Grey as he stood there in the uncertain light of the oil lamp, that he was witness to a personal tragedy. But even if there might be a way in which he could help, Dr Grey knew from experience that he could not involve himself in every tragedy his profession brought him into contact with. If one did, then one would surely go mad.

29

Vincent was dead. For a while, it was almost harder to contemplate the significance of such news than even the mere fact of it. Coming so soon after the news of Helen's death, it seemed to underline how little a human life meant to those who traded in human life for their own ends; and how fragile was the world, the universe, that each human being created in his inner self as his perception of the world, and his place in it in life. When he died, his universe was also lost. He had wept when he heard the news about Helen. Despite all that had happened, despite the darkness that had been revealed in the rift between them, she was still the love of his life, the love of so many memories. However much bitterness there had been, he had not wanted her dead – did not want her dead. For a while, his grief was visceral in its intensity; but he grieved not only for Helen, but also for what they had lost in the last few months of their lives together, bitter months that had destroyed everything that had gone before. And now also for Laura, whom he would probably never see again.

But with Vincent's death, the darkness returned, that incomprehensible darkness that had driven Helen from him. He was filled with alarm and dismay, even before anything was certain. But he had known, almost from the beginning. It was mid-morning when he had been called to the secretary's office. The secretary and bursar had established quickly enough whom Mrs Fitzgerald had come to see; but not the reason for her visit. As soon as he saw her, however, John knew that she could only have come about Vincent. Mrs Fitzgerald told her story again for John, and although he could not follow everything she said, the main message was clear.

He thought for a moment. Today was Thursday. In conscience, he could not wait until the weekend before taking any action. Mrs Fitzgerald was confused and distraught, and needed some response and reassurance, if not immediately, then certainly that day. He spoke to the secretary.

"May I use the telephone?"

Permission was grudgingly given. He phoned for a taxi to take Mrs Fitzgerald home. Replacing the receiver, he turned to the secretary again.

"I'm afraid I'll need to take tomorrow off."

Mrs Allen, the secretary, was unsympathetic.

"You're perfectly well aware of the rules. You must make any request for leave of absence to the Head at least a week in advance. Under the present circumstances, the granting of leave at such short notice is almost certainly out of the question."

"Well, if the Head feels confident that the school can manage with the loss of one more member of staff, I'm sure he'll do what he thinks is necessary."

As it happened, the Head wasn't in that day, so he could not have been appealed to in any event. As far as John was concerned, it was an emergency: he would justify it later. He was having to think on his feet. He would have to make some arrangement for Mrs Fitzgerald that day. Even in the short term, she was dependent on Vincent for such requirements as food and fuel, while Vincent paid the rent for the flat they lived in. He vaguely remembered Vincent mentioning brothers in Australia and Canada. But in Ireland? He recalled the conversation in which Vincent had spoken of the expectation that one would leave Ireland to make one's way in the world.

Had he been the only one to stay? A question to Mrs Fitzgerald revealed that Vincent had a younger sister in Glasgow, but that Mrs Fitzgerald had not seen her for some time. There was an address, however. He would send off a short note, asking if she could help. He would have to do that now, so that Mrs Fitzgerald could add a few words and her name. He must contact the newspaper for which Vincent worked as a freelance contributor, in case they had any news of him. If they hadn't, he would have to go to Galway to try and find out for himself. He would need to go to the bank to draw money out for any of this to be possible. He had about ten shillings in his pocket – he would have to give that to Mrs Fitzgerald to see her through the next day or two.

He would need to use the phone once more. He turned to the secretary again.

"Mrs Allen, if I'm off tomorrow, I'll set work for each class, which I will require to be finished for the end of each class. They'll require only minimum supervision, and for the work to be collected at the end of each class for me to mark on Monday."

It didn't seem to make much impression, but it was the best he could do.

"I'm afraid I'll need to use the telephone just once more."

Any conciliatory progress he might have just made was lost.

"The cost of any telephone calls will have to be deducted from your salary, of course."

"Of course."

He put a call through to the newspaper which Vincent contributed to as a freelance writer. He was through to the newspaper fairly quickly, but there was then what seemed like an interminable wait until the features editor was brought to the phone. After explaining who he was and the nature of his query, John was told that no communication had been received from Vincent for at least two weeks, and that they had no information about where he was. He had not been sent anywhere at the newspaper's behest. John was more than a little dismayed by the man's evident lack of interest. The most he got at the end of the conversation was: "Well, if anything has happened to him, you'll let me know, will you?"

But it sounded more like the interest of a newspaperman in a possible story than any personal concern. He put the receiver down and turned to Mrs Allen again.

"I'm afraid that confirms my need to take tomorrow off. It was possible that the newspaper might have known where Mrs Fitzgerald's son was, but it seems that they don't."

He didn't want to say any more while Mrs Fitzgerald was present. He found some paper and quickly drafted a short note to Vincent's sister, then asked Mrs Fitzgerald to add a few words of her own. There was a knock at the door. It was the taxi driver. John saw Mrs Fitzgerald out to the taxi.

"I'm going over to Galway tonight or tomorrow morning to look for Vincent," he told her. "I shall see you again tomorrow evening or Saturday. If I'm any later, I'll send you a wire – a telegram."

She nodded, but said nothing. John felt helplessly inadequate in the face of her trust, or resignation. He squeezed her hand gently.

"I'll do whatever I can."

Again, she nodded, but said nothing. Her frailty, the frailty of the elderly, was not only physical, but also because she had to rely on others, even strangers, in matters of the greatest importance, whether they served her well or not.

There were still a few minutes left before the start of the next lesson in which he might do what he could to try and salvage his position with Mrs Allen. It was not that he expected much sympathy, even when he was able to explain the situation more fully. The school was now seriously short-staffed because of the number of 'patriots' who had volunteered for service with the British forces and, in truth, the Head could no longer afford gratuitously to sack teaching staff. Replacements were scarce – the great majority of teachers from the Irish state schools were unacceptable because of their religion, and not a few would refuse even to consider teaching at St Mungo's anyway.

At lunchtime he cycled to the bank, and then to the railway station, where he confirmed that there was a train that could take him to Galway that evening. One further thing remained. He would need to tell someone where he was going and for what purpose. Now that Helen was gone, there were few left whom he could tell. The only interest at St Mungo's if he failed to turn up on Monday would be to discharge him from their employment. He had already broken the rules concerning absence, and a further breach would terminate his contract of employment as far as they were concerned. They would not regard it as part of their responsibility to try and find out what had happened to him. He had made no friends at the school, and there were none who would risk their position for his sake – not even the not-quite-closet-republican Carter. The police would be no better. For the Dublin police, Galway wasn't their patch; and the fact that the Galway police had tolerated the Bradys and their activities on their patch was as much as he needed to know as far as they were concerned.

After some consideration, he decided on the landlord of the Queen's Hotel in Bray, Tom Redmond, whom John had got to know quite well over the past year or so. He wrote Tom a brief note, saying he was to open the enclosed inner envelope if John had not made an appearance by Tuesday evening. The letter inside the inner envelope gave brief details of where John was going and with what purpose.

30

John finally ran old O'Grady to earth in a bar near the college. John didn't approach him in the bar – he knew better than that by now – but bided his time in a secluded corner where he could watch the door, waiting for O'Grady to leave. It was nearly nine o'clock before the old man got up to leave, nodding to one or two of the others in the bar as he walked towards the door. John followed him at a distance until he was sure that he was not being followed himself. He quickened his pace suddenly so that he was upon O'Grady before the latter had time to do more than half turn in surprise. He gaped in fear as he recognised John, who grasped him by the coat lapels to stop him from bolting off.

"For God's sake," the old man wheezed, when he finally managed to speak, "have you no pity? They'll kill me if they find out I've been talking to you."

"Well, maybe I'll kill you if you don't."

But O'Grady didn't look very convinced. John shook him none too gently by the lapels.

"Where is he?"

The old man shook his head, but said nothing.

"Where is Vincent Fitzgerald?"

"Oh, God, no, no ..."

The old man's face twisted as he tried to turn away.

"I need to know where he is. If he's in danger, I've come to help him."

"If you'd wanted to help him, you should have told him to stay back in Dublin."

"I'm not his guardian or keeper. I don't tell him where he can and can't go."

"He was a fool to have come back, and he must have known it."

"For God's sake, where is he?"

The old man turned his head away again as he spoke.

"He's dead."

"Dead? I don't believe you. Dead when? How? You're lying to get rid of me. Where is he? I want the truth of it."

"Well, Mr Englishman, here's your truth, then. Vincent Fitzgerald is dead. It happened two nights ago. I told you, you should have warned him to stay in Dublin."

"Two nights ago – where?"

"Where do you think? He couldn't keep away from the Brady girl, and so he came back. He must have been crazy out of his mind."

"What happened?"

"I didn't see what happened. I wasn't there."

John shook the old man.

"If you know he's dead, you know what happened."

"I'm not a witness. I can't be called as a witness. I only know what I've heard. Old Seamus Owen told me. He saw what happened." O'Grady looked away before speaking again. "They beat him. They beat him with clubs and staves, spades, iron bars, anything they could lay hands on. Even after he stopped moving, still they struck at him. Seamus said that his head was smashed in so that he couldn't be identified. It was a terrible thing. The man was a fool, but he didn't deserve anything like that. I've known the Fitzgeralds most of my life, and I wouldn't say they were bad people. But they knew the way things worked in Kilkirrin, and Vincent Fitzgerald must have known what he was walking into." O'Grady looked up.

"You wanted the truth, mister, so now you have it. I've nothing more to tell you, so you might as well let me go now."

John released the old man, but continued to hold him with his gaze.

"How is it possible for such things to happen? Is there no law in this country?"

The old man sneered.

"This isn't England, mister. It isn't even Dublin, where Vincent Fitzgerald should have stayed if he'd had any sense. It's different here, as you should know yourself by now. There is law in Kilkirrin – Brady's law. But, like any other law, you stay on the right side of it if you want to keep out of trouble."

John said nothing for a moment, then asked: "What … what happened to the body?"

"I don't know. If you've any sense, mister, you won't go poking around trying to find out." As an afterthought, he added: "You'd likely be wasting your time anyway. I don't know what happened to the body, but if you know Kilkirrin, it wouldn't be hard to guess. Most folk there have a boat. It was most likely wound up in an old fishing net, weighted with stones and dropped out to sea. No-one will ever find it now."

John shrugged, as a gesture of resignation.

"Well, I suppose you can go now. Thanks for that anyway."

The old man turned to go, then looked back.

"You'll not be thinking of going to Kilkirrin will you?"

"I don't know what I'll do. But have no fear – I won't make any mention of you, whatever I decide to do. In any case, you've only confirmed what I already suspected, and I'm no friend of the Bradys."

O'Grady would have to make do with that. Up to that point, John had assumed that he would probably have to go to Kilkirrin just to confirm what had happened to Vincent. He had intended to spend that evening looking for O'Grady, and it was a piece of luck to have found him so quickly. The old

267

man had told him everything he had needed to know, including what had most probably happened to Vincent's body. Nothing further of consequence could be gained from going to Kilkirrin now, especially with all the difficulties such a venture would involve. Tomorrow, he could return to Dublin; perhaps even in time to retrieve something of the day at St Mungo's.

But he would not go back to Dublin. He had passed the point where such things weighed much in the balance. Or rather, other matters now weighed more heavily, and could no longer be ignored.

Why had Helen abandoned family life to return to a war which had nothing to do with her or with them, and which she had little understanding of? It was surely not the war itself. She had not been drawn away by silly, ignorant patriotism, or even by the general tendency of women to conform to what was expected of them. She had felt herself driven away from him, by something that was stronger than love, stronger than family life, and perhaps, as it now seemed, stronger than life itself. It was a fundamental difference between them as individuals. For him, it was the difference between reason and instinct. It was clear to reason that the best and safest future for their life together as a family was here in Ireland. He could see nothing of the instinct that was not simply destructive. But what had happened was his fault because of what he was. However much he might try to lessen the pain of his loss by telling himself that Helen's action was as much that of an individual as his own, the barb in the wound she had inflicted on him had gone deep, and he no longer had the confidence to believe that anything he had done was right. But now, in this dark street in Galway City, it seemed as if another perspective on the matter had opened, suggesting that what he had felt constrained to imagine as being no more than a construct of his own mind, was indeed more than that. He needed to know the truth.

31

John climbed down from the bus to the wheezing and clattering sound of its engine as it idled. He had asked the driver to set him down at the bend in the road where it turned inland before running through the village. He did not want to get off the bus in Kilkirrin. The fewer people who knew he was there the better. From the bend in the road, a rough track or pathway continued along the line of the shore, running along the top of the machair, the grassy foreshore above the sand and shingle of the beach. As the bus pulled away, John set off along the path, wanting to get out of sight as soon as possible. Ahead of him, as he walked, was Kilkirrin Bay, the low hummocks of its islands dark in the morning light against the cold grey of the sea. To the north, the hills of Connemara were dim, half-imagined shadows in the mist. At first the wind was against him, and before him it pushed the wave tops over into whitecaps as it blew them into the bay. As the path followed the shoreline round into the bay, he turned until the wind blew from his left, flattening the machair as it swept down towards the sea's edge. At length, as he walked on, he began to see the roofs of some of the cottages in the village beyond the tops of the machair. At that distance, he was too far from even the nearest houses to be recognised from the village. He might be identified as a stranger, but that was a risk he would have to take. A little further on the path divided, with one track going up over the top of the machair and into the village, while the other wandered down towards the bottom of the machair and the edge of the shingle. He followed the lower path to keep out of sight. At one point he thought he could identify the roof of the Fitzgeralds' cottage, but he couldn't be sure. His memories of that day, the last time he had been in Kilkirrin, were distorted by the events surrounding their escape from the village. The tension and the fear of that day were with him now as he walked past those same cottages just beyond the top of the machair. It was bizarre that the most tender of emotions should also be the cause of such violence and bitterness; but here in Kilkirrin, however tranquil things seemed on the surface, it was not difficult to believe.

He found her on the beach below the Bradys' farmhouse, which was almost out of sight beyond the machair. He caught sight of her while she was still some distance away, walking alone, out on the sands below the shingle, her long auburn hair blowing freely in the wind. His resolve strengthened once he was sure it was her, as he remembered Vincent's photograph of her. Whatever had happened, seemingly they had not managed to restrict her liberty entirely; but in truth, he knew nothing about her.

Would she even let him approach? Surely she must have some sense of apprehension after what had happened? But was she not safe here? Who would dare to enter the lion's den alone to exact revenge? She became aware of him when he was still some distance away, and watched him cautiously as it became evident that he was making for her. When he was some thirty feet away, she called out for him to stop.

"Don't come any closer. What do you want?"

John told her who he was, and watched her face set hard as she understood.

"Vincent Fitzgerald – how dare you even mention his name in my hearing?"

"Is there nothing more you can say about him? He died because of you."

"He died because he was a fool, and because his friend, if that's what you call yourself, did nothing to stop him."

"I didn't know anything about it until afterwards. But he came here because of his love for you."

"He'd been told to stay away, and that's what he should have done. I can't be held responsible for what happened."

"Have you no feelings at all for him? You cared for him once."

"Once! I was a girl – hardly more than a child. What did I know about love then? Puppy love, that's all it was. And that's all he ever knew, which is why he was such a pathetic creature."

"He loved you as profoundly as any man can love a woman."

"No! He knew nothing about love. When I went to America I grew up and became a woman, and then I found out what love is. Love is when you want a man; and before he can earn that love, he has to prove himself a man. He has to show that he's strong, that he can hold his own with other men. In other words, that he's a real man. Then a woman will love him."

"And in your case, more than one woman, perhaps?" It was a shot in the dark, but she flushed with anger.

"I suggest you mind your own business, mister. But I'll tell you this: I'd rather share a man, a real man, with another woman, than allow myself to be defiled by a deadbeat like Vincent Fitzgerald."

"Why can you not accept that what he felt for you was love?"

"Because he wasn't a real man. He was a whelp, a cur, a boy who never grew up, because he didn't have it in him to be a real man. Such creatures deserve only contempt from a woman; and if they press unwanted attentions on a woman, they surely deserve to be whipped back to where they belong by real men."

"As Vincent Fitzgerald was whipped and beaten?"

Her lips parted in a slight smile. She understood him now.

"Yes, if you want to know. He knew what the score was if he was stupid enough to come back here. He tried to kill my father and my cousin back in January, so what happened was only justice. He was a whippersnapper who didn't know his place, and I was glad that true justice was done."

Her smile was one of triumph now, and she met his gaze with hers, her wide hazel eyes alive with pleasure in the knowledge that she had returned his barb and more, and in a way that vindicated her contempt for him and his kind. And in her eyes, her pretty, hazel eyes, he could see nothing but an abyss. Was it thus, then? Was there nothing else?

But now he knew another truth, back here in Dublin, in the little flat overlooking Rialto Street as he faced Mrs Fitzgerald, the old lady's blue eyes faded with age, yet bright now with tears, but also with pride that Vincent, with both his faults and his strengths, his kindness, his loyalty, his gentle intelligence, and above all, his love, had been her son. John saw, in those faded blue eyes, that there was another truth. The lion might roar, might conquer; but it could never destroy this truth.